It is with deep gratitude that I dedicate this book to Mrs. Perdue's beautiful daughter, my lovely wife, Patti.

Oct. 16/2011

Vicky
May all your favorite
dreams come true!

Love

Mighty Oaks

A novel by
Lorne S. Jones

© Lorne S. Jones (lornesjones@hotmail.com)
All pertaining rights reserved

Author's note:

This book is a work of fiction and, although I have used the names of real people, I make no claim that any of the events in this account ever actually occurred. Many of the characters are composites, and places and situations have been created or altered for dramatic purposes. This is not an absolutely accurate memoir; it is a story constructed for the purpose of entertainment only.

Cover artwork by Glenn E.C. Brucker

4

Contents

I have to thank all the Librarians who have dedicated so much time and effort to the massive job of keeping the fragile flame of human intelligence burning. Without their help Mighty Oaks, and many thousands of other books, simply would not exist.

Introduction:

Some things, sometimes, simply must be done. Sometimes, like, when the roof leaks, the attic must be entered.

And, sometimes, the entry into said attic results in the unforeseen, unexpected discovery. The observation of something that stands out, like a cardboard box that has become slightly sodden and likely to crumble.

If left untouched.

And so, touched it must be.

And, once touched, this particular box must to be opened, examined, and the contents found to be...

Well, let's start with: most of the contents had been in the box for closer to five decades than four. But how to describe?

Lined notebooks, with the brand name Hilroy on the front and row upon row of my tortured handwriting on the pages inside. Do kids still use those in school to learn how to print with a pen? I know I did. I know I did because my name was on the front cover of these.

Lined notebooks, an old report card from Fern Avenue school in Parkdale, a note from a speech therapist assigned to me in Grade Four.

A Teacher had reported my stuttering.

I was instructed by the therapist, when I got caught in a stutter "loop," to stop, then say ahhhhhh... for a second or more, then continue with what I was trying to say. It worked, and I stopped stuttering. But I developed an awful habit of saying "Ah" and "Um" a lot, and I mean a LOT, throughout all my speech until well into adult life.

I beat that habit with the help of a public speaking club, called Toastmasters, but after all those years, the stuttering came back. Of course, within a few weeks I had that old habit beat again. But it was an odd feeling to have the stutter return after so many years.

It was also an odd feeling to be looking at all those old notebooks in the attic after all the time that had passed since they first went into this box.

More lined Hilroy notebooks from grade five, more report cards.

I failed grade five, and we moved again. Back to Toronto Island... again.

A few more clues in the box triggered a flood of memories.

Grade Five at The Island Public School, then Grade Six.

There was a copy of The Dharma Bums, a school library book that wasn't technically overdue because it had never been checked out. Then another notebook and, pressed between its pages, a poem I had written entitled Sharkhawk, along with a couple of Sports Day ribbons and a writing assignment with red pencil marks indicating the spelling errors.

I thumbed my way through half the box and found that I had traveled a quarter century from the time of Sharkhawk and the rest of the items at the front of the box, forward in time to a Globe & Mail newspaper clipping dated December 2, 1987. The headline cried out: **Poet Won Governor-General's Award**.

The time-yellowed first paragraph read: "Gwendolyn MacEwen, a Canadian poet who won the Governor-General's award for English-language poetry, died Sunday in her Toronto home of undetermined causes. She was 46."

I was troubled by that phrase, "undetermined causes". To me, it meant that somebody in the coroner's office hadn't done their job, hadn't looked carefully enough for the true reason for her death.

I quickly dropped the clipping back into the box. I wasn't ready to be browsing that far ahead. The hurt was still too fresh.

I riffled back through the earlier pages.

Back to those once oh-so-important pieces of paper.

Back to the Island.

Back to a cold February morning, the day we first met, and that writing assignment with red pencil marks indicating the spelling errors.

Chapter 1
Holler

Holler. I got a mark deduction because I used the word "holler" in a sentence. It didn't seem right. I knew the word existed. I had heard people use it many times, in a lot of different situations.

"Stop your damn hollering in the house!"

"But he won't give it over and it's *my* turn!"

"I SAID STOP HOLLERING INDOORS! Take it outside or I'll lay a lathering on you!"

Or: "Holler across to them from the port side."

"Okay, Dink. HEY, DOOLY, WHICH WAY ARE YOU DOCKING?!!!"

Holler: verb, to talk loudly and distinctly. To holler requires raising the volume of the voice while talking as opposed to a shout, which uses the yelling voice. You holler to people, you yell at them.

I knew that definition had to be in a dictionary.

But The Teacher insisted that no such word existed. He smugly watched as I frantically thumbed my way through first the thick little blue-bound Concise Oxford dictionary from my desk, then the big red Funk & Wagnall's at the back of the room with the large print, then the really fat, heavy Webster's in the front corner.

"The word isn't in any dictionary, therefore it's a spelling error and that's your mark."

I knew that word had to be in a dictionary somewhere.

The library was the opposite way from the door our class was supposed to exit through to go out into the playground. When the recess bell rang and the whole class jumped up and dashed for the hall and then turned right, I turned left. The Teacher was standing there and was quick to move in front of me. This hall error had been made before. "That way out," he said.

"I'm going to the library," I said.

And: Wham! There was one of those sudden moments of telepathy, when you know that the other person knows that you know what they're thinking, because, as you looked into their eyes, they just suddenly knew what you were thinking.

He looked knowingly at the rolled up paper in my hand and, confident that I wasn't going to find the elusive word in any dictionary in the library either, stepped aside.

The library was three doors up on the left, past the two open doors of the next class which was now exiting their room and all diligently trying to turn left to exit at the other end of the hall. I jostled with them as I crossed through the flowing current of bodies, forced my way to the left to where the big old brass fire extinguisher hung dutifully in its bracket on the wall, the hose crusted with a few white crystals of some corrosive nature. Someone on my right shoved me and I bounced off the extinguisher and back, a bit of the white crystal stuff scratching my bicep, a wee burning sensation and a tiny droplet of blood going unnoticed as I sped up to slug the guy in the back who had shoved me.

The library, rows of yellowish steel shelves bearing pitifully few books, was on the left, across the hall from The Principal's office on the right. Both doors were open, and, just before I could bring my fist down and give the kid who had shoved me a thump between the shoulder blades, I caught sight of The Principal at his desk. I barely stopped before landing the punch, got my fist down and unclenched, turned the other way and went straight into the library while the other class continued up the hall.

I walked straight up to The Librarian, each step a careful balancing act, feeling The Principal's eyes boring into the back of my skull, certain that, at any moment, that eagle-talon of his was going to pierce my shoulder; thinking only of how to stay upright if he jerked me left, or right, or pulled me backward.

I came to a halt at The Librarian's desk. I hadn't felt anything yet. Looking backward would just anger him all the more because, by looking, I'd be admitting that I'd done something wrong. I waited. Would it be my left shoulder or right this time?

"Yes?"

"Um-m, yes?" I shivered.

"Yes, can I help you?"

Sometimes you can be listening to music, or birds, or children playing through a window or something, and be concentrating on it so much that you don't realize, don't become aware of something else right in front of you until you've tipped your cup of coffee over so far that a small, hot drop lands in your lap.

"Are you looking for a book?"

I shivered again as I realized that I was staring right at the chest of the new Librarian.

At that moment when you feel the first hot drop of coffee hit your lap, you're likely to be so startled that you reflexively jump and spill quite a bit more, possibly scalding yourself.

And as I was startled to realize that I was staring at her chest, I reflexively jumped and looked at her eyes.

And there was another of those sudden moments of telepathy, when you know that the other person knows that you know what they're thinking, because, as you looked into their eyes, they just suddenly knew what you were thinking, and what I was thinking about were her nipples, which stood out like Hershey's kisses. You would get roughly the same visual effect if you put 2 of those conical foil-wrapped chocolates on top of sunny-side-up fried eggs, then hung them on a girl's chest and loosely draped them with a thin layer of purple cotton. All concealed yet all revealed at the same time.

What I was thinking about were her nipples, and that wasn't good.

I needed to make her think that that wasn't what I was thinking at all.

"Holler," I said, and then it hit me.

Wham!

Ice-tongs aren't used much any more, people simply don't have iceboxes, they have refrigerators. But picture a tool with handles like sheet metal cutters, or big scissors, with big steel hooks instead of scissor blades. Picture them pinching together, designed to bite into a block of ice and hold. Picture those two hooks coming together with enough force to hold a one hundred pound block of ice. Picture those two hooks coming together on a part of your body with enough force to pierce mortal flesh to the bone. Picture that amount of force, that amount of concentrated pressure, coming together fast as a snapping rat-trap on my left shoulder, and me spinning around, off balance, suddenly staring at The Principal's face, staring at that spot between his eyes.

I knew that spot so well, I could still draw it on a moonless night if I had to. That spot where two craggy face lines came down from his forehead, between his eyebrows, but one of them only half way, and at that point they were intersected by a horizontal line, as thick as the other two, and the little clump of coarse hair that grew there in the square formed by the upper portion of the lines, between his eyebrows, like a letter "h", but upside down and backwards.

I knew that spot because it was the only thing that I could look at that would make it seem like I was looking him in the eye, while avoiding looking him in the eye.

"What are you doing, Jones?" His voice, that awful voice that could rip and shred and crumple and crush. It wasn't loud at the moment, but that could change, oh so suddenly. "He said 'holler' when he came in," The Librarian interjected.

"What?"

"Holler," I said. I held up the page I'd written, showed him the red underline, the mark deduction. "I want to find a dictionary that has 'holler' in it."

"Oh, I think this one might be a good place to look," she said, turning away.

The Principal watched The Librarian as she pulled out a big brown dictionary. He didn't say anything, just released his grip and turned and walked away.

"I know it's got to be here somewhere," she said, and said again, and then around the third or fourth reference book, she noticed that a trickle of blood had run down my left arm. It wasn't much, but she insisted that I go to the nurse's office and even walked along with me. To make sure that I didn't just dash out the door and off to the playground, I supposed. By the time I got a Band-Aid on the tiny scratch, recess was over.

It was quite a while, almost a week, before I had reason to venture in the direction of the library again.

Thursday afternoon was arithmetic.

On Friday afternoons our class had current events.

Monday afternoon was art.

And when Tuesday rolled around again we did a "library time" march down the hall from our classroom.

The young Librarian was chatting with one of the mothers who volunteered to help around the school. I slipped past unnoticed and browsed among several of the inter-language dictionaries, then the encyclopedias, looked through the H's, couldn't find the word, tried to find another dictionary. Mickey came over and, snickering, showed me a National Geographic with pictures of bare-

breasted black women in some African village. We spent
the rest of the period looking for more "smut".

As we filed out and went back to class I noticed her name
tag: "Mrs. Acorn". She seemed so young, not much older
than the girls in school.

Older, but not much.

How could she be married?

So young?

Chapter 2
Frosted

During that year, over the winter, I had tried again to learn to skate.

One of my great embarrassments was that, despite being surrounded in winter months with some thirty thousand acres of smooth, clear ice, I had never been able to skate worth a damn. Not for lack of trying, mind. My uncles, my Grandfather, friends, neighbours, everybody and their dog had offered me advice and hand-me-down skates that, they assured me, had worked just fine for them.

I tried, ankles bending like over-cooked spaghetti, and got laughed at, and tried some more. I was persistent, but not fond of ridicule.

I figured that I could probably find some ice somewhere down around Centre or Hanlan's where nobody could witness my clumsy attempts to stay up on the blades. I walked, on one especially frigid day, in street shoes inside bulky galoshes that fastened with metal snap clasps, down the frozen lagoon all the way to Centre Island. It was right around New Years, and a few souls were out strolling over the Manitou Bridge. I kept going under it, down Long Pond, where small groups of people were taking turns skimming around on an iceboat, a triangular wooden contraption with skate blades and an enormous sail.

Long Pond is just about exactly one mile long and, at the Western end of it, I turned left, to the South. Finally satisfied that I was out of sight of anyone, I strapped on my skates and made my wobbly way around Blockhouse Bay, towards Toothpick Island and the Filtration Plant.

I just needed to strengthen my ankles. That's what everyone told me. And practice would do that, I hoped. So I tried, I really tried, as I had done so many times on so many other frosty afternoons.

Two, maybe three hours of lumbering along, pain radiating up my shins, the ache increasing all the way up to my groin, and I was ready to call it quits for another day. I turned toward the bank, surveying the shore for a log or something to sit on to change back into the shoes and galoshes that I had tied together, hanging around my neck.

"Just go over to the shore and take my skates off," that's what I thought.

The ice was so clear and blue that, where the snow had been blown from it by the wind off the Lake, you could see that it was well over a foot thick… in most places. But there was an outflow pipe that came from the Filtration Plant, and I'd forgotten about it. The current from that pipe warmed the water, melting the ice dangerously thin there while wisps of snow on the surface hid any clue from above to the danger.

One moment I was hobbling, sore-footed, toward the shore. And the next I was up to my armpits in the cold, cold lagoon, the thin crust of ice cracking away under my elbows as I tried to keep myself from going under.

I stayed perfectly still.

Ever so slowly, despite my urge to panic, I got myself turned around, facing back the way I had come, and managed to lay my arms out on top of the ice.

Then, by small, incremental degrees, I hauled one inch of my body up onto the still-solid part of the ice, then another, then another, until I was finally able to stand and look back at the hole, finally allowing myself to be terrified at what had almost happened.

But I wasn't home yet.

And the laces of my skates were wet and about to freeze together. I could feel the cold in a way that I never had before, but managed to get my hand into my pocket and pull out the small penknife that I always carried.

There was no time to untie the laces, I ran the sharp little blade down under them and got the skates off and stuffed my feet, wet socks and all, back into my shoes and galoshes. The seat of my wet pants had frozen to the ice in the time that it took me to change and it required a supreme effort to tear them away so I could stand. The penknife fell from my unfeeling fingers, and proved impossible to pick up with hands so numb. I left it there and walked all those miles home with my jeans frozen into denim tubes, hard as concrete.

How I made it I'll never know. Chalk it up to just plain stubbornness. I just would not give up.

I made it home, stripped off and stood in the shower, my fingers and toes burning in the water that was only slightly warm.

I was very lucky that I didn't actually freeze any extremities, I didn't have any frostbite. But I had become awfully sensitive to the cold. I just couldn't seem to fully warm up the whole rest of that winter and on into spring.

Chapter 3
Hercules and the Uptown

Across to the city on the ferry boat, then uptown to Yonge Street.

Simpson's.

Eaton's.

Yonge Street.

A huge movie theatre used to stand at Yonge and Bloor, Leow's Uptown.

Movie houses today are split up into multiplexes, theatres where two or three hundred, maybe even as many as six hundred people can watch a movie at the same time. If the modern multiplex has a blockbuster on their hands, they show it on more screens to accommodate the bigger demand.

So it's kind of hard to describe to someone who's never seen one what it was like to sit in a showplace crammed with more than three thousand rowdy kids at once. There may have been only fifteen hundred seats, or somewhere around that number, I never actually counted them. But on Saturday morning any kid with a quarter could get in from eight until noon to watch old Three Stooges and Roy Rogers shorts, interspersed with cartoons. There was plenty of room in the lobby and extra standing room in the aisles and on the floor in front of the front row of seats. Lots of kids never even went in to watch the movie, just stood around in the lobby, talking, milling about, bumping into each other and trying to be sociable, with all of the good and bad (but mostly good) connotations that you can read into that word.

Yeah, we were loud, and that was okay. There was an occasional fight, but the ushers were plentiful.

And we made physical contact, social contact; met each other.

After the show, outside, thick pedestrian crowds mingled on Yonge Street, elbowing to be somewhere else. Sam the Record Man's, full of shoppers, browsers, kids mostly, looking to pick up the latest forty-fives and albums at bargain prices. The Hercules army surplus store. Hercules was one of this gargantuan store's incarnations. It had gone by many names, and would stay the same, more or less, through many more. They played the bankruptcy game, so I was told. Changed names every few years and bought up the old company's stock at a fraction of the cost and then started selling all over again, but super cheap. So I heard.

They sold war surplus supplies, like drilled-out hand-grenades and old .303 Enfield rifles in big bargain bins. Anyone with eight dollars could buy a bolt-action .303 (with twisted sights and a warped barrel) from the pile; ammunition in aisle 4, next to the crossbows. There was a deep bin of 8-inch stiletto knives. They'd had their springs removed. Without spring loaded push-button action, they weren't switchblades anymore. The blade swung free, though, so you could swing it out and it would lock in place just as fast, but they were legal. We called them flick knives.

Old gas masks and army boots on pallets to the right of the checkout counter.

And behind that, up a wide set of worn wooden steps, over there, between a horse-stall sized rack of oily smelling tents and a ceiling-high stack of heavy rectangular metal boxes all painted army green, behind some heavy dark blue overcoats hung on a rack display that had to be rolled out of the way to get through to them, there was a whole back section on the second floor with piles and piles of bamboo poles. That's what I was looking for!

I got a bit tangled in shelves piled high with parachutes, but managed to leave with five of the most perfect bamboo poles to be found in the city.

I know.

I had looked.

I had looked through Chinatown, through the Kensington market stores and Honest Ed's, even tried Eaton's and Simpson's (though I hadn't really expected to find any there).

Sold as "ten feet and over," their true measures averaging somewhere between eleven and twelve feet long, roughly an inch and a half in diameter at the thick end. I picked out only the ones that were perfectly straight, as green in colour as I could possibly find. No cracks, tiny end splits or flaws of any kind. Hercules sold them as ten feet and over expecting, I supposed, that the purchaser would, like me, re-cut them down to ten in order to have a good, square, freshly sawed end at the bottom. The top didn't matter, so long as it wasn't dried out or splintered. I'd gotten a bamboo splinter off a dried-out brown pole once, and that splinter hurt almost as much going in as it did when Dink pulled it out with a pair of pliers.

Green and smooth, that's what I wanted.

I'd learned from experience that five was the maximum number I could carry. At a length in excess of eleven feet, I couldn't get them down to the ferry dock on any bus, streetcar or subway train. I had to walk all the way down Yonge Street, across to Bay and then down to the docks with the poles on my shoulder, tied together in a bundle.

I could only vault six-nine, but Dink could already sail over a seven-foot crossbar. I knew, if I just caught the hang of it, that I could master this pole-vaulting thing.

So I practiced.

And I broke poles. Four or five impacts with the chock and they'd start to splinter lengthwise back from the tip. Hockey-stick tape around the joints and the tip helped slow that down, but only a little.

So I returned to the Hercules surplus store and bought five more poles, and I practiced.

I broke those poles and went back to Hercules and bought five more, and practiced.

A speech impediment is an embarrassing thing. On top of a stutter, imagine what it's like to not have what is generally considered to be the correct vocal sound for the letter L, and to have one of those in your name, like Lorne. When I first started school I got teased a lot for the way I talked. I beat those speech impediments eventually, but not before my inability to say Lorne had won me the nickname Thor.

As soon as school started in September we got out the old stands and crossbar and dug a little trench and planted the stop-chock. Holding a pole for the first time felt kind of familiar, something I was used to, from smelt fishing. I already knew I could sprint pretty good. On my first attempt, the very first time I tried to pole-vault, somebody, I don't know who it was, hollered, "HEY, LOOK AT THOR VAULT." That got the attention of the whole schoolyard as I sprinted toward the chock, pole wobbling in my hands. And, as I jumped, somebody else hollered "WHO'S THORVAULT?"

I cleared that bar, and got a new nickname.

One day, bringing poles home, I got some help from Fram Ward, who offered to carry the bundle on top of his bicycle, from the ferry dock as far as Fifth Street and Channel Avenue, lengthwise from his seat to the handlebars. As we walked away from the dock he asked how high I was clearing. I told him I'd cleared six-nine. Six-ten, actually, once. But the pole followed me through and knocked the bar off, so that one didn't count. He asked me what got me interested in pole vaulting.

"Back last summer," I told him, "a bunch of us did a 'walking on your hands' competition. Gronk won that hands down, going all the way from the Algonquin Bridge, along Omaha Avenue to Nottawa, up to Seneca, then over to Ojibway and back down to the bridge again. Dink almost

made it the whole way, falling over part way down
Ojibway. I was third... had to quit because of broken glass
in my palm, part way along Seneca.

"So we figured that a guy who could do a good, steady
handstand, and sprint really fast, would probably be pretty
good at pole-vaulting."

"Yeah," Fram said, "you're probably right. Makes sense
to me."

We reached Fifth, where he was turning, and I lifted the
bundle and thanked him for lending a hand.

As I hefted the long, tied bundle of poles to my shoulder,
Fram paused before getting on his bike and said, "You
know, I remember, we used to have pole vault in school,
too."

I nodded from under my load.

"Yeah, and the fellows who were doing the best were
making the pole bend, kind of like a spring, to throw them
higher."

I thanked him again for his help and continued down
Channel while he headed along Fifth toward Lakeshore.

With my arm raised like that to hold the bundle, the wind
found an opportunity to slide icy fingers up under my
jacket, all the way to my right armpit, my whole right side
slowly turning numb. I quickened my step and shifted the
bundle to my left shoulder, exposing vulnerable flesh on
that side.

I carried them past the back door, went on around the
corner of the house and laid the bundle on top of the frame
that held the fuel-oil tank. As I came in the back door,
Barry stuck his head up above the counter that divided the
living room from the kitchen and greeted me with, "Hey
Thorvault! Dinner's ready, wash up."

Chapter 4
Pool Night In Canada

Hockey came on after dinner, and I didn't have any cash left. I didn't have much time.

The game was going to start at 8:00.

It was already 6:47.

I didn't have any cash left, but I had five sheets of writing paper. My dilemma: do my homework or make two dollars and fifty cents?

My books went on my bed, the chicken casserole that Flo had been cooking for hours from "an old family recipe", went down my throat, and I was out with the scissors, a pen, and out the door with a basket and fifty slips of paper, each numbered by hand: 1, 2, 3, 4, 5, 6, 7, 8, 9, 0.

Knock on Mr. Search's door.

"Hockey pool tonight, 25 cents each."

"Same payoff?"

"That's right."

Then show him ten slips of paper in the basket, each with a number. One full draw of numbers.

Allow me to explain the game.

If you pay me 25 cents, you can draw one of the slips from the basket. Whatever number you draw is your number on the final score of the game.

Example:

Final score is 1-0, add them and you get 1. You win if you have a "1"

Final score is 2-0 or 1-1, add them and you get 2. You win if you have drawn a "2"

Final score is 3-0, 3 -1 or 3-2, add them and you get 3, 4 or 5. You win if you have that number.

On up to something that totals 10, like a 5-5 tie or 7-3 or 6-4, Then 0 wins (0 also wins if the game ends in a scoreless tie). And after that, 5-6 would total 11, drop the first number and 1 wins. Only the last number counts. So for a total score of 18, the last number, 8, counts.

And if you are holding one of those five slips of paper that I wrote an "8" on this evening, you know that I am going to be at your door with 2 dollars in my hand within minutes of the end of the game.

Period.

If you buy a ticket, I write your name and the number you've drawn into my little notebook and move on to the next door.

Tickets are twenty-five cents each and there are ten of them in each draw. I pay out two dollars on every draw.

You and I both know that I made 50 cents on the deal, and that's okay. I walked up and down the street, knocking on doors, and put the deal together, making wages from wagers. With a total of 10 numbers sold in each of 5 draws, and $2.50 profit for me.

I had a sufficient set of sales on First, Second, and part of Third to sell 10 tickets, one full draw.

Move on up Third and Fourth and sell 10 more, another draw.

Keep going up Fifth and over Lakeshore, back down and across to Bayview and back up Sixth.

A good night, five draws sold, going fast, and then back home by the start of the game.

Hard to do homework on a night when the smallest man in the league has been called a bunch of foul things by a sports-writing blowhard who says that Dave Keon has no business playing in a big man's game. Shouldn't be allowed to waste space on the bench unless the Leafs would rather forego a Stanley Cup in favour of just another Lady Byng.

And the names of all the capitals of the Southern hemisphere had to be correctly identified on the map in today's homework assignment, due tomorrow.

There is also the weekly homework that we were assigned on Monday, but that's not due until Friday and can wait.

"Faster Foster" and "Faster Foster's Father" have wrapped up the pre-game banter.

And "The Game" begins.

And just the way his father, Foster, had done before him, Bill Hewet has

just

become

the

only

voice

I

can

hear

on

the

face

of

this

planet.

And Barry smokes Rothmans and Flo, DuMaurier.

And I brazenly reach for the pack, tap the bottom hard with a snap of my thumb and one pops up and does a full flip in the air, and I catch it with my lips, filter end out. And Barry laughs and I spit the brown tobacco out, sheepishly turn it the right way around and, before I can light up, Red Kelly gets stripped of the puck and Montreal scores.

Montreal.

The dreaded Habs.

Number one in the standings and snotty about their lead, confident that second place Toronto will finish the season behind them, second rate.

And the traitorous officials seem to be out to get the Toronto good guys too, calling a very questionable Leaf penalty.

Keon had been under attack before, in the press, and, somewhere around the middle of the season last year, Dave Keon had put on a clinic, shown them how it should be done.

The Leafs had a penalty, penalty killers went on the ice. Leafs won the draw.

Puck went over to Keon.

He skated back of his own net.

Bower looked back at him.

Keon skated up, carried it out over the line. Took the puck deep into the other zone, spun around and came back again, right through all the traffic going the other way. Short-handed, Keon owned that puck. Nobody could take it away from him. He skated back and forth, this way and that, up over the line, back into Leaf territory. Around and up to centre ice. Back down the ice into the Leafs zone again, around his own net, back up again.

Always controlled the puck.

Never passed. Never had the puck taken away from him. For two full minutes!

Dipsy-doodled around everyone on the ice and killed that penalty off single-handed!

Couldn't be touched!

At that moment, last year, when he skated off the ice ending a long two-minute shift, the crowd at the Gardens exploded to their feet in mighty cheers. Fans went wild everywhere that hockey was seen that night.

Non-Leafs fans cheered.

People who didn't even like hockey cheered.

I don't remember the final score of that game, but I'll always remember that moment, and from then on I was sure that nobody would ever question whether Davey

Keon, smallest man in the league, had a right to be in the NHL.

But that was last year.

And here, now, coming down to the end of the season, some sports-writing nitwit has done it again, has said that the only logical reason the Leafs could have in keeping him on the team would be that they'd rather win another Lady Byng than the Stanley Cup! Keon was going to show them! I just knew it!

Montreal was ahead by seven points in the standings and off to a 1 - 0 lead, with Johnny Bower and Eddy Shack on the injured list. Don Simmons looking shaky in goal in that first minute, and Dave Keon had the puck.

Bobbing, weaving. Was he going to do it again? Single handedly kill off another penalty?

But there is a tactic in the game of hockey that is even more spectacular than single-handedly controlling the puck for two minutes.

That tactic is:

Leafs short handed and Keon gets a breakaway, blows past Bernie (Boom-Boom) Geoffreon, swoops down from the right wing, across the Montreal goal, Jacques Plante stays with him... stays with him... and, just when it seems that he's left it too late, Keon flips the puck up over the sprawling Plante and scores! Short handed!

The Leafs dominated the Habs the rest of the night, final score a convincing 5 – 2.

So the final score was 5 to 2, the total was 7, and there were 5 number 7 winning tickets out there. I had a list of the winners, and needed to go back out into the night and, at 5 different doors, deliver 2 dollars each.

But, though the game was over, Carl Brewer shoved Jean Beliveau in the face. I kept one eye on the screen as I got my jacket on, then finally tore my eyes away from the TV, forcing myself out the door.

Ten bucks paid out and back home in less than a half-hour, not needing to ask at each stop along the way how the fight was going. Every nuance of the game had been audible through all the neighbourhood while it was on, and now the post-game antics were just as plainly heard emanating from houses all up and down the streets. The same coordinated blue flicker radiated from all living rooms as one.

I had made $2.50 to pack with me to school tomorrow.

Tired and cold, I half-heartedly tried to remember which city went where on the maps of South America, Australia and Africa before I crawled under the covers and rubbed my legs and arms trying to get warm enough to drift off to sleep.

Chapter 5
Mandrake

Once the ice in the Bay thawed sufficiently, the unpredictability of the commuting schedule went with it and the big fat ferryboats went back into service.

The gangplank came down, people walked off, the way was clear, we were waved on and I trotted down the starboard (right) side of the wooden-walled passenger seating area, around the bow and down the port side, meeting the crowd of people who were still getting on, made my way around the corner and up the stairs to the second deck, around the bench seats, and back down the other set of stairs toward the bow.

Inventory: several Globe and Mail, two Star, and two sections of the Telegram. I headed quickly down the Port side and slid into the seat right beside the incomplete Telegram. Among all the folks filling up the boat, a girl sat down at the same time on the other side of the paper. Just another passenger I thought without looking up. As I put out my hand toward those two sections of the Telegram she did likewise, and we did one of those weird "deja-vu" kind of things as we instantly and simultaneously recognized each other as well as our intent.

"I'm sorry, go ahead Mrs. Acorn," I said.

"Oh, no. No. If you want it go ahea..." she almost replied.

"You going to read that?" Bill Stevenson asked, reaching for the paper. He was being jostled from behind. Looked like it was going to be a pretty full ride.

"Um, Yeah, yeah..." we both stammered in unison. She pulled one section away and I the other as Bill took the seat between us.

I thumbed through the section I had, feigning interest. The ferry whistled off and we departed Wards. Less than a minute out she made a barely perceptible course change. "Hmmm..." I thought, "not going to be a straight run..."

This wasn't the 4:40 regular, it was a schedule addition. A 4:30 or something. I didn't remember the marquee in the front of the boat saying: Ward's/Centre. Did it say Ward's/Centre? I couldn't recall.

But we certainly weren't going straight to the city.

I thought this ferry seemed early, but didn't have a watch to be sure. Oh well, add fifteen minutes for the extra time to get to Centre before the city and I'd still be getting to town at five. Same thing, almost.

I dozed, then felt the syncopated "THUMP-thump" of the boat as she nosed into the dock. Vaguely felt the surge of bodies as the moving crowd of, who knows? Twenty? Forty? Fifty or more passengers disembarked. Port and Starboard had just switched sides. Maybe somewhere in the middle of the boarding process I sensed that more than a hundred were getting on, felt the calm mob-serge form into a standing blob of sandwiched-in humanity.

It felt warm. Good to be warm. Pressed among so many warm bodies, steam heating under the smoothly curved wooden bench seats, heat rising up my back.

A thought occurred.

I found a pen in my pocket and scribbled in a margin of the Telegram: "Oh, the humidity!" I thought of the dirigible "Hindenburgh" going up in flames and the voice of the radio announcer, proclaiming on the loss of life with that same inflection, that same delivery, when he uttered that now-famous wailing line: "Oh! The humanity!"

But what if?

What if that man had made a slip of the tongue? I started to chuckle. What if he'd actually said: "Oh, the humidity!" instead of: "Oh, the humanity!"

I dozed.

I dreamt of gentle THUMP-thumps in the night, cradled in the swaying rhythms of the engines.

I dozed.

I felt the THUMP-thump of the city dock. No need to get up yet, it was going to be a few minutes before all of these people disembarked.

I waited.

And dozed.

The crowd in front of me steadily thinned as folks exited over the gangplank.

Finally, groggily, I got to my feet and started off to the right, to the exit. But everyone else was going left. What was going on?

I quietly panicked. What time was it? I didn't have a watch on. I ran the numbers in my head while trying to get through the thick crowd of passengers who had left the boat before me.

If this boat had been out of Wards at, say, 4:35...

Then we had done 4:50 at Centre, plus a, let's see, 5:05 from Hanlan's, which meant that it might probably be somewhere around...

I spotted Bill Stevenson.

"Hey Bill, you got the time?"

He took a quick glance at his wrist watch and hollered back, "HALF PAST FIVE," trying hard be heard above a scratchy announcement coming over the public address system, telling people on the other side of the chain-link fence that separated those getting on from those coming off the ferries that a boat for Centre was now boarding.

Damn! I was going to be late.

I saw a Bay streetcar just leaving across the street in the loop. It looked like I was going to have to hike up to Union Station if I wanted to make up any time at all. But if I did that, and another car came down to the loop, I'd be between stops and wouldn't be able to get on.

What to do? What to do?

I had to hike across to the loop anyway so, keeping an eye out for signs of any more streetcars coming down through the underpass, I dashed past Mike's Diner and was trying to cross the busy lanes of Queens Quay without becoming road kill when I thought I heard the squeal of steel wheels coming from the underpass. I veered to the left, towards the streetcar stop with its small wrought-iron TTC shelter, got across several lanes of blacktop and joined about a dozen folks waiting there for the next car.

"Well, hello again,' Mrs. Acorn said, then added: "this certainly is Kismet."

I didn't know the word.

Wham!

There it was. Another one of those sudden moments of telepathy, when you know that the other person knows that you know what they're thinking. And she knew I didn't know the word, Kismet.

A fat banana-coloured streetcar slid out of the underpass, around the corner and into the loop, swiftly squealing around to the stop in front of us. The doors opened and people got off. We got on and, somehow, the question was still hanging over us, un-answered. I felt like saying: Okay, I don't know that word, Kismet. Would you like to explain it to me? But the moment hadn't yet ended, because she already knew that I thought of asking that, and I knew, the same way, that she felt like slipping into school-mode and explaining it to me. After all, it was obvious that I wasn't familiar with the word, it wasn't part of my vocabulary. And she looked at me with those giant eyes, eyes that could see more than her tiny frame could digest, and I knew what had to be said.

And so did she.

In unison we spoke a single word: "vocabulary."

And we broke out laughing.

I mean, what else can you do when something like that happens? Other passengers stared at us but we didn't care. And then, just like that, the telepathy was gone. And that was okay. The streetcar started to move, carrying us back up into the underpass. I stood up. On the other side of the underpass, at Union Station, if I ran really fast along Front Street, and if... Oh... if..if..if..if..if there was a subway train just about to leave waiting down there, I might still make it.

As the streetcar came to a stop, just before the doors opened, a thought occurred. "Um, did you want to read this?" I asked, holding out the part of the Telegram that I still carried.

"Oh, no, I..." she looked at the crumpled section, "...well, maybe. Yeah."

I handed it over and made a motion to the section of newspaper she still held. The doors opened. She made the trade and I dashed off, across Bay Street and down the stairs, through the turnstile and down more stairs, across the platform and just, and I mean *just*, through the doors before they could close.

It was a fairly empty subway car, lots of vacant seats. I had time enough to read a bit before my stop. I unfolded the paper and found the object of my quest: The Comic Section! At last I held it in my hands! And...

And...

Something was definitely wrong here!

Mandrake the magician was missing!

Cut out!

What had happened to him?

I read the rest of the funnies with a heavy heart, knowing that not even the Katzenjammer kids could have made me chuckle that day.

Chapter 6
Windows

Our seats faced North, and the windows of our class looked out to the West, into the girl's playground. I sat at my desk on the far left side of the room, fourth from the front, next to the window. The playground was totally deserted, of course, during class time, except for a few errant leaves tossed about and occasionally lifted from the pavement by mini-cyclone breezes. A chain link fence defined the far side of the playing area, and beyond that a thickly wooded tangle of poplar saplings that everyone thought was haunted. The play surface stretched North from where I sat staring out through the window. It was walled on its East side by our class, the next class, and then the library. There the building went left, to the West. Along that North wall of the girl's playground were the windows of the Island Natural Science School.

The Island population had been diminishing for decades as the Parks Department, at the vindictive direction of Tommy Thompson, expropriated and bulldozed the Islander's houses. At some point in time some bright mind with the school board had come up with a plan to save the school. Part of it was turned into a learning centre for rudimentary natural science studies, and every grade six class in the city came for a week to tromp around in rubber boots through marsh and grass, collecting bugs and pond creatures to examine under microscopes. For a week. Every grade six class in the city. One week each. They ate in the school cafeteria which, if I turned around in my seat, I could see behind me as it formed the South wall of the girl's playground.

And they slept in the dormitories.

Every grade six class in the city.

Except ours.

We already lived on the Island, so we didn't get to eat in the cafeteria or sleep in the dormitories. When it was our turn, when it came time for our grade six class to spend a week attending the Island Natural Science School, we had to bring our own lunches and go home on the school bus each night, same as usual. We had regular Natural Science classes during the day, but we didn't get to sleep in the dormitories, didn't get to have late night hot chocolate sessions with ghost stories or a pre-breakfast hike to the shore to watch the sun come up.

I felt cheated.

From my seat, facing forward, in through the high windows in front of me to my left, I could just see the ceiling and upper portion of the girl's dormitory.

One time, back in the fall, I caught sight of a girl standing up on top of one of the top bunks. Just for a moment. A girl standing on a bunk. Visible only from the waist up, through those high windows, in her bra! Just for a moment!

But from that moment on nothing The Teacher ever said or did at the front of the class gained my full and undivided attention. Whatever was being written on the board, whatever I was supposed to be writing in my work book, no matter how hard I tried to concentrate on the lesson at hand, my gaze was constantly drawn, as surely as the needle on a compass, back to that magnetic set of high dormitory windows. Just in case.

On Tuesday in the afternoon, before recess, we usually had French. After recess, our class was scheduled to make our "library time" march down the hall from our classroom.

But this one particular Tuesday, when we came back in after recess, The Teacher announced that we'd be doing something different. The Librarian, Mrs. Acorn, was going to come in and read us some poetry.

Any change from the monotony of an ordinary day was a welcome relief, squirming and murmuring ceased, eyes on the door, as Mrs. Acorn walked in, up to The Teacher's desk. Navy blue corduroy jumper over a full-sleeved deep purple blouse, very demure.

She thanked him and turned and scanned across our collective faces, and I thought she was going to hurl or something. She quickly swallowed, though, looked down to the book held open in her hands and then back up again, then spoke.

Her first syllable caught in her throat, but she only stuttered that once that I've ever heard.

"Goo - gUhf! - good afternoon everyone."

I heard a noise behind me to my right, but The Teacher was still standing beside her. I didn't want to get punished for turning in my seat. I stared unblinking at her huge, wide eyes.

She looked down at the book again, "I have come here to tell you about," she closed the book and looked at its spine, "... the Dewey Decimal System."

And tell us about the Dewey Decimal System she did.

She stacked an imaginary set of books on an imaginary set of book shelves at the front of the class, explaining how each section of the shelves could be labeled with a number, which would represent a topic. She explained that all the topics of everything that had ever been published, or ever would be published, could be placed into its appropriate Dewey Decimal System category and then later looked up and found with ease. The Teacher had slipped out of the front door and she was alone now at the front of the class.

We moved around a lot during my earlier grade school years, and every school I ever attended had a Mickey-like character. Everywhere there was someone sort of like him. Mickey was the guy who "knew stuff."

There was always a kid in every school who knew everything about sex. You've heard adults talk about how kids should get proper sex education in school instead of hearing about it in the schoolyard? Well, Mickey was the guy that kids heard about it from in the Island schoolyard.

He had the coolest of everything: tan shoes, suede collar. He could explain any dirty word, all dirty or racist jokes. He could completely hide a cigarette in the shock of bushy hair above his ear, and often did.

This particular Tuesday, at lunch, he had shown me a pocket-sized "Art" book (photographs of naked models in classic poses with all nipples and pubic hair air-brushed away) wrapped in the fold of a CHUM Radio Chart.

And Mickey raised his hand.

Mrs. Acorn looked startled. Like she wasn't sure what to do.

"Yes?" she asked.

He stood and said, "I thought you were going to talk about poetry?"

"Oh, are you interested in poetry?" she asked enthusiastically.

"Kind of..." he said, half sinking back into his seat.

"Well, if you'd like..."

"Mickey wrote a poem," one of the Snoopies said, pointing her pencil at his desk. "Why don't you ask him to read it for you."

There was a phony sound of jealous attack in her voice. Mickey got along too well with all the Snoopies for it to be real. This could get entertaining, I thought, noticing in my peripheral vision to the left a flicker of shadow on the ceiling of the girl's dorm across the playground.

"Yeah, read it..." "Read it Mickey..." was beginning to become a scattered request from several voices in the room.

"Well, If you wrote it, then I suppose it would be okay. Go ahead, Mickey, read your poem to us, please."

We applauded faint-heartedly as he got to his feet. This was too easy.

He glanced a smile at the Snoopy girl to his left and then back to Mrs. Acorn, confidently lifted the page, took a deep breath, one great inhalation, and rattled off:

"There once was a man from Nantucket..." and we gasped just long enough for the potential to hit. Then, so quickly that he couldn't be stopped: "Who brought home a trout in a bucket." He went on with: "His wife said: This fish will make a fine dish..." Then, with perfect timing, "But there's a hole in the bucket... so chuck it!"

We roared! Mickey bowed deeply and quickly to the front of the class, then to the side, then to the back, and the laughter stopped.

Instantly.

The Principal rose from a seat at the back of the room and The Teacher rose from his seat beside him. The Principal strode quickly out of the room through the back door as The Teacher hurried to take his place at the front of the class.

Mickey was informed that he had an "appointment" in The Principal's office as soon as the bell rang (I suspected that he was going to get the strap) and The Principal wanted to see Mrs. Acorn right away. She hurried out, the doors were closed and we got punished with an extra French assignment. Back to memorizing: "Mon, Ma, Mes, Ton, Ta, Tes, Son, Sa, Ses..." until the bell.

Chapter 7
Gwendolyn

"Gwendolyn," The Librarian said, "you can call me Gwendolyn."

"Okay, Mrs. Acorn," I said, not even thinking about it.

The Sam McBride was pulling away from the city-side dock and there were only a handful of passengers on board.

"I found that word, Holler, in one of my own books. I've got it at home, and I could bring it in to school tomorrow. Would you like to see it?"

Would I? The chance to regain my mark? To prove the Teacher wrong? Oh yeah, I wanted to march up and rub that book right into his face!

"The book I found it in lists it as a Southern bastardization of the word Hollow. It comes from the origin of people shouting across a valley, a hollow, to each other. From that the mispronunciation split, so that you have the 'holler', which is a noun, the hollow that they yell across, as well as the verb, to holler: the act of calling loudly, hollering. That's the second meaning."

I hadn't heard a thing after she said "bastardization". I was floored the school librarian could swear that way and make it sound like it was just an ordinary word, not a swear-word at all.

"Where did you pick it up?"

"Pick what up?"

"The word, Holler?"

"Oh, I don't know. I guess I've always just sort of known it."

"Have you ever been to the Deep South?"

"I've been to Florida. That's not really the Deep South though, is it?"

"Well, yes, it's pretty far down there."

"But people don't talk with that funny "Sow-thurn draw-well" there. Not the ones I met, anyway, except for some of the black folks."

"Did you know many blacks there?" There was something about her eyes, their largeness and their tranquility, like the surface of calm lagoons, perfectly reflecting me back at myself. She radiated a warm, comfortable calmness.

"Only two really well. There was a kid, Jummy, who was my age. We used to fish and throw stones into the swamp water and catch chameleons together and stuff like that. And there was one old black man..." I trailed off as the ferry whistle blew.

"What is it. Was there something wrong?"

"Hmm? Oh, no, no. I was just listening to the whistle blow. That note, that sound. I've tried to play it but just can't quite get it right."

"Play it? You play an instrument?"

"Yeah, harmonica, but I don't have one with me. When we lived in Florida, where we lived, it was in this place that had a whole bunch of houses that were all owned by a company. It was kind of like a motel, but instead of the cottages being all in a row, they were, like, all these houses with no fences around them, just lawns in between. A Motor Lodge, they called it.

"And this old black man would go around all day long on this ride-on lawnmower cutting the grass. When he'd stop for lunch he'd rest under a tree, and after he'd eaten he'd pull out a harmonica and play for a half-hour or so before he went back to work.

"My Uncle Barry bought two harmonicas, somewhere around North Carolina, on the long car ride on our way down there, one for himself and one for me. The rest of that trip we both tried to play along with every song that came on the radio. I got pretty good at 'Sixteen Tons' and 'Ain't A Gonna Need This House No Longer.'

"So anyway, me being a little kid and all, I carried my harmonica over to this old black man sitting in the shade of a palmetto tree and told him that I played harmonica too. Then I played him what I knew. I put my fingers on the holes to block the notes I didn't want to play. I played like that, moving my fingers back and forth along the sound holes, sucking and blowing with a bunch of bad notes and pauses and re-starts, and then asked him if he could teach me the song he was playing."

Gwendolyn made it so easy to look into her eyes and just talk on and on.

"He showed me how to tongue block, how to spread my tongue wide to play high and low notes together at the same time, and got me to learn all the notes to 'Way Down Upon The Swannee River', but he called it 'Way Down Upon Suwannee River'.

"I thought he played it way better than the Al Jolson recording I heard on the Radio. There was something more about the way he played, the way he made the notes sound. I asked him to teach me how to play like that, how to get that sound out of the harmonica.

'Kid,' he said, 'Ah cain't tech you dat. But ah kin tell you how you kin lun it. You save up yo own money and buy yousef a bran new harMONica.' He pronounced it that way, with a heavy MON sound in the middle.

'...buy yousef a bran new harMONica. An you put it in yo pocket. An don't play it! An you wait. Sumpin's gonna happen, like you'll hurt yo toe, or yo dog's gonna die, or your momma's gonna spank you. And you gonna want to cry. Don't!

'Don't you let yosef cry!

'You holds it back, hold in dem tears, and you go off somewheres all by yosef, somewhere where you know dere's lotsa echo, like in a stairwell or unner a bridge.

'Then you take out that harMONica and you play, and you cry. You let that cryin' out then, and you lurn how it feel, how it sound, to be cryin wit your harmonica.

'You lurns how to cry fust, then you lurns how to laugh, just like you done wit yo talkin voice when you was a baby.

'And after you lurn that, you lurns to sing, wit yo harMONica, and then you lurn to talk.'

"And that's how you play harmonica?" she asked me.

"Aw, I'm not that good. But I do like to sit up on the upper deck when there's no-one around on the boat and play. That sound, though, the sound of the ferry whistle blowing, that's something I'd like to catch. I'd really like to be able to play that."

"Why?"

I was surprised by the question.

Why do anything? I wondered.

"Well, because it's something I think I should be able to do, to make that sound. I mean, I can hear it, so why not..." I trailed off. "Like, um, something that I've tried, and it should be easy, I think, but it isn't. If it was easy, I'd probably get bored."

She thought for a moment. The sound of the engines dropped from a churning rumble to a quiet murmur. We were approaching the dock.

"Then you should probably keep trying," she said, getting up from the bench and starting to hoist several Loblaw's shopping bags.

I offered to help and carried two of the bags toward the bow as the fat old ferry boat turned to starboard and the engines rumbled louder, in reverse now, slowing our entrance into the slip.

As we came within fifteen feet of the end of the slip we both sat again, bracing ourselves. The engines picked up the pace, throwing a big plume of water forward, forcing the boat to slow further until she touched her nose to the dock ever so gently. The engines ceased their labour and the Sam McBride slowly rode up and down in her own wake, her bow bobbing less than an inch from the steel lip of the dock.

The bow crew looped massive hawsers over the bollards on the dock and secured the ship in place. The gangway was lowered and we joined the small group of islanders walking off, passing those patiently waiting their turn to get on board for the 15-minute ride back to the city.

"So you think I should keep trying to play that sound of the ferry whistle just because it's hard to do?"

"Not everything that's hard to do is worth trying," she said, a mix of seriousness and a bit of a mischievous smile crossing her face. "I mean, you could try to become a great boxer, or hockey player, or mountain climber. Those are hard to do. But if it's not something that you need to do, for your self, then just doing them because they're hard is kind of dumb."

"But what if I want to be a great boxer?"

"You'll know, inside, whether it's something you need to do or whether it's something you just want to do."

"Huh? I don't get it."

"Inside. It's like, when the man who taught you to play harmonica told you to go somewhere that you could be alone to play, he meant to go inside yourself."

"Naw, he told me to go somewhere that there's lots of echo."

"And what echoes louder than an empty space. That place inside yourself where you can withdraw to and just be. That's it, to just *be*, you have to turn inward."

We walked on in silence, up Channel Avenue, past Fourth and Third. There was something cold inside one of the paper grocery bags and the condensation from it was making the bag soggy. I was getting worried that it might fall apart in my arms.

"I hope this isn't taking you out of your way," she asked.

"Naw, I live right here," I replied as we turned the corner of Second. I nodded my head to the left, the cottage at the corner, 3 Channel, corner of Second and Channel.

"Oh, I'm right up the street, number 10 Second, a couple of doors up on the right."

"I think you'd better get this one into the fridge quickly," I said, pointing out the wet corner of the bag.

I started to walk a little faster and she also quickened her pace. In a few seconds we were at her door and she fumbled her keys out and opened it. I handed off the bags and she was gone behind a brass number 10 on a closed red door.

Chapter 8
Beauty and the Beasts

There were two playgrounds, East side of the school for
Boys, West side for girls. When the recess bell rang we
bounced up out of our hard wooden seats and filed out of
the classroom, turning right and down the hall, then boys
off to the East, girls to the West, out into our respective
playgrounds. I supposed that the girls skipped and played
hopscotch and whatever else girls did for exercise.

In the boy's yard, a hard concrete surface enclosed on 3
sides by the school building, we played catch with soft
rubber balls. And tag. And we played marbles in a chalk
circle, and threw chewing-gum package cards against the
wall. Sometimes four or five guys would join together in a
line and cross the playground like robots, swinging their
fists down like windmills, chanting, "We don't stop for nobody!" Four, five or six abreast, a straight line of them,
arms flailing like a thrashing machine, and woe be to
anyone who stood in their way.

One day somebody tried. Hobie stood his ground,
wouldn't budge, and one of the Fitzgerald brothers, in
formation with five other kids, walked slowly up, arms
spinning, fist clenched, and brought his swing arm down
and struck. Hobie punched him back, and the fight was on.

In a short time they were both hauled away to The
Principal's office, and they probably both got the strap.

We all figured that it wasn't so much that they had done
anything wrong, but because the Principal enjoyed giving
the strap to kids. I mean, really, *really* enjoyed it. There
was the grade three girl who got the strap five times on
each hand for peeing in class. She'd been waving her hand
desperately to be excused to go to the bathroom, but her
Teacher refused to acknowledge her need until it was too
late. I'd gotten the strap, ten on each hand, for farting in

class. I don't know how I was supposed to handle that, but somehow I'd done it wrong, and off to the office I went. Two or three times a week, somebody was marched off to the office and strapped, and we knew that there wasn't any good reason for most of these punishments, The Principal just had some deep need of his own, and we somehow satisfied a part of it.

The paved portion of the boy's playground was enclosed on the East side by a high chain-link gate that was locked at night but open during the day. We were allowed to go out, during recess and lunch, onto the sandy triangle area that was defined by the Filtration plant and Lakeshore Avenue on the North, the school behind us to the West, and a row of tall poplar trees that lined Lake Ontario to the South.

Out there, with the sand and a pile of old gym mats to break our fall, the older boys practiced pole-vaulting and high-jump, hundred yard dash and a host of other track and field sports, getting ready for the big competition between schools that would be coming up in May.

There was a lot of cheering and encouragement, and the highest compliment for doing something really well, like getting over the crossbar nice and clean and setting a new "personal best" height record, the single greatest thing you could say about someone's achievement, was "Beauty!" With a heavy emphasis on that middle "oo" sound. Run a hundred yard dash in twelve seconds?

"Hey! Bea-oo-ty, eh?"

Fun as it was, I knocked off early, with 2 minutes still left in the recess period, dashed up to the door to the right of the playground, the one my class was not supposed to use to re-enter the school. One of The Teachers was there in the doorway, looking at the clock on the wall, big brass bell in her hand, getting ready to go out and start ringing to call us all back in.

She looked up, surprised to see me coming, and stepped in front of the door to prevent me from going in early.

"Bathroom?" she asked.

"No, library."

She stepped aside and let me pass into the nearly empty building, down the hall to the left, left again and then a right into the library.

Mrs. Acorn wasn't there. But one of the parent volunteers was in attendance at the librarian's desk, Mrs. Perdue. The Island guys used the word "beauty" to describe things that were achievements of great athletic prowess. Mrs. Perdue had that other kind of beauty. Tall, elegant, with the self-assured grace that you might expect of a movie star or royalty. A Doris Day, Elizabeth Taylor, Grace Kelly sort of beauty.

"Can I help you?"

"Um, I'm looking for Mrs. Acorn."

"I'm afraid she's in a meeting right now. Perhaps I can... Oh, wait you're Lorne, aren't you? She left a book here for you. Now, where is it?" Mrs. Perdue rummaged around under the desk for a few seconds, then came up with a battered old book with a torn spine, full of various irregular bits of paper here and there between the pages. "She asked me to ask you not to lose any of her place markers."

I thanked her and hurried back to class as the bell rang.

I stood at the side of The Teacher's desk, while everyone else took their seats, and showed him the page, my finger pointing at the word, "holler".

"It doesn't make any difference," he said, trying to gain control of the class so he could get back to the lesson at hand.

"But it's there!" I protested. "It really is a word!"

"Look," he said, exasperated, and pulled out his big book of student marks. "Here, your final mark on that assignment was a C. you had 7 spelling errors. I change that to a mark of 6 errors, and..." He ran his finger across to the grading scale. A+ for no errors. A for 1 or 2, B for 3 to 5, C for 6 to 8. He took out his pen and changed the 7 to a 6. I still got a C.

"Satisfied?" he asked. "Can we please get back to work now?"

There was nothing left to do. I carried the book back to my desk and dropped heavily into my seat.

I learned the meaning of another expression that day: "hollow victory".

Wham!

There it was.

Felt like the Principal's pinch in my shoulder, but in my gut.

"Ah, poor Thorvault," I heard Tiny snicker.

The way Tiny said "Thor-vault" had a lot more cutting dig to it than I could ever fully describe on this page. Funny thing, that you could put more meaning into saying someone's nickname a certain way than you could by using their proper name.

Nicknames just sort of caught like a firecracker going off or a bit of static electricity when you walk across a rug and then touch a doorknob. Just suddenly, Zap! And there it was.

I was watching a baseball game at Ward's one hot afternoon, Willy Wilson at bat, and Randy Scott-wood yelled out from the bleachers, "Come on, hit it Dooly!"

And that nickname stuck.

I asked Randy later, and he hadn't a clue, it just popped into his head as he was saying it. Didn't know where the idea came from.

There was Dooly, Chisel, Starchy, Hobie, Weasel, and Gronk. A whole host more, including Boy, Peno, Tiny, Dink, and me: Thorvault.

The nicknames had no rhyme or reason and couldn't be chosen. Or shaken. No matter how hard some guys tried, they just didn't end up with a nickname. And, no matter

how hard you wanted to shake it, you couldn't lose your
nickname either. And, though most of them were short,
they didn't have to be. A generation later there was
Michael-Michael-Motorcycle. To the best of my
knowledge, that one never did get shortened down to
anything else.

There were a few girls with nicknames, but for some
reason they were never complimentary. Two that I recall
were Sea-Hag and Bucket. Then there were the Snoopies, a
bunch of girls who just had to know everybody's business.
But you couldn't let them overhear you calling them that or
you'd be spitting out teeth.

I don't know why the nicknames for girls were so cruel,
but I have my suspicions. I think it might be because the
Island guys thought that Island girls were cruel beyond the
norm.

The population of the Island was small, and getting
smaller, what with all the houses on Hanlan's and Centre
having been torn down, and those few of us who were left
all knew each other. Island girls didn't think of the Island
boys as attractive at all in the possibility-of-dating sense.
They knew us far too well for that. We were more like their
brothers, boys who were just irritating, crude, barbaric
beasts.

Years later my wife, looking through some old school
photos with me, laughed at one of the pictures I had taken
of the guys in our class and said, "What a bunch of horny
creeps!"

She meant it in a humorous way, but in truth that's how
Island girls saw Island boys back then. There were a few of
us who grew beyond that barrier in later years, when we
matured and became more like reasoning adults. But back
then, trying to get too friendly with an Island girl was a
sure way to get slapped down, at least verbally.

I remember an Island dance at the AIA Hall a few years
later, girls sitting on the one side of the dance floor, boys

on the other. I mustered all the courage I had in me and strolled across and asked Michelle Finney if she'd care to dance.

Michelle Finney wasn't really an Island girl. She was an actress, same age as us, who starred in a TV show opposite a puppet named Howard The Turtle. She was trying hard to fit in, to be part of the community, and, in response to my invitation to dance, looked up from her seated position, eyed me slowly from head to toe and curled her lip in a sneer. Then, without even responding, went back to chatting with the other girls. As an actress she'd learned the Island girl's reaction to an Island boy exceedingly well. She was already known as "Mitch the Bitch." I suspect that that nickname outlasted her celebrity. But she was cute to look at, and could instantly turn into the most charming and attractive girl around if she knew there was a camera on her.

Michelle Finney was cute, and Mrs. Perdue was beautiful, but Mrs. Acorn was sort of funny looking, like she still had a lot of growing to do, as if her face hadn't grown fast enough to keep up with her eyes.

I've done some things instantly and intuitively in my life, things that, if I'd thought about them for even a split second, would have turned out quite differently. Sometimes those impetuous decisions have been for the better, more often they've made things worse, and I've tried to control those impulses, tried to get that knee-jerk reaction under control.

I have only occasionally succeeded.

Out in the school yard, during lunch break, after finishing my cheese sandwich and thermos of cream of mushroom soup, playing catch with a red and blue rubber ball in a circle with some guys, Dink asked me what that was all about, that thing with the book after morning recess. So I told him about trying to find the word holler in a dictionary, and that Mrs. Acorn had brought one of her dictionaries from home for me to show The Teacher.

"You mean the new Librarian?'

And somebody else said "Toady Face?"

Like I said, I've done some things instantly and intuitively in my life, things that, if I'd thought about them for even a split second, would have turned out quite differently. And Mrs. Acorn was in real danger of getting tagged with a nickname. At that moment my instinct kicked in and I yelled, looking at the sky, "HEY! IS THAT PLANE IN TROUBLE?"

We all turned our heads skyward and, sure enough, there was a thin wisp of smoke puffing out from the silent engine of a small plane gliding overhead. Then the motor coughed and sputtered back to life. It circled away, and we got on to talking about something else.

And Mrs. Acorn never got tagged with one of those uncomplimentary girl's nicknames.

Chapter 9
Mr. Acorn

The corner of Second and Channel had a permanent rut in the ground on each side of the sidewalk. There was no road, just a paved sidewalk, and service and delivery vehicles had to make their infrequent rounds with one wheel on the pavement and one in a dirt track. Quite pleasant for walking, once you learned where all the places where that the roots of gigantic trees had thrown up the pavement.

Oh, and remember the places where chunks of concrete walk had been broken off by overweight vehicles.

Quite pleasant for walking, briskly, on a frosty game night, with few working streetlights, and 50 tickets to sell in a hurry.

I had a waiting list of people wanting to get in on the action, but limited my sales to only 5 draws. I'd tried more, but it just took too long to get around, especially on a school night. So, if someone wasn't home, missed my knock, I just went on to the next door. No time to lose. My night began with a knock on Mr. Search's door.

"Hockey pool tonight, 25 cents each."

I liked to start with Mr. Search's door. It wasn't the most efficient route to take, but it always started my mood off just right for going around to all the other doors. Even if Mr. Search wasn't home, I still went off ready to spring through the rest of my steps that evening because, when I knocked on Mr. Search's door, there'd be a rustling of someone rising inside, then the sound of footsteps, a turn of the knob, and there she was: Diane Search. A most extraordinarily beautiful girl. Way out of my league.

If he was home, I'd say, "Hockey pool tonight, 25 cents."

She'd turn and holler, "DAD. POOL TONIGHT," and he'd come to the door.

If he wasn't home, I'd say, "Hockey pool tonight, 25 cents."

And she'd say, "Sorry, he's not here, but he left his quarter on the counter for you." Then she'd give me the coin and I'd let her pick his ticket. I'd thank her and go on to the next door on my list.

Diane Search. 17? Maybe 18? Way out of my league. But drop-dead gorgeous. I was sure that any day now someone from some sort of big production type place (I just knew that one had to exist somewhere) was going to discover how beautiful she was and she'd just suddenly be a star. She'd be on magazine covers and in movies and things, and mere mortals like me were never going to be able to get up close to someone as beautiful as her ever again.

I'd still be as fired-up, as charged and ready to get the rest of the evening's job done, whether Mr. Search was home or not because I had a chance to see Diane. But even if she wasn't home that night, as long as her dad was, I'd at least have my first sale under my belt and a good start to the evening. Of all my choices, sort of like a chess move, knocking on Mr. Search's door had become my favorite opening.

Then I'd cut through between the houses back to Second, to John McLarty's, where his new black-lab pup, Tina, would bark greetings to me at the door. Up Second to Lakeshore, left and down First, then back along Channel and on from there, splashing through iced-over puddles in the dark.

I ended up at Parson's, facing the ferry dock, chilled to the bone, with one ticket left, and headed back towards home.

Tommy English wanted a ticket, I knew. The English's home was near Lakeshore and a strong North Easter was coming off the Bay. I got hit with the least of the blast by going straight up Fifth to the path just before Lakeshore, and then East.

But Kathy English said Tommy wasn't home yet, and she didn't want to buy one.

Shivering, with cold wet hands and numb to the core and all the waiting list customers I had left were blocks away on the other side of the park, I contemplated just packing it in and taking only twenty-five cents profit from this last draw. I went along the path behind the houses facing Lakeshore and down Second for home, badly in need of warming up. Along the way there was Number 10 Second on the left, and at least worth a shot. I knocked on the Acorn's door.

"Hockey pool tonight, 25 cents each."

"What's that?"

"Hockey pool. Twenty-five cents a ticket. Would you like to buy one?"

"How's it work?"

And so I explained about the way the final score on the game determined the winning number while a trickle of wet snow melted down the back of my head and inside my collar.

"So you make fifty cents on the deal?"

"Yes, sir, I do."

He glared at me. "I give you my quarter, and then I'll never see you again."

It wasn't a question.

"Well, um, if your number comes up, I come right back with your two dollars."

"Yeah, so you say. What's to keep you from just disappearing?"

"I - um - I live right there." I pointed my hand at the house on the corner. "If your number comes up, then, tonight, as soon as the game's over, I'll walk right over here and deliver it. Honest."

"Honest?" he mocked me.

"What is it?" a woman's voice called from inside the house.

"Shut the damn door," a man called out. "You're freezing the house!"

"Okay," I said, "I guess I'd better go. Sorry to have bothered you."

"No wait," he said as I turned away, "Gimme one." He flipped a quarter at me and I held up the box.

He put his hand in, pulled out the slip and read his number.

"Hey, wait a minute," he called as I ran down the street, "THERE WAS ONLY ONE TICKET IN THERE!"

"THAT'S RIGHT!" I hollered back as I went in through our back door and slammed it tight against the weather.

Chapter 10
Mighty Oaks

Another day, another boat ride, about a year earlier, coming home from the city on the Thomas Rennie, biggest ferry in the fleet. We went to Centre first, and came from Centre with nearly a half load, but still a fair bit of room. Folks randomly gathered in groups, Barry and Flo on my right talking with Peggy Aitken. Seems she had this awful problem.

Across from me sat a tired looking group of city folk with picnic baskets, plus a pair of worn out parents and two bratty boys having a slapping and crying match.

A bunch of oddball beatniks sat to my left, all in drab, dark colours, continuing a conversation obviously hours old on the merits of Stalin-ism, Da-Da-ism, Nihil-ism and a bunch of other -isms.

"Sam," I heard Peggy say. "His name is Sam."

"And he's pure white?" Flo asked.

"Yes, except for the exposed pink skin where they operated, but they say the hair should grow back in over the scar, so you'll hardly be able to see it."

As we carried on across the Bay from Centre to Wards in calm water, the bratty kids dropped to their respective bums in triumphant huffs, arms folded tightly across chests, backs to each other.

"I'M NOT SPEAKING TO YOU!" one of them yelled.

"WELL I'M NOT SPEAKING TO YOU!" the other one screamed back.

Within a minute they both fell over, asleep, in fetal positions. Their parents lifted the eye-rubbing little clumps up onto the polished wooden benches.

"Oh, I just love him to bits," Peggy was saying, "But it turns out I'm allergic."

To my left the question of the state of human existence was getting heated. "You are only a figment of my imagination" someone said. "When I close my eyes, you cease to exist."

"You wish," one of the other beatniks scoffed.

"So," Barry went on as the crowd of standing non-islanders swayed as we docked, "you say he's been neutered?"

That had been about a year earlier.

Deja-vu on that same Thomas Rennie as the engines rumbled deep in its belly and voices were raised to be heard above the throaty din, but this time on a straight run from the city to Ward's Island.

Sam had lived for the past year in our home, a pure white feline of extremely haughty attitude and the most finicky food preferences. Dry food? Forget it! Canned cat food wasn't good enough for Sam. Canned tuna? Just barely acceptable. Steak? Cooked rare and only when offered by hand, it might occasionally merit a wee nibble.

During that year we found that there was only one type of tuna that he'd eat in any quantity and, fortunately, it wasn't a very expensive brand.

Barry and Flo again sitting on my right, sharing jokes with Peggy Aitken. We stood up and forced our way through the throng of people staying on the boat.

Then off the ferry and across the park to Channel, the crowd from the boat thinning as people disbursed toward their various homes. As we strolled past Sixth, Fifth, Fourth, Peggy talked about Darwin's ongoing gig at the Victory Theatre. He had a real shot at getting a permanent gig at the Inn On The Park, which would be quite a prestigious step up from the Victory, a strip club where he had been the piano player in the band for what had seemed like forever. All his years of study and improvement were finally about to pay off, they hoped. Much better money and quite a few more students for him. He was still going to

go down to New York City every week to study under
some great piano master whose name I didn't catch.

As we were approaching Third, there was Mrs. Acorn
coming the other way, and we all stepped over to the left to
let her go by on the narrow pavement. She recognized me
and stopped to ask if I'd seen Lucifer.

"Who?" I asked, not certain that I'd heard her correctly.

"Lucifer," she repeated. "He's a big black cat with a tuft
of white fur right at the tip of his tail."

Barry, Flo and Peggy were going on ahead.

"No, I haven't seen anything. I just got off the boat. How
long has he been gone?"

"Two days," she said, starting to head up Third.

"Well, If I see him I'll be sure to let you know."

"Thanks," she called back as we went our separate ways.

As I came in Barry was making up three tumblers of Tom
Collins and gin and, while I got my jacket off, asked if I
wanted a Coke. Then he smirked and asked who that
beatnik chick was. I told him that it was the school
librarian, Mrs. Acorn from up the street, and Peggy started
to laugh.

"Acorn?" she asked. "Sounds a little nuts to me."

"Well, if she ever has kids," Flo added, "they would
probably be knotty."

"No, probably not knotty pines," Barry chuckled. "It's
Mighty Oaks that, from little acorns, do grow."

"Do you suppose she'll find Satan?" Flo wondered.

"Satan?" I asked.

"Yeah. Wasn't she looking for the devil out there?"

"Oh, you mean Lucifer," I said. "That's the name of her
cat."

"Well," Barry joked, gesturing with his drink for effect,
"you know what they say? Speak his name and he will
appear!" He took a large swig while Peggy laughed and Flo
got frozen pork chops out of the heavily frosted up freezer
compartment of the fridge.

Chapter 11
Sharkhawk

Mrs. Acorn came back to our class many Tuesday afternoons after that initial embarrassment at the hands of Mickey and the Snoopies. The first few times The Teacher stayed in the room. Then, as his confidence in her ability to handle us increased, he'd take off. To the teacher's lounge for a smoke, I guessed, while she talked to us about rhyming couplets, sonnets, Iambic Pentameter and Limericks, foreshadowing, rhetorical questions and double entendres.

She familiarized us with names like Rudyard Kipling, Robert Service, Emily Dickinson and Lewis Carrol.

I noticed that, as she read a poem out loud, she barely glanced at the page. After "Jabberwocky" I asked if she recited the piece from memory.

"Yes, I memorize as much as I can," she replied.

"So, even though you're holding a book, you're only pretending to read it?"

"That way, I can keep my eye on all of you," she smiled. A mild giggle went around the classroom. "It's true, and a really good point to bring up. When you're reciting," she said, "try to look at your audience instead of a book or, worse still, your feet. You always want to memorize your poem thoroughly. Practice until you've got it perfect, then go out and watch your audience, look them over, see how they are reacting to your presentation. The poem has to be the interesting thing for them, but you have to find the audience interesting for them to find you and your poem interesting. You can express so much more that way. You'll be less nervous when you recite and so much more comfortable in front of an audience."

She went on to talk about the different ways that thoughts could be communicated, and how words could have many meanings.

Then she wrote on the chalkboard: woman without her man is nothing

Just like that, no punctuation.

Then she went on to punctuate those words as: "Woman, without her man, is nothing."

Then: "Woman! Without her, man is nothing!"

Completely opposite meanings, from the exact same words.

Then she made a game of combining unrelated words into new ones, showed us how "any one" changed when it was made into "anyone", then gave us fifteen minutes to come up with our own compound words.

Silence of diligent student labour descended on the room. At the end of fifteen minutes I was still trying to complete my page while Dooly read his list.

It was with an exhaustion similar to running a sprint that I finally put my pencil down and waved my arm, but Mickey got to go next and read out a list of a dozen or so word inventions. Inga had her hand up and read her list next, without me waving my arm in competition. It had just dawned on me that I had misunderstood the assignment. "Lorne," Mrs. Acorn asked after a few others had read their lists, "I believe you had your hand up earlier?"

"Oh, um, well. That's okay."

"No, we'd like to hear what you've got."

"Well, um... you see, I didn't understand the question."

"How's that?"

"Well... ah, I didn't know you wanted us to write a list of words."

"So, what did you write?"

"Well, I thought we were supposed to write a poem with a bunch of made-up compound words in it." I was folding the sheet while trying to stuff it into my desk.

"So you wrote a poem?"

"Yeah," I said, sheepishly.

"I'd like to hear it, if you'd read it out for us." There was something both comforting and commanding in her manner. Though I didn't want to, I found myself standing, dry throated and quaking at the knees. I unfolded the foolscap page and read:

"Sharkhawk patrols the reefcanopy of the oceanicforest.
Questing behavior of the overconfident,
    Vulnerable nestlings
        an everpresent possibility.
Above, beneath and within the aquaforest
    with fluid movement,
        swimming through air and flying through water
            landing and nesting and feeding on the flyswim.
Perchswallow flying, swimming, feeding, seeking insectminnows,
    finding many,
        needing more.
Darting, dashing, spirals and loops
    spirals and loops,
        and ever, back at the nest, the cry:
            "Where's my dinner?"
                "Hey! It's my turn!"
                    "No! It's mine!"
                        "I'm hungrier than you!"
Then, suddenly, it's not Mom or Dad at nestedge!
It's Sharkhawk! And somebody's gone!
And the banquet goes on.
    Bigbird devours littlebird
        and bigfish likewise,
            and occasionally they cross paths,
                as heroneel and pikeduck gobble each other.
At some point, they all converge on the seedeater.
    lillyalgae digester

who bares the biggest litterschools of them all."

"That doesn't even rhyme," Mickey smirked.

Heather was looking around at my desk. "He's only got seventeen double words. I've got twenty three." Her tone, the way she said it, made it sound like she was sticking her tongue out.

"Not all poems rhyme," or "A poem doesn't have to rhyme," or "Poetry isn't just rhyming," are things that Mrs. Acorn might have been about to say, if she'd had the chance.

In just the briefest split second, she got out the words, "That's rather..." as the bell rang and the rumble of the class rising from their seats began. Dink and Chisel were putting their unread lists of compound words away in their desks. Heather was already stuffing her arms into her coat as The Teacher walked back into the classroom and loudly reminded us to read pages 217 to 222 in our geography books. Then, with a great banging of desks, clatter and chaotic mayhem, classroom emptied into hall, hall emptied into schoolyard and schoolyard slowly emptied into waiting schoolbuses.

I headed for the back of the bus. The preferred seats.

We sang loud rude songs in the back of the bus.

We sang loud pop songs.

We sang loud folk songs.

We sang loud.

Very loud.

As a singer, I was pretty bad. But I certainly was loud. Loud enough to hear my own voice against the background volume of everyone else. That's how I knew I was a bad singer, because I could hear that I wasn't quite on the note a lot of the time. But I tried. And, at the back of the bus, anybody who tried could just pipe up and join in.

"Roll Me Over In The Clover" followed by "Great Green Gobs Of Greasy Grimy Gopher Guts" and, of course, anything on the radio that we could remember most of the words to.

"Charlie On The MTA"

"Big Bad John"

"The Man Who Shot Liberty Valance."

There was a pause, followed by the shrill, so-high-pitched-as-to-be-almost-inaudible sound of: "weeeee-e-e-oo-weeeee-e-ee-e-eee-oo-weeeee-e-ee-oo-mum-mawaaay"

We started chanting: "Uh-Weemaway Uh-Weemaway..." and, since a lot of boy's voices were cracking, sang an absolutely dreadful rendition of "The Lion Sleeps Tonight".

Then Weasel started Elvis's "Can't Help Falling In Love". But he sang, in exaggerated Elvis style: "Wise men say..." and then looked around, saying/singing nothing. He's pretending to be Elvis: Elvis isn't saying anything: ergo Elvis isn't a wise man. We all laughed a big jack-ass dumb-guy laugh.

At least we thought it was funny.

Chisel and I looked at each other and, on the same wavelength, started into "Wolverton Mountain".

We sang in over-accentuated hillbilly drawls and slurs and finished with a fade-out round of:

"I don't care about Clifton Clowers,

I'ma gonna climb up on his mount-ayn

I'ma gonna get the one I lo-ove

I don't care about Clifton Clowers..." Interlaced with another round starting on the second line, then three, and finally four, rounds of:

"I don't care about Clifton Clowers

I'ma gonna climb up on his mount-ayn

I'ma gonna get the one I lo-ove

I don't care about Clifton Clowers..." Quieter and quieter until the sound of our singing faded so much you could actually hear the tires thump-thumping on the segments of concrete pavement. Then, in one big unified shout louder than anything else we'd sung so far: "I'M-A GONNA GET THE ONE I LOVE!"

We laughed and swayed back and forth trying to make the bus fishtail as we went around the corner at Hooper Avenue. Somebody hit me with a spitball and I went charging up the aisle to try and find them.

"English Country Garden" started and I went back to my seat to join in.

Then "My Old Man's A Dustman" and "Does Your Chewing Gum Lose It's Flavour On The Bed Post Overnight?" Oh how we slaughtered and made fun of those British accents.

We were blissfully unaware of so many things.

We didn't know physics or algebra.

We didn't know calculus or trigonometry.

We didn't know that a few days ago somebody named Tony Sheridan released a record with some back up guys who's names were known by maybe about as many people in the world as those who knew mine. They called themselves The Beatles.

We didn't know that an equally obscure bunch of musicians had gotten their first paid performance that month. They named their band "The Rolling Stones".

We didn't know any of that.

We just knew that British accents were fun to mock, same as Hillbilly's.

We broke into a machine-gun fast: "I'm Leaning On The Lamp Post At The Corner Of The Street In Case A Certain Little Lady Comes By". George Formby never sounded so raucous.

Half the bus got out at Algonquin and I swung out with them, then got back on the second bus. The driver wanted to know if I'd been kicked off.

"Naw," I said, shoving past him, "Somebody farted and it just stunk too much."

"It was probably you!" Mickey shouted.

"Yeah, you need some paper now?" Dooly jibed.

"What's the definition of a big surprise?" I shot back. "A fart with a lump in it!" I shook my pant-leg in their direction and they jumped back in mock horror.

We started singing:
"He was coming round the mountain
Doing ninety miles an hour
When the chain on the motorcycle broke!
They found him in the grass
With a sparkplug up his ass
And his prick was playing Dixie
On the spokes!"

Then I noticed Mrs. Acorn sitting in the front seat, right across from the driver. My back had been to her as I got on.

She was staring out the front window so intently that I wondered what she saw out there in the distance that was so engrossing. The bus bounced around the sharp turn at the loop, throwing us all forward as the driver hit the brakes hard at the Ward's Island stop.

She was the first one off, and I was only a few steps behind but hadn't caught her eye.

The guys behind me went noisily bounding off the bus in all directions. Someone threw a gum wrapper that hit me on the back of the head. I spun around and flipped a middle-finger salute at nobody in particular, then quickened my pace to catch up with her. Behind me Mickey was singing at the top of his lungs:
"Chicken soup
Makes you poop
Down your leg and in your boot!"

She wasn't running, but walking so fast that I didn't think I'd catch up to her. I called out, "Mrs. Acorn... Mrs. Acorn! Hi... um... GWENDOLYN!"

She slowed her pace and turned.

There was a look of sheer terror in her eyes and I instinctively looked around behind me to see what it was that she was so afraid of. "What's wrong?" I asked, having almost caught up to her now at the corner of Channel and Sixth.

In the instant that I asked the question the whole cloud of fear disappeared from her face, her shoulders slumped and relaxed, and, quick as a snap of the fingers she smiled and said, "Oh, hi Lorne. How are you?"

I heard running footsteps coming up behind me and, once again, there was just the briefest flicker of fear in her eyes.

I heard the oncoming rush of feet, a slight variation, and guessed that the runner was coming up on my left. As he ran by me Mickey thumped me on the back and shouted, "You're it!"

I swung my left arm and, between the words "you're" and "it", slapped him hard in the belly with the back of my hand while bellowing out: "YOU'RE IT! NO TOUCH BACKS!"

He slowed a moment, confused, then went running after Dooly.

I wondered, ever so briefly, if she'd been afraid of Mickey, or of me, or maybe of rowdy boys in general. But she was smiling again, like someone in total control of every variable in the whole universe. She asked me where I'd gotten the inspiration for the poem I wrote in class.

I told her about seeing a Disney special about fish that live in and around the coral reefs of the ocean and how, sitting in class that morning, I was struck by how similar the birds in the poplar thicket beyond the schoolyard looked as they flew in and around the trees. When she asked us to combine unrelated words into compounds, I just started to write down what I saw.

"Flow of consciousness," she said.

"Huh?"

"It's what you get when you relax and just let creation happen."

"Yeah, I guess."

"Some people try all their lives to attain it."

"Why?" I kicked a pebble ahead as we walked past the ancient wooden public washroom building on our right, a grove of absolutely gigantic willows rising high above its roof. The heavy mat of branches from these giants was so thick that, even with only buds that promised a new growth of spring leaves, their twigs were still thick enough to darken this stretch of Channel Avenue to a cavernous hue.

She explained something about the curve of the universe, a never ending source of power, a stream of consciousness that ran through all space and time, all the while looking out to the distance as if she was reading the words somewhere in the sky just above the houses. The leaves thinned out and it brightened a bit as we approached Fourth. She turned to me and all I could see was how extraordinarily huge the pupils of her eyes had become in the darkness under the willows. It was like gazing into a pair of binoculars, and I had to resist the urge to put my face next to hers and just look in.

I tripped and stumbled on the broken pavement between Fourth and Third, caught my balance and recovered with a quick 2-step and spin. "I guess that was sort of a stream of unconsciousness," I chuckled.

She laughed at my stumble and recovery and together we turned the corner on Second. I went towards our back door and, as she continued up Second (two more doors, on the right), she asked if I'd maybe like to drop by some time and see their place.

"Sure," I said.

In through the screen door, letting it slam behind me, I quickly turned to the right and dropped my books in my room with Aunt Flo calling after me, "Supper's at 5:30!"

I bounded back out, letting the steel spring slam the screen door shut behind me with a loud: "SPROING-OINg-OIng-Oing-oing!" as Flo yelled: "And quit slamming the door!"

Chapter 12
Septics and Skeptics

Gwen staggered back a step and I knew, from fifteen feet away, why she had paused.

"What's that smell?" I heard her call ahead.

"The damn can's acting up."

I heard him before I entered the house and saw Mr. Acorn, a knotty burl of a face looming out of the bathroom in a thick cloud of cigar smoke. Then, with a grin and nod to me, he said, "I'm trying to figure out where the draft's coming from, but it all just keeps blowing back in. Could you hold this?" he asked, handing me a flashlight.

As I shone the beam Mr. Acorn blew thick billows of cigar smoke all around the toilet.

"Lorne, this is my husband, Milton Acorn," she said. "Lorne's one of the students at the school."

There was a distinct sound of pride in her voice as she said his name, like he was special, a man of importance. Milton gave a perfunctory wave. He looked more to me like one of the Three Stooges. Milton, I swear, If you bumped into him on the street, could have been mistaken for Moe. Except for the hair. Milton had the worst splat of greasy hair hanging down his forehead. He kept trying to wipe it away with the back of his hand about every ten seconds.

He looked like Moe, but with Curly's mannerisms and body language. Right down to Curly's "MMM-mmm-phh!" and the swipe of his palm down over his face. It was the natural reaction to trying to hold your breath against the utterly foul stench.

"You're looking in the wrong place," I said.

"What do you mean? The draft's coming in right here," he pointed a finger in under the rim.

"Yeah, but that's not where the problem is."

He looked like he was likely to take me by the scruff of the neck and throw me out the door.

"The back of the toilet, there..." I squeezed by him, "Goes out the wall, there, see? And outside, running up above the roof..." I turned my head and breathed in some air from outside the bathroom door. "...there's a vent pipe. It pulls the air out. That must be blocked somehow. If we go outside..."

I looked for a back door. With a glance about I saw that there were several stacks of boxes of books filling up about half the kitchen. The stove was accessible, but you had to lean over a stack of books to get water from the sink. Going through the back door would mean moving them. "It's, um, easier to go out the front," Gwen said.

We went out the front door and around the side.

John McLarty's wheelbarrow had fallen over and bashed the rusty four-inch vent pipe connected to the back of their toilet. Tina barked excitedly as we snooped around in the narrow space between the houses, bringing a stick in hopes that one of us would throw it for her.

I pulled out the crumpled portion of stove-pipe, banged it straight as best I could with a length of firewood from John's pile, then forced the misshapen pipe segments back together.

"It'll hold for a while," I said. "And the house will air out in about an hour."

"Doesn't look like a very good job to me," Milton grumbled.

"Ah, Milt, quitcher bitchin." Gwen laughed.

Milt got down on one knee and scrutinized the pipe I had replaced, scratching at the rust with his fingernail, then finally stood up, pronouncing, "I guess it'll do for now." Then, apparently satisfied with the temporary repair job, lead the way around the side and back in the front door.

"Milton's a poet," Gwen went on. "Milt, Lorne wrote an interesting..."

"Now let's see if this works," Milton said, cutting her off in mid-sentence, puffing his cigar into a smoking fury.

"...poem in class today," she finished, undeterred by his gruff manner.

"Is that so? A poem? Nobody around here wrote a poem today except me," Milton called back from the bathroom. Then: "Well I'll be damned. It works!" Looking around him I could see the thick smoke being pulled down into the toilet hole.

"But it's still really gross," Gwen said.

"Yeah," I said, "that smell will go away in a little while."

"Not the smell, the whole concept of that type of toilet... looking down the hole at a pyramid of poop. It's just so... primitive."

"Oh, listen to the princess," Milton teased. "Most people through all history would die of envy. They'd fight wars for a toilet like that! An emperor wouldn't have it so good! Indoor crapper? Just the thing to prove that civilization is capable of getting some things right!"

"But dear," Gwen cooed, feigning pity, "I'm so sorry to have to be the one to inform you, but they now know how to make one that, dare I say it... flushes!"

"Ah, phony trappings of the bourgeoisie! You wait and see! No more flush toilets for only the elite! Come the revolution, everybody will have a can like that!" he declared, pointing toward to bathroom.

"Doesn't sound like a very good argument for *the revolution* to me," Gwen shot back. Then, to me, "would you like some tea?"

Milton was almost choking on his cigar. I got the impression he was easily angered, and that Gwen somehow found him funny when he blew a fuse.

"Sure. Or pop, if you've got it."

"Sorry, no pop."

"Tea's fine."

"So you think you're a poet?" Milt challenged me. "Hold out your hands."

I held my palms out for him to study. "Nope, no poet here," he scoffed. "Too young, Too soft. When a man's hands begin to lose their beauty, that's when his poems start to gain theirs."

"So what about a woman's hands?" Gwen teased, waiving her hands in the air.

"That is why women can never be great poets the way men can. Because really talented women will always have some beauty left in their hands."

"I don't know whether to be flattered or insulted," Gwen said with a pout.

"And that," Milt boasted, taking a big, flamboyant bow, "is the best result a great poet can evoke with his words."

There was a large easel taking up most of the space in the centre of the living room, and on it a painting, obviously not yet finished, of an elegant looking woman with a long neck and a high, fancy head dress of some sort. Gwen saw me studying the painting and said: "A work in progress."

"Yours?" I asked. She nodded, picking up a small plastic figurine that was sitting on the counter. "My model," she said, "Queen Nefertiti."

"Ah," I said, as if I knew who that was. I noticed a chess set, some sort of woven spider-web/mandella thing hanging on the wall, a thin book with what looked like cascading hair and the word "gas" or "gad" or "gao" or something like that on the cover. I couldn't figure out what that last letter was supposed to be. Was it an "O"? Gwen shut the water off and put the kettle on the stove. She noticed me picking the book up.

"Have you heard of the Tao?" she asked.

"The what?"

"Tao. That's the book of Tao."

"Ta…Oh! I thought that was a g."

"I guess that T does look like a small case G, doesn't it?" She took the book from me and held it close for him to inspect. "Milt, what do you think?"

"About what?"

"About the way this letter T looks on the cover."

"Hmmm, yeah."

"Or it even could be an S," I said.

"Jeff did ask you what you thought of it," Gwen said to Milt. "You should tell him that the graphics make it hard to read the title."

I took the book back from Gwen and read the cover: "The book of Tao" and beneath that, in smaller red letters, all caps: KEY TO THE MASTERY OF LIFE. I flipped it over and the back was just the same thing repeated. I put it back on the counter where I found it.

"You should read it," Milt said.

"Well... I guess. Is it any good?" I asked, picking it back up. "It doesn't seem too long. I guess I could."

"You sure do a lot of guessing," Milton growled as he seated himself at a dark coloured wooden desk with a typewriter prominently placed in the middle. He turned the knob on the side of the carriage, rolled the paper that had been in it up and out of the machine. He turned to Gwen, obviously expecting something.

"Well?" he asked.

"Well what?"

"Where is it?"

"Where's what?"

"You know." He eyed the case she'd brought home from school.

"Oh!" she jumped up, suddenly fathoming his meaning. "Sorry, I forgot."

She unzipped the case, slightly larger than a standard briefcase, but thinner, and carefully passed him a small stack of blank Ditto machine sheets, carbons attached.

"You got them!" he beamed, happy as a kid with a birthday present. Then with a flurry of the wrist that would do a stage magician proud, she pulled from the case a stack of about a hundred sheets of printed pages.

He engulfed her in a big smothering bear hug and she nuzzled her nose into the crease where his jawbone and ear met his neck and they breathed in each others scents and, I'm not kidding, I think they actually purred.

I sat on a wooden chair at the table, opened the book of Tao somewhere in the middle and silently read:

"The concept of Yin is ever present. It is the Mystic Female from whom the heavens and the earth originate.

"Constantly, continuously, enduring always.

"Use her!"

The kettle came to a boil and Gwen rushed to catch it as a blast of water belched out the spout onto the burner. "Oolong?" she asked.

"Plenty long enough," Milt shot back.

She poured about a cup of scalding water into the teapot and swirled it, then put the kettle back on the burner and looked at me. "What kind of tea do you like?"

"Oh, Salada, I suppose."

"Hmm, haven't got any of that. How about Jasmine?"

"I don't know what that is."

"It's the flowers of the tea plant, instead of the leaves," Milt said, sounding like I was dumb for not knowing.

"Now Milt," Gwen scolded, pouting her lips as she spoke.

"Yeah, you're right. I suppose," He said as she finished swirling and dumped the hot water out of the teapot. "It's just a case of something you didn't know before, but you do now. Sort of like how I didn't know that it wasn't the breeze blowing in from the toilet that was causing the smell, but how the vent pipe wasn't pulling the air out. But now I do."

"Oh, Please don't remind me of that thing," Gwen said. She threw a small handful of loose tea into the pot and then quickly tipped the vigorously boiling kettle into it. A tempting aroma wafted about the room.

"Mmm... Smells better in here now," I said.

Milt turned to the typewriter and spun a sheet of Ditto paper into it. He set up a steady staccato rhythm, pounding hard to indent the blue backing layer of the Ditto paper through the white top sheet, making the whole desk and floor reverberate with shock-waves.

Chapter 13
Past or Future

"Have you ever had your tea leaves read?" Gwen asked.

"No, I can't say that I have."

"Well," she said as she poured, "I could do it, if you like. It'll be fun. Would you like me to read your past or your future?"

I tried to take a sip. "I haven't even started yet. It's still too hot."

"Well," she said, sinking into a big overstuffed green corduroy armchair, "If you want me to read your future, hold the cup with your right hand, and if you want me to read your past, hold it with your left." She blew across the top of her cup and took a sip.

I transferred the cup to my left hand and tried another sip. It was still too hot to get more than a tiny bit, but quite tasty.

"So you'd like me to read your past?"

"Just to see if you really can do it. I already know my past, so I'll know if you get it right."

Milt set his cup down beside the typewriter and leaned over, putting his face down to it, slurping noisily as the cup sat there in its saucer. "Ah," he challenged, straightening up "what can you tell me if I drink it no-hands?"

"That you're a fool," she laughed.

"Every court needs its fool," Milton said, carefully tugging the Ditto sheet from the machine. I took another sip as he fed the worn old Remington another and the hammering started again.

"So you're a poet?" Milt asked while continuing to hammer the keys.

"Ah, well... I don't think you can call me that."

"Lorne wrote an interesting poem in class today."

"Indeed. Do tell us."

"I don't have it with me."

"Where is it?" Milt barked.

"It's at home. I could get it, if you like."

"Sure," Gwen said, "Why don't you do that. Your tea needs to cool a bit anyway."

I was out the door and onto the sidewalk in four big strides, a cold whip of wind in my face. The thickest of the ice had been gone from the Bay for weeks but it still felt like we could get frost tonight. Sam ran in the house, the screen door slamming as I went in.

Karen was awake from her nap and screaming, the big red "map of Canada" birthmark on her forehead standing out as she cried.

I turned to my room on the right and heard Flo yell something as I opened my bag and found the folded poem. "What was that?" I yelled back, tossing the Book of Tao on my nightstand.

"Would you mix the margarine for me?" she called louder as I came out of my room. I folded the paper twice more and stuffed it in my pants pocket. As I went to the fridge she yelled, "Wash your hands first!" from the living room. I turned from the fridge to the sink, soaped up and rinsed off and got my hands sort of dry on the towel hanging from the fridge handle, opened the door and found the margarine box.

Two bags left.

I slid one plastic bag of white goo out of the box, turned it over and squeezed the dot in the centre until it popped, making the red die capsule burst inside the bag. The margarine was hard and stiff and it took me a good five minutes to massage it until it was all a consistent yellow colour. I tossed the bag back into the fridge and took off out the back door with Flo yelling after me, "Remember, supper's at 5:30! And don't slam the damned door!"

Back to number ten, front door still slightly ajar.

"That took you a while," Gwen smiled across the surface of her tea.

"What'd you do, re-write it first?" Milton scoffed.

"Naw, I had some chores to do." I unfolded the sheet and Milton took a glance, then stared harder.

"What's this say?" He asked.

"Um, where, there? Sharkhawk."

"That's a k? Man, your handwriting is bad. Here, you'd better read it." He handed it back to me.

"Okay, um... Shark..." I coughed.

"He can't even read it himself," Milt said in Gwen's general direction. Gwen was behind the easel scratching paint into the canvas.

"Give him a chance," she insisted.

I took a mouthful of luke-warm tea, cleared my throat and started again, this time reading the poem all the way through with just a couple of pauses to be sure, myself, of what I'd written. Milton was right, my handwriting really was awful.

"Hmm, not bad," Milt said when I was finished.

"See, I told you," Gwen said to Milt. Then, to me: "I see you're still holding the cup with your left hand. Almost done?"

I hadn't thought about it, but there I was, wrinkled sheet of foolscap paper in my right hand, a half-cup of almost cold tea in my left. I tipped it way back and gulped it down, then held the empty cup out to her. She looked at me in wide-eyed surprise.

"You're not supposed to drain it," she said, "You're supposed to leave a little bit."

"Oh, sorry. I didn't know."

"I mean," she said, staring into the empty cup, "how am I supposed to read your tea leaves if there aren't any leaves left in the cup?"

"So, we've got a man without a past here," Milt laughed.

"Well," I said, feeling a bit of tea leaf between my teeth and chewing on it," I've got a few stuck between my teeth.

I guess I could spit them back in." Gwen shook her head and wrinkled her nose in a grossed-out-girl sort of way.

"That's the spirit!" Milton boomed, "Find a way to make it happen! Never give up!"

"Or maybe I could have another cup?"

"Well now your just taking advantage of our hospitality," Milt jibed.

"Pot's empty," Gwen said, going back behind the canvas. "And the kitchen's closed."

"Any further thoughts on the matter?" Milton searched my eyes.

"Well, it was good tea."

"And that's a damned good answer! And," he added, "probably the most accurate thing about the past that you're ever going to get from a tea cup."

It was Gwen's turn to be on the defensive. "Shut up," she smiled, "I really can do this."

"I believe you," I said. And I really did.

"I believe! I believe!" Milt chanted, waving his hands in the air.

"How about this?" Gwen asked, leaving the easel to pull a purple and gold cardboard package from among the clutter at one end of the table. She flipped it open and produced an over-sized deck of cards. I'd never seen anything like them before, a bit too large to hold in the hand for playing, say, Cribbage or Euchre or Poker. And thick too. The cards were made of a stiff cardboard material. I wondered how you could possibly shuffle them.

"Shuffle them," she said.

I looked at them again. Way too thick and stiff, but I tried.

I took the deck, slid it apart into two stacks, interlocked the corners, and tried to riffle them. They fell together in large clumps, hardly mixed up at all.

"How am I supposed to shuffle this deck?" I asked.

"That's the one thing I can't tell you," she said, a mischievous glint in her eye. "You have to put your own mind to it."

I tried a downward slide shuffle, right hand to left, but they were too big for my hands and wouldn't mix. In exasperation I spread them all around on the table, scrambling the order as best I could, then tried to get the pile organized back into a neatly stacked deck. From outside I could hear a distant shrill whistle.

There is a kind of whistling you do when you're whistling a song, and then there's the shrill sound you make when you whistle through your teeth. This was that sort of high, piercing kind of whistle. The sort of whistle you make at a pretty girl from a distance: "Wheet-wee-oo!" The kind of whistle that I had never mastered, though I had tried. Oh how I had tried. One index finger at each corner of my mouth, two fingers from my left hand and one from my right, or the other way around. Middle finger and thumb of one hand. All I got was a whooshing air noise.

That high, shrill whistle that I heard at that moment, sounding like: "Whittoo-whittoo-whitteeeee," that was the family whistle. The Jones whistle.

Whenever my Grandfather or my uncles, Barry or Jimmy, made that whistle you could tell it from all other sounds in a noisy background. When we all went to the CNE you could hear that distinctive whistle calling us together, cutting through all the noise and mayhem of a crowded midway. Despite all the traffic noise of downtown Toronto at rush hour, you could hear that whistle and know that it was a member of our family hailing you from blocks away. That whistle could be distinctly heard against a background of thunderstorms and loud televisions and shouting crowds and of course, as it did now, through the thin walls of an Island house.

I heard it again, closer, and left the scrambled deck of cards on the table and made for the door.

Uncle Jimmy was out there, just coming up Second, whistling: "Whit-too-whit--too..." He saw me and stopped. "Hey, come on," he yelled.

"I gotta go," I called back to Gwen.

"Okay," she said, looking slightly disappointed. "Another time, okay?"

"Yeah, sure."

"Nice meeting you," Milton said. He continued to type and, as I closed the door I heard him say: "What was his name again?"

Chapter 14
Honeydippers

Flo was looking into a small paper bag.

"They didn't have any Magic Wood," Jimmy said, hanging his jacket in a hook beside the door.

"Barry said that's the only brand that works," Flo said, pulling a one-quart can of wood filler from the bag and looking skeptically at the label. The receipt had stuck to the bottom of the can and fell to the floor. I took a step to my right to get a better peek down her blouse as she picked it up.

"The guy at Tom Taylor's said this stuff is just as good," Jimmy said. He looked at me looking down Flo's top and said, "Don't..." Flo stood up and he paused, then finished with "...tell Barry if you see him first. Just let me handle it."

I heard someone walking on the street outside. Through the window I could see Cliff Hadrall going up Second. The 4:25 boat must have come in. I heard Barry wipe his feet on the mat, then he opened the door.

As soon as he saw Jimmy he asked, "Did you get the Magic Wood?"

There are some times when there's a pause, a natural opening in a conversation, and they usually pass, and the conversation goes normally on. This was not one of those times.

From the moment I heard Jimmy say, "They didn't have any Magic Wood," I knew what I was going to say if I just got the chance. And this was one of those times.

This was one of those times when I won that lottery. One of those times when I got what I wanted. One of those golden moments when all the sweet fruits of the world fell into my lap.

Barry asked, "Did you get the Magic Wood?"

And Jimmy hesitated, just ever so slightly.

And I said: "No, but he did meet a man who gave him seven magic beans for his cow."

Barry and Flo burst out laughing. Jimmy was wide-eyed, incredulous, and started laughing. For just that briefest of moments I was the most clever, witty person on the face of the planet.

Barry wiped at his eye and Jimmy looked at me like he'd never known that I had it in me, and he said, "That's really good. You got any more?"

But I didn't. I had thought it through to this moment but, now that they were all looking at me, I didn't know what to do next. And, just like that, all the sweet fruits of the world ripened and spoiled right there in front of me.

"Ah, I didn't think so," Jimmy said, then went back to the business of explaining to Barry why the guy at Tom Taylor's thought this stuff was just as good.

The phone rang and Flo got it.

Barry was insistent that Magic Wood was the only stuff that worked. Flo told him that it was Bob Fulford on the phone. Barry took it and I went to the bathroom.

When I came out the decision had been made that we weren't going to patch the hull of the launch in Jimmy's back yard today after all. Bob Fulford's septic tank was overflowing.

Forty dollars was what Barry quoted him, and that was a lot of money for a couple hours work at a time when fifty bucks was a decent weekly wage.

"Just keep thinking about the money," Jimmy said as we dug.

"That's right," Barry agreed between shovel scoops. "Just think of that thing as overflowing with cash."

There was an old English term for this kind of work, probably thought up during the Victorian era. They called it honeydipping.

Whether I thought of that tank as overflowing with cash or with honey, either way, it stunk.

I stepped on the shovel, drove it in, pried down on the long handle and lifted with my knees.

Chunk! Lift. Heave.

Chunk! Lift. Heave.

"Yo -o heave ho!" Barry chanted.

"Yo -o heave ho!" we all sang.

Chunk! Lift. Heave.

Chunk! Lift. Heave.

Six feet by eight feet. Four feet deep, if we could get it. If not, we'd have to extend a side by a foot or more. Barry checked his watch.

The Island sand vanished from the ground into two mounds on each side, not too far away because it was going to have to go back in.

When the hole was finally big enough, Jimmy used his shovel to pop the fourteen-inch lid off the septic tank, then inserted the hand pump into the soggy thick mass. Two feet. Three feet. Four feet down the end of it stopped at the bottom of the tank. He took the T handle on the end of the plunger stick in his right hand and pushed and pulled a few quick strokes to prime it. The greenish sludge filled the three-inch tube and began to dribble out the spout. Then he started to work in earnest, pulling and pushing on the handle with a steady rhythm, fifty strokes with his right arm, then fifty with his left. The thick sludge flowed out of the tank and into the hole we had just dug. Then it was Barry's turn. Then mine.

"Just keep thinking about the money," Jimmy said again.

I couldn't help thinking that if I got a dollar for every stroke, then maybe it would be worth it.

Once we had the tank empty Barry checked his watch again. We put the metal lid back on the tank and tossed a few shovels of sand over the pit, which now contained the fermented effluent. Just enough sand on top to keep it from smelling overly much. We put planks across the pit so no one would fall in.

Jimmy hosed off the pump and shovels and we headed home, Jimmy taking off on his bike while Barry and I stashed the pump and three shovels under our house.

I had to wait outside until Barry finished his shower, then it was my turn to strip down to my gonch and dart to the bathroom for a thorough wash-up.

Flo plunked down a couple of plates of something resembling bronzed shoes.

"Supper was at 5:30!" She barked.

I looked at Barry, and he looked at me, picked up his knife and fork and said, "Just keep thinking about the money."

One third of forty bucks? I couldn't help thinking that even if I got a dollar for every stroke of the pump, *plus* every shovel full of sand, it still wouldn't be worth it.

We finished dinner and dessert and then it was my job to go back with a flashlight and see how much the pit had sunk.

I came home and told Barry that it was down a good foot and a half. He phoned Jimmy and, when he showed up, we got out the shovels and went back. We tossed sand into the pit until it filled up level with the ground around, then kept going until there was a mound about a foot high where the pit had been. That would sink away by morning.

We stomped around on top to tamp it firm and Barry went to the door, talked with Bob and brought him out to show him that the job was done. Satisfied, Bob pulled out his wallet and gave Barry some bills, nodded a smile to Jimmy and me, then went back inside.

When we got to our back door Jimmy didn't want to come in. Barry pulled out his wallet and gave him a ten and a five.

From a forty dollar job? I wondered...

Jimmy's parting words were, "Just keep thinking about the money."

And I did.

I'd been thinking about that all night. Forty dollars divided in three was thirteen thirty-three each.

Barry handed me a ten and went in ahead of me, wiping his boots on the mat and asking Flo what was happening on the TV. I didn't wipe my feet. I didn't take my coat off. I just went to my room, fell on my bed, rolled myself in my covers and wondered what the hell my worth really was.

I had shoveled just as many shovelfuls as each of them. I had pulled exactly as many strokes on the pump as they had. I had done every bit as much work as them on every single aspect of that job. Why the hell wasn't I worth a full share of the wages?

Barry knocked and opened the door.

"Here," he said. I had my head under the covers.

"You all right?" he asked. I didn't look.

"Anyway," he said, "Bob gave us a five dollar bonus for getting the job done in one night. I didn't have change on me, but here's another five, the rest of your share. I'll just leave it on your dresser, okay?"

I didn't look.

He went out and closed the door behind him.

Okay, I thought. I was wrong.

It wasn't the first time.

And certainly wouldn't be the last.

Chapter 15
Ditto

On the schoolbus in the morning I suddenly remembered that we had a test coming up and tried desperately to read pages 217 to 222 in my geography textbook while bouncing along the pot-hole pocked road.

I did lousy on the test. Worse than lousy. The Teacher had us put the tests in a pile at the corner of his desk as we finished them. He marked the papers already handed in while the rest of us finished. The only pupil he looked up to acknowledge was Christine. I think it was because she wore an incredibly bright yellow dress that day.

I read through the window the elongated words on a banner in the window of the girl's dorm across the courtyard. "Happy Bir..." the rest of the banner hung at an angle below the level of the frosting on the lower half of the windows. I got to wondering...

Happy what? Happy Birthday? Maybe.

Or maybe Happy Birds day.

Or Happy Birch trees. Or...

Tiny nudged me in the leg and Chisel nodded to draw my eyes over to the other side of the room. Mickey passed Ralph something for me. A CHUM chart. I got it into the pages of my geography book without getting caught, then waited.

The Teacher was studiously marking the pile of tests. About half the kids in the room were still writing. Silence prevailed.

I held my geography textbook up at an angle with my thumbs, then cautiously turned a few pages. I checked to see that Heather couldn't see over my shoulder, turned the page, opened the CHUM chart and began to study the top 50.

"Lorne!" The Teacher bellowed. I jolted, the CHUM chart slipping out of the textbook and fluttering to the floor. "Come up here!"

I rose and carefully stepped over the fallen pamphlet. That's when The Teacher saw it, rolled his eyes toward the ceiling and then instructed the rest of the class to keep writing or be quiet and read something if they were already done. He pointed his pen at my test page. At my mark.

I had gotten three right out of twenty.

"Shit," I said. Then realized what I'd said.

The strap? I wondered.

"Detention," he said. I started to return to my seat. "Recess detention," he said to my back. Heather snickered. The CHUM chart was gone from the floor. I slid back into my seat feeling mad at the whole damned world.

I usually spent recess detention perched on the hard wooden bench in front of The Secretary, hoping that The Principal wouldn't see me there and speculate on whether more severe punishment might be necessary.

But The Secretary wasn't at her desk. She was in the little cubbyhole of a printing room. I could see her in there from where I stood at her desk and so I went across the hall and reported to her. She looked at me, looked at the big Ditto machine, and told me to start turning the drum.

I took hold of the black handle and started to turn, the drum rotating, sheets of blank paper being pulled one by one onto the drum, making one full rotation in contact with the Ditto sheet, and then going onto the stack of printed pages on the other side of the machine. As I turned the drum around again and again, the stack of blank paper slowly diminished and the stack of printed pages increased. Round and round and round the drum turned, and I counted: twenty strokes with my right arm, then twenty with the left.

She stopped me, took the ink-soaked Ditto page from the drum and clipped a new one in. I resumed cranking the handle, now making a stack of some different document.

Then another.

Then the bell announcing the end of recess rang and I headed back to class. The Teacher was just coming out of The Principal's office, saw me and told me to go in.

There aren't many things that one can experience that feel truly life threatening, but that feeling, at that moment, came pretty darn close, then eased into just a feeling of being unjustly picked on by fate when told that, for my obscenity, I would have to serve an afternoon recess detention as well.

Okay, I wasn't going to get the strap, but I was still mighty pissed off.

Afternoon recess found me sulking into that place, frozen to that hard wooden bench before The Secretary's unflinching scrutiny, hands folded, perfect upright posture.

The Secretary did not tolerate fidgeting.

Mrs. Acorn leaned her head in, said a few pleasant words to her about the weather, and turned to leave, saying that she had some copies to make.

"I could turn the drum for her," I said, eyes still straight ahead at The Secretary, fearful that my outburst could backfire into a week's detention, or worse.

She looked puzzled for a moment. I think she thought that making copies was a worse level of punishment than just sitting there, but it did seem like a good idea. She told me I could go and help The Librarian, but reminded me that she could still see me from her desk.

Round and round and round the drum turned, and the printed pages piled up.

A report on books damaged or missing from the library, ten copies, then a list of 200 titles available for inclusion in the circulating books, ten copies.

A form with blank spaces for kids to fill in with names of books they would like to see in the library, one hundred copies. The Secretary looked in to see how things were going, scowled at me, thumbed through the copies that had been made, suggested that I could manage a better pace than that, and went back to her desk.

A list of top ten books that had been checked out that year, ten copies. A list of top ten suggestions for kids to check out. Ten copies. A poem with the title: The Fights, fifty copies. Another poem entitled: The Island, fifty copies. I tried to read them as they went around on the drum, got dizzy, and the bell rang to announce the end of recess.

There was the sudden roar of bouncing, boisterous kids piling back into the building. Mrs. Acorn thanked me for my help and, with a conspiratorial wink and a smile, said, "You won't tell, will you?"

She turned at the library and I kept going on up the hall to my classroom wondering, "Tell what?" I didn't get it.

After school I headed over to the pole vault run. I hadn't had a chance to practice all day, having missed both recesses.

And Dink topped eight feet! I was impressed.

I got one of my bamboo poles from the bushes, waited and watched.

Dink made it over eight feet again. The guys raised the crossbar another inch.

He knocked the bar off and it was Gronk's turn. He had them set it at eight foot one and made it. Went for eight two and knocked it off. It was my turn.

I told them to set it at seven feet and bounced on my toes. I thought about what Fram said about making the pole bend, like a spring. I got running, the pole bouncing, looked down at the tip, aimed for the stop block. Picked up speed. Stabbed the tip into the chock and felt the instant stop of the pole's momentum, but my own body carrying on, still running, driving all of my weight straight down instead of up, at a spot just a foot or so above the chock.

When performed perfectly, the pole coils into a spring and then releases that energy upward, projecting the vaulter up and forward with greater thrust. Combine that with doing a hand-stand, feet to the sky, and you can throw your body higher than the place where you hold the pole.

And I could.

And did.

But my timing was off and I made that perfect handstand feet-first right into the crossbar, sending it flying way over the landing pads. Lucky it didn't break, but I had soared higher than I ever had before. It was just a matter of timing. I was certain. I could do this.

While waiting for my next turn I took a good look at Dink's pole. Funny sort of bamboo, joints seemed awfully far apart. I looked again. There weren't any joints at all! It wasn't bamboo!

He started his run and got a tremendously deep bend and fantastic spring, but missed eight foot, one inch.

"Fiberglass, sixty dollars," he said proudly as he walked back to his place in line, holding it out for me to take a closer look. Slightly green in colour, smooth and lightweight. No chance of splinters. Great spring action.

The first bus left.

The second bus left.

Dink got on his bike and headed off for home, his new fiberglass pole in the crook of his arm like a jousting knight.

I cleared seven foot one, seven-two, seven-three. Went for seven-four and didn't make it. Broke my best pole and pulled out another and practiced until the late bus was ready to load, then stashed my pole in with the others in our spot in the bushes.

I got on the late bus, riding with the Teachers and staff and kids who had served after-school detentions, staring out the window on a very quiet trip home. Compared to the rowdy behavior on the early buses, this was downright

creepy-quiet. The only one talking at all was Claire
Chantler, up front, cheerily chatting away with the bus
driver.

I had just one okay pole left, and even it had a bit of
peeling near the grip. I had another that had split at the tip
and I'd used it the other way around, thick end forward, but
it wasn't very good that way. I didn't have any really good
poles left at all. I needed to go back to the Hercules.

Chapter 16
Eyes On Backwards

The boat pulled out from the slip, into the open air of the Bay.

What had been a slightly cool but calm afternoon whipped suddenly into an Eastern blast that quickly switched to the North, then came ripping back from the West, all confused, no doubt, by the great length of long warehouse buildings on the city's piers. It really was too foul a day to stand out in on the windward side. Bob Mallory joined me in the lee, pulled out a pack of some weird oval-shaped French cigarettes, lit up and offered me one.

They were a lot stronger than the brands I was used to and I leaned out toward the rail and horked a big cough and spit out to be carried over the rail by the blast of wind. I pulled my heavy blue topcoat tighter around my neck.

Bob took a ballpoint pen from his pocket and opened a sketchbook, a lined tear-out sheet pad, about the size and shape of the ledger book that The Teacher kept our marks in.

"Whatcha drawing?" I asked.

He showed me the page, a mixture of images and words.

It was a rambling diatribe about sweat in the armpits of the strippers at the Victory theatre, accompanied by drawings. Simple, evocative drawings, capturing the essence of what he wrote with just a few pen strokes.

"That's kind of neat," I said when I was done looking at it.

He shrugged, tore out the page and wadded it up into a tight ball, then leaned out and tossed it overboard, followed by a big snot-spit of his own.

"Wadja do that for?" I asked, rather incredulous.

"Water and fire," he answered. "Ways to send a letter, a thought, off to the universe."

"Okay…"

"All art is but a transient record," he said, "like the sand pictures that Tibetan monks make, then destroy. Given enough time, everything vanishes. And that, making things vanish, you should know, is the art of the magician."

"Ah-ha…? So you're a…"

"A magician. Yes."

"So you can do that "gesture hypnotically" thing like Mandrake the Magician?"

"That's cartoon stuff," he scoffed, "Although there is a bit of truth at the heart of it. You can make a hand gesture and get somebody to do what you want, but only if they know what the gesture means ahead of time."

"So you can't, like, wave your hand and put a bunch of strangers in a trance?"

"Yes and no. If you put someone in a trance before, and tell them that "this gesture will put you back under," then, yes, you can make a hypnotic gesture and put that person in a trance. But it's the gesture, not the hypnotist, that puts them back under. So, if one magician hypnotizes a bunch of people, and gives them the post-hypnotic suggestion that "This gesture will put you back in a trance", then another magician who knows that gesture can make those people fall under his spell, yes.

"But you can't just make some stranger fall into a hypnotic trance with a wave of the hand, no."

"Hmm, I see."

"But there's more to magic than hypnosis," he said. "To be a magician, you do have to know some entertaining party tricks, sleight-of-hand stuff. But you also have to be an alchemist and a herbalist, and at least a half-assed decent artist as well."

He wrote a rambling dialogue on the page that looked like poetry, interspersing the words, To, Rue, The, and Day here and there with images, a leafy plant on one side of a balance scale, then a pregnant woman, pushing a baby stroller on the other side.

I watched as he drew, the cold starting to get to me. I wasn't going to be able to stay up here on the exposed upper deck much longer.

He wrote words over the pictures, adding descriptions of smells of the city. Then some odd stuff about Greek gods being crucified by businessmen in suits. Then he tore the page out, balled it up and threw it overboard

There, out in the foul weather of the upper deck of the ferry coming home, he sat and wrote and filled pages.

And, one by one, as he filled the pages, he tore them out and crumpled them and tossed them away with the wind. Into the sludge-ball polluted scum of the harbour.

The weather continued to deteriorate, the white-cap waves becoming especially rough. I huddled from the wind in the shelter of the life-jacket box and smoked the French cigarette and shivered and read over Bob's shoulder as he drew and wrote.

"I traded the gold fountain pen that my cousin gave me, on the day that he married, for a cigarette." He wrote. "And god! How I needed that smoke!"

I read the words and wondered at some deeper meaning as he threw it overboard and began another page.

"You come up the stairs to the blast of chill spray on the deck," he wrote. "You stride over to the rail. Your back is to me and I don't think you see me there. Then you wave to me, before you turn around. You know that I wonder if you've seen me, then I remember that you put your eyes on backward today."

A swift flurry of the pen and there was a simple but exact depiction of a girl at the rail of the ferry facing the other way, but with her eyes in the back of her head.

Just a few pen strokes.

I recognized the girl in the drawing as Gwen.

His pen stopped and he smiled, tore the page from the pad and handed it to me. I read it again while he drew another, then crumpled and tossed that one to the wind and spray.

"It's kind of like making something more detailed than a wish," he wrote, "because, to make a wish, one must put the thing you desire into writing, then destroy it, usually with fire." His pen paused until he was sure that I understood. "But, when you write something down and then destroy it in water, you can put a lot more into it. But be careful! It sometimes comes back in a reverse way."

His pen stopped again until I indicated that I had read all that. "If you want to cleanse the minds of people who feel that the armpits of a stripper on stage at the Victory Theatre are disgusting, you write it down and cast it to the waves. Then people think about them differently. The Stripper's armpits are just as sweaty, but now people think they are a little less unattractive. This power comes from Neptune, and he likes to be kept informed." He stopped writing.

I still held the page with the drawing of Gwen with her eyes on backwards, and asked if I could keep it.

"Sure," he said. "Giving it away and throwing it out to Neptune to fetch amount to the same thing.

"Actually," he hoarsely whispered, using the back of is hand to shield his mouth from the waves, as if there was someone there that he didn't want hear his words or even read his lips. "He's just plain hooked on going for anything you throw into the water, kind of like a dog waiting under the table for a scrap of food to fall."

His eyes bulged and I had to keep from laughing, thinking about god the dog, wagging his tail, drooling anxiously while awaiting a treat, and Bob knew what I was thinking and couldn't keep from cracking a smile himself. "But you have to be very cautious not to ask for anything just for the sake of selfish vanity. If you do, you'll always somehow get punished for it. You have to be careful because, you know, he bites!"

We both broke out laughing and I asked him to put this "power" to the test. Make a wish come true.

He said, of course, that it didn't work that way and I said that, yeah, of course, that's the usual lame excuse.

"So," he said, "okay, let's try it. What do you want to wish for?"

I thought long and hard, then, with complete confidence, looked him in the eye and said: "ten bucks."

"Well," he said, "that's certainly is specific. Let's see…" He wrote "Ten Dollars for Lorne" In large letters on the page.

"Seems like I could write a lot more on that much paper," he said after tearing it out. "But, here goes." He crumpled and threw it over the rail just before we pulled into the calmer waters of the protected route into the dock at Centre.

"You know," he said, contemplating the pen in his fingers, "it seems to me I could write a lot more with this pen." He tossed it with a quick flick of his wrist off over the railing. "The fate is the same for the pen as the paper," he said. "Neptune can read what has been written equally well from either."

We had some moderate shelter from the harsh East wind, but I was still chilled all the way through and turned toward the stairs.

"Ah, could I ask you just one thing before you go?" he asked me.

"Yeah, sure, what?"

"Do you, ah, have a pen I could borrow?"

I already had my hands in my pockets and started to pull my right one out, paused and asked, "Am I likely to get it back?"

"Probably not," he sheepishly admitted.

I pulled my left hand from my pocket, saying, "Will a pencil do?"

"Hey, even better," he said, taking a step towards the white metal garbage can with its swinging lid that was bolted to the side of the lifejacket box, "pencils float!"

He took a small, red plastic pencil sharpener from his pocket and started sharpening the tip, carefully making sure that the shavings went into the can. "Um," he said, pausing, "I wouldn't want him to get any wrong ideas."

"I understand," I said. I was shivering uncontrollably and headed down stairs to the shelter of the first deck to sit beside my bundle of new poles as we docked at Centre. Bob stayed topside.

When I got home I put the drawing of Gwen with her eyes in the back of her head between the pages of my Atlas.

Chapter 17
Stanley Cup and Slushy Ice

I began my run.

Put on a tremendous burst of speed.

Planted the pole and swung.

Aimed myself as hard as I could. The pole split lengthwise in the middle and I landed hard, scraping my back on the cinder track.

I was clearing over eight feet now, but I broke more poles. So I bought more, carrying the awkward bundle home on the ferry among the commuters and tourists.

Word got around the Island that I was selling my pool tickets for track gear, and suddenly everybody wanted in. I had to start earlier in the evening on game nights, but the hockey season was winding down and there weren't many games left to go, so I increased my efforts and sold more and more draws on each game.

There never seemed to be anyone home at number 10 Second on game nights, so I never sold Mr. Acorn any more pool tickets.

The play-offs were about to start when I thought up a new game and started selling another wager. I called it a "Double".

Allow me to explain.

There are four double numbers on each slip of paper that you get: 44, 55, 66 and 77.

I've made them double so that there can't be any confusion between the slips of paper with these numbers on them and the tickets for my regular draws. Everything goes down in my book anyway, but still, to avoid any chance of an argument, I make the tickets for this bet look different.

Instead of drawing a number at random, though, you get to choose which one you want. What you're betting on is how many games the series will last.

So, the Leafs are going up against the Rangers in the semi-final, and you know that it's going to be a best-of-seven series. Before the drop of the puck in the first game, you can choose, say, a 44 (like I said, the numbers are only double to eliminate confusion). What you've got is a number 4. And what you're betting is that the series is going to end in 4 games, no matter who wins. You have four choices, the numbers are 4, 5, 6 and 7. Tickets are a dollar, and the payout is two dollars. You've got a 1 in 4 chance of doubling your money.

There's more risk in it for me, I might sell all number 5's, and five could be the number of games that series takes to end, which means I've got to cough up double whatever was bet in order to pay off. But the odds, I thought, were way in my favour.

The players knew it, and didn't mind taking a bigger chance in order to help me get new poles. I was actually getting encouraged to keep at the sport of pole-vault by guys like Johnny Peat and Preacher John, guys who were sports legends from their own generation in the Island Canoe Club glory days. Even Bill Ward, who I didn't think even knew I existed, asked if I'd come to his place across the park on game night to see that he got a pool ticket.

Winter had lost its grip. Just a few weeks ago I would have risked crossing the over ice to Algonquin from the ferry docks at Ward's to the foot of Nottawa. Now that stretch of lagoon had turned into open water, though still cold enough to hold ledges of ice on its shores. I had to go all the way around to the Algonquin Bridge and then come back towards the Queen City Yacht Club to start my Algonquin Island sales. Besides selling more tickets, there was a secondary reason for taking this longer route: the tree-swing.

At the foot of Nottawa, where it meets Omaha, stood one absolutely gigantic poplar, quite possibly the oldest tree on Algonquin, with root gnarls like giants knees some five or six feet up. It had a stout branch twenty five feet or more from the ground, aiming West, from which hung a two-inch thick hawser rope.

Swinging on that rope was the best exercise I could imagine for pole vaulting. I'd climb up onto one of that tree's knees, grip the rope, swing out and invert. Then, while swinging out and back, feet up and head down, do pull-ups, running shoes gripping the rope, sliding it between my feet, my head a few feet from the ground.

Pull up.

Swing and pull up.

I'd try to do ten, twelve, fifteen or twenty repetitions.

If there were other kids playing, waiting for their turn, I'd have to flip off after a few reps, land in the soft, shifting sand, and then wait my turn again. Often, though, on a game night, I'd have the whole tree to myself and could spend a good half-hour on the rope swing before heading up Nottawa, around Seneca and back up Ojibway. Then I'd come back and do another set of pull-ups on the rope before getting around to as many more houses on Algonquin as I could before game time.

But, of course, all seasons surrender to their successors in turn.

And, just as all of nature's seasons must pass, so too must all hockey seasons.

Toronto beat New York in the play-offs in 6 games, and 26 of 54 players had chosen 6 as the final number of games. I paid out 52 dollars on the "double" pool and pocketed only 2 in profit. Chicago had also beat Montreal in 6, but I only ran pools on Leafs games.

The finals started, with sixty double tickets sold, and Toronto won the first two games. Then Chicago won one. Number 4 was out of contention in the doubles pool. Chicago won again and then Toronto won another and 5 was out.

Thirty one of my customers had gone with 6 this series. I'd sold 60 tickets in all, and only 3 of them were on number 7. If the series ended in 6, I'd lose two dollars. But if it went to 7 games, I'd make $46.

I wanted Toronto to win the Stanley Cup so badly that year, but just not yet. As much as I was a died-in-the-wool, true white and blue Leafs fan through and through, I wanted Chicago to hang in there for just one more game.

And, televised from Chicago, I knew before the game even started that Toronto was going to win it tonight. Somebody in Chicago screwed up big time. Whoever was in charge of playing the national anthems played a lame few bars of "The Maple Leaf Forever," realized their mistake, then went into the Star Spangled Banner.

Nothing could have fired the Leafs up more!

Every Canadian watching that pathetic display was ready to take up arms and go down there and, just like in the war of 1812, burn their White House down again!

We watched them go through the first period.

Scoreless.

And the second period.

The same.

And then the third...

Bobby Hull was tired, worn out, and scored!

The Chicago fans dumped about three tons of rubbish on the ice! I guess their thinking was: "If we're ahead, and there's no more ice, then there's no more game, and we win!"

But it doesn't work that way.

And so three tons of eggs and old hats and cigars and spit and such got scraped away and the puck finally dropped back into play.

Oh how I wanted Toronto to win, eventually, but for now I hoped that they'd be unable to put the puck in the net for the rest of this game, then bring the series back home. But the Leafs weren't getting tired. If anything they looked

fresher than when the game started. Hull and Makita tried
to keep it together, but Chicago just didn't have the legs.

Nevin scored. The game was tied one-all!

I could hear the cheering from dozens of houses all up
and down the block, feel the thump, the universal
shockwave as hundreds of fans leaped from couches and
feet pounded floors. I was torn, jumping and yelling a
grateful cheer along with the whole Island, but with a
sinking feeling all the same.

Eddie Shack rushed around the Hawk defensemen, threw
them off their pace. They couldn't figure out what he was
going to do next, who he was going to pass to.

And Nevin got a breakaway!

Nesterenko, Chicago defense, was beat, desperate, and
tripped him!

It should have been a penalty shot!

We shouted from our living rooms so loud that we were
sure that the officials in Chicago that night could hear us
calling for a penalty shot! But such was not to be.

The puck dropped and...

It's Keon...

To Armstrong...

Who waits...

Stops at the line...

Passes to Kelly,

Over to Horton,

To Duff,

Back to

Horton...

Hard fast pass back to Duff and an explosion from our
couch as... there it is!

It's Behind Hall!

The Leafs ahead 2-1!

At 14:14 of the third period!

And I wished I could be as happy for that goal as I
wanted to be. I jumped as high as everyone else did, and

cheered as loud. But my heart just wasn't fully in it. It wasn't honest elation. I was cheating. I was pretending to be happier than I really felt.

But Barry's exuberance was genuine. He kept looking at the little slip of paper in his hand. Shoving it in my face and saying: "Look at that! 14:14!" Showing it to Flo. "Can you believe it!"

14:14 was the time he had in his pool from work. If there was another goal, he'd win at least twenty-five dollars for this ticket. But, if this stood up as the winning goal, he'd be collecting about the equivalent of three weeks wages!

And it did stand as the winning goal. Barry was so ecstatic, I thought he'd burst a blood vessel in his forehead or something.

Toronto won the Stanley cup in 6 games.

6 seemed to be a significant number that year. If all the players in my "Double" pool had chosen the number 6 I'd have been in really big trouble. As it was I considered myself lucky to have only lost two dollars.

I wasn't going to do that again.

I thought of changing the rules next season, maybe splitting it and increasing the payout. That is, total number of games, same as before, but with a choice of teams so that you'd be betting on one team or the other to take it in that number of games. That would give me a total of eight numbers to sell. But I'd have to increase the odds, maybe pay out 3 or 4 for 1, but the possibility of losing big time scared me into thinking that running this type of pool wasn't such a good idea after all.

Worst of all, it had made me cheer against my beloved Leafs.

A chilly breeze slapped a fine spray of rain in my face as I went about paying off the winners. The Leafs had won the Stanley Cup, hockey was over for the year and, along with it, my main source of income. Still, for the moment, the whole city was celebrating.

Honking horns wafted their joy from across the Bay and rowdy cheer spilled from every home. There was a loud party going on at Bill Durnan's and I had to wade through the jostling crowd to find him and give him his winnings before heading back out into the drizzle to finish my rounds.

I heard later that Bill's dog had gotten drunk and someone had lifted it up on the piano bench where he banged his paws on the keys and howled his own drunken dog-songs to the delight of the equally drunken revelers. Bill made the mistake of passing out in that dangerous situation. My mother and Laurel Stevenson shaved off half his beard and half his hair. The poor bastard woke up to find himself bald down the left side of his head.

It took me quite a long time to make all the payoffs but, since it was Easter Sunday, at least there was no school tomorrow.

I got home cold, soaked, and tried to sleep, only to be jolted out of bed by a horrendous boom that shook the house like an earthquake.

Barry was up in his bathrobe and out the door with a flashlight, as were several of the neighbours. An orange ball of flame was still slightly glowing across the Bay beyond the turning basin. We went back to bed knowing that the car crusher at the scrap yard across the Bay over that way had encountered another vehicle with a full tank of gas. The tanks in the cars being crushed were supposed to be empty but, about once every week or so, they would hit a full one and we'd get a blast louder than the boom from a jet breaking the sound barrier. I went back to bed wondering why they were working over the holiday weekend.

Two in the morning went by.

Three AM.

I just couldn't get back to sleep.

Three fifteen.

Three thirty, the rain no longer drumming on the roof. I got up, dressed and quietly let myself out the back door. I walked over to the Eastern Gap and out the concrete causeway to the end, staring out over the Lake. Sluggish waves rolled gently, the surface emanated a soft hissing sound as a fine mist, slowly thickening into a chilly fog, descended. I sniffed the thick city air coming down from behind me, diluting with the clean cool air off the Lake in front.

Among the millions of scents, now thinned out enough that I could actually differentiate them, I caught a whiff of something half-remembered, from somewhere far away and long ago.

A tiny hint of a memory.

Saw Palmettos and Daytona Beach surf! Remembered so clearly from just that faintest trace of an aroma! I stared off into the southern reaches of a thickening low-level fog.

I knew some things about the weather, things I had learned from watching Percy Saltzman.

Percy Saltzman was the only man I'd ever seen who could write with both hands at the same time, with chalk, on a piece of glass, backwards. With two wildly swirling arms and sixty seconds left at the end of the newscast, drawing the whole weather picture for the Toronto area, he would explain what the clouds and winds and high and low pressure areas were doing. Then, with a flourish, he'd toss the chalk into the air, pronounce his closing tag line: "And that's…" and catch it coming down "…the weather!"

He was right, most of the time. More importantly than whether or not his forecast was right, he showed me how to understand the charts and diagrams, the high and low pressure patterns, and how to relate them to the cloud and wind patterns I could see in the sky with my own eyes.

I'd stood there many a night, at the end of the Eastern Gap, looking up and seeing in the sky what Percy Saltzman explained on TV.

I watched the weather unfold, usually the way he predicted.

But he wasn't always right. I started listening more to the lake and the sky, watching the clouds and smelling the wind. I still studied the weather charts in the papers, but often didn't agree with those forecaster's predictions.

I knew, or felt, that sometimes those big lumbering weather systems would just sort of lay themselves down and stop trying. And then, I felt, I could sort of tug on them. Just ever so gently, I could raise my arms and give a little pull, and that would begin a momentum that would grow until it hauled a whole mountain of weather over me. I'd done it before, I was pretty sure, though I could never prove it. But I couldn't disprove it either. Nor, do I think, could anyone else.

I just felt like I could will the wind to rise, to come towards me, and that feeling had grown, had been reinforced during my summers sailing in the QC Junior Club.

As I stood there, at the end of the Gap, I raised my arms and pulled, feeling just the faintest suggestion of a breeze touch my face through the fog, bringing droplets of condensation to my eyelids.

But it was enough. I turned and headed for home, feeling that, even if my whole heart hadn't been behind my hockey team tonight, at least I had pulled the wind.

I believed a lot of strange things back then.

I suppose I still do now.

But nobody has ever disproved what I thought, so I'll just comfortably cling to it now. And what I thought was that, in the same way that I could actually push against a ship in its berth, a ship that weighed hundreds of tons, and see it slowly, steadily move away and tighten ever so slightly on its lines, I could also, sometimes, take hold of a large weather system and give it a pull and start it moving towards me.

Sometimes.

And tonight I had had enough of hockey and of winter and had fastened my grip on a big blob of hot weather somewhere down around Florida.

I was just so sick of being cold.

Fog, they taught us in school, was the result of cold dry air meeting warm moist air. I felt the edge of the warm air as it swirled with the cold in the fog that night, felt the surge of it as the heat started to move, and somehow knew that warm weather was coming and believed that I had caused it. I had put the whole of it in motion.

No, not warm weather. What I was conjuring was hot. What I wanted was a real, true heat wave!

It was just a week ago that I'd stood out here and felt the presence of a wicked, nasty weather system that meant harm to anyone who got in its way. The centre of that weather system was a low that drifted across Northern Ontario and then stalled over the Ottawa area. At its outer rim, as it spun counter-clockwise, it pushed the wind West across James Bay, pulling all the Arctic cold air down out of Hudson's Bay. Then it swirled South, driving snow and severely cold wind the entire length of Lake Superior, then East across Lake Michigan and, unimpeded, that cold flow ran the whole length of Lake Erie. It spilled its icy contents over the Falls as a South West wind that snarled its way across Lake Ontario and slapped my face with fresh, wet snow. I had stood out there and watched the weather happen, but ignored it. I just knew, in some primitive part of my understanding of the universe, that if I did anything to attract its attention, that malevolent blob of bad weather would come barreling down on me like a runaway freight train.

Now, one week later, this wind from the South West was carrying the smell of Saw Palmettos and summer.

There were still slushy ice chunks flowing out from the Bay, grinding their snow-cone texture against the concrete walls of the gap. The pack ice was long gone from the Bay, the winter ferry schedule had surrendered to Spring's in its turn. This parade of small ice chunks was coming from the polluted old Don River. The faint scent of industrial chemicals wafted to my nose.

I went home feeling a deep confidence that a real heat wave was on its way, and indulged in the fantasy of believing that I had caused it.

I paused to wonder for a moment if what I had done really was selfish vanity?

If it was selfish, and if I really had caused a change in the weather, then, according to Bob Mallory, I'd probably somehow get punished for it. All I could do now was go home, try to get to sleep, and see what would transpire in days to come.

Chapter 18
Line Squall

When a piece of paper is punched to make it capable of being held in a three-ring binder, there are three little, round pieces of paper left over, waste. When a lot of pieces of paper have to be punched this way, a heavy-duty piece of office equipment is required, and that paper-punching device has a holding tray in its bottom for catching all those little round bits and pieces of paper. A waste paper box, if you will. It wouldn't be good practice to just let them fall to the floor and make a mess now, would it? They could be rather difficult to clean up.

Yes, quite a difficult mess to clean up.

Worse still if you were to open the windows and toss all that waste paper out into the street. That could be a terrible clean-up problem. Yes indeed.

But such was the case and such were the circumstances that the otherwise neat, civilized, tidy folk who worked in the office towers along Bay Street were compelled to throw all that office waste; all the contents of three ring paper punches, plus yards and yards of yellow ticker-tape paper from stock quotation machines, even all the rolls of paper that could be scavenged from the washrooms, down onto the street below.

And, yes, I joined in that wanton display of environmentally catastrophic proportions, that disregard for the planet.

But, really, come on. Wouldn't you?

After all, it was a warm, sunny day. Short-sleeve weather. And the news was that it was snowing in Montreal, where the Habs had finished the regular season first in the standings.

And, of course, on that note, the Leafs had incidentally JUST WON THE STANLEY CUP!

Somewhere out on Bay street, beyond that surging throng of fanatical True Believers plugging the street, there was a motorcade of the best hockey team in the world going by! Lampposts and hydro wires were hung thick with the ever-growing tangle of paper strands.

I tried my best to add my bag of store-bought confetti to the knee-deep drifts piling up on the pavement in some significant and meaningful way. My big, loud, "singing at the back of the bus" voice added my cheers to the rest of the throng until my throat went hoarse. Then I managed to squeeze through and shake hands with Eddy Shack and Red Kelly without getting shoved under the wheels by the press of fans behind me.

I headed back for home hoarse of throat and happy of spirit.

There were a lot of smokers on board, so it was pretty stuffy down in the enclosed first deck of the ferry, despite the fresh air blasting in the few wooden framed windows that had been lowered. Then someone stood up and pulled one of the open windows closed. The wind was picking up.

The ferry began to rock and somebody closed another window. Other passengers down each side followed suit until they were all closed. One of the crew came down the aft staircase, checked that all the windows were closed securely and headed back toward the bridge up the bow staircase. I went up toward the bow to stand close to the steel grate. A couple of deck hands lounged on the bench out in the "Employees Only" area at the bow where it was reasonably sheltered from the wind coming now from the stern.

As we turned, lining up with the Ward's Island dock, a line squall blast hit us like a freight train on the Port side. The whole ferry lurched and I had to hang on to keep my feet. One of the deck hands looked and pointed ahead and they both stood up. I could see past them, over by the QCYC, some commotion of keelboats, guys who had been trying to get in an early sail. The warm weather had lured a few of the members whose boats had been stored in cradles nearest the launching winch to try to jump the season.

I went back up on the upper deck in the open air and, as the ferry turned slightly to Starboard to line up with the dock, I watched the formation of four boats stretch out, three motoring ahead at full throttle while frantically dropping sail. The last one was still under sail, lagging well back. That boat wasn't going to make it into the shelter of the lagoon.

It was not going to outrun the blast.

The outline of the vicious little line squall's progress showed in the flattened tops of the white-capped waves as it ripped across toward them like a tornado lying on its side.

Then, as it hit, the boom of the boat at the rear of the pack swung over and she jibed with a force that laid her whole mast and main sail completely flat on the water, laying her hull over, keel up, right on her side. In less than a second she was on the bottom, only a few feet of the mast sticking up above the waves, her unfortunate skipper swimming for his life in the cruel froth.

As we docked at Wards I could see him being grabbed by the arms by other yachtsmen and hauled out onto the QC clubhouse lawn. I stayed on the upper deck and gauged the wind, the moment the ferryboat would make her first thump against the bumpers of the dock on her Port side. I didn't want to waste time elbowing my way through the other passengers, going off over the gangplank. I glanced back across the Bay to the weather beacon on top of the Canada Life building. The wind was about to drop.

I jumped over the railing and down the four or five feet to the bumpers, then onto the dock. I was off and running for home before the crew even got the bow line thrown. There was no time to lose.

No one was home and I let myself in with the key hidden under the mat (nobody would ever think of looking there).

I couldn't remember the number for the payphone at the QC and lost precious seconds looking for where it was written in black ink inside the front cover of the huge phone book.

There was no answer for the first ten rings.

Then, finally, somebody picked it up.

I asked whoever it was that answered to get the owner of the boat that had just gone down on the phone and, over the roar of a blustery wind still blowing in the background, I could hear him telling The Owner that he thought it was maybe a reporter on the phone. The Owner of the sunken boat came on the line and I got his name, introduced myself and asked if he had any plans on how to get his boat back up.

He told me that there was the number of a diving company taped on the wall in front of him and he was about to give them a call.

With my heart pounding I said that I knew he was in need of a diver, and offered to do the job for him. He sounded uncertain, but I reassured him that I was very experienced and told him that I'd be right there and hung up the phone.

I got the kitchen chair over beside the back door, climbed up onto the countertop over the stove and, standing on it, lifted the ceiling hatch and slid it to one side. I stuck my arm up and felt for the old pink table lamp that was sitting up there, already plugged in to an extension cord that I uncoiled and ran down the wall to a plug-in in my bedroom. I hoisted myself up into the attic and, hunched low to keep from getting spider webs in my hair, made my way along over the loose boards randomly offering precarious protection from going through the pressboard ceiling panels.

I rummaged through box after box until I found the one I wanted, pulled out my diving fins, mask and snorkel, got myself out of the attic and re-coiled the extension cord, tossed it back up and closed the hatch. I put my swim-trunks on under my pants and took off out the door as fast as I could.

I felt a phenomenal sense of urgency, there was an opportunity here… if this was going to happen the way I wanted it to, then I had no time to waste. I didn't want to go all the way around and over the Algonquin Bridge and back. Instead I headed straight to the shore facing the QC, stripped out of my jeans and, flippers on, holding the bundle of dry clothes above my head with one hand, swam across to the Junior Club jetty.

A few of the members saw me coming and came down to question what the hell I thought I was doing. "This is a private dock," one of them said.

As I pulled on my shirt I explained that I was here to see the guy whose boat had gone down and they said they hadn't heard anything about that. Then Bill Stevenson and Al Rae recognized me from the second floor of the clubhouse and came down to introduce me.

So, The Owner of the sunken boat asked, why did I think that I could save his boat? He had quickly determined that I was just some loopy kid and dialed the dive company that had a business card posted on the wall beside the payphone at the foot of the stairs.

I waited while he talked to a woman on the other end, picking up from what I overheard that their company was based in North York, could be here in about three hours, and would probably be able to do something for around, maybe, a hundred and fifty dollars. He gulped visibly as he repeated the price.

The commitment was made, he gave them the number of the payphone and hung the receiver back on its cradle. I waited for him to write down some details and turn around.

"Look," I said, "They want a hundred and fifty and can't be here for three hours. By then it's going to be completely dark. They'll tell you that they can't dive after dark and you'll have to wait until morning. By then your boat's going to be really bashed up after rocking on the bottom all night."

I could see him hesitate, thinking.

"I'm here right now, and I'll do the job for ten dollars."

At this he scoffed, and the phone rang. It was the North York dive company. They just figured out that, in three hours, it would be a night dive. They'd have to charge extra if he wanted them to bring in underwater lights, or he could wait until morning if he couldn't afford that. He was looking at me as he told them that he'd maybe wait until morning, then hung up.

"How do you propose to do this?" he asked.

As we went out to the dock I explained that I had been a QC Junior Club member for years, knew the bottom quite well, as well as the hauling ability of the club workboat, the Lillian. Where his boat was sitting, I said, was all sandy bottom, as was the entire stretch over to the small boat hoist.

"That hoist is only rated for two tons," He said. "It isn't strong enough to lift my boat out of the water. Her dry weight just over three."

"It doesn't have to pull it out," I replied. "All it has to do is lift your boat in the water, not out of it. As long as she's underwater, she weighs less. The Lillian can drag her along the sandy bottom causing little or no damage at all to the hull. And, once we get her under the hoist, we only have to lift her gunnels up to the surface. Once she's up that far," I explained, "we can put the electric pumps that the club has in the maintenance locker into her and pump her out where she sits. It will take hours, but she'll float as long as her hull isn't holed."

To The Owner and other members gathered around it sounded just possible, and so five of us loaded into the Lillian with a length of good thick rope.

I wasn't very familiar with his boat and asked him about her layout. I didn't want to get tangled in any lines or guy-wires that might be attached in odd places. I asked where the decks met the mast and how it was set to her hull, how she was rigged, if she had an inboard motor or outboard (she didn't have either).

He described her quite well and, as we came up to windward of the mast tilting back and forth from still-nasty waves, told me that he wanted me to tie the rope off to the forward bow cleat.

The wind pushed us toward the spar that protruded about four feet out of the water, and I asked the skipper at the helm to bring us around to the leeward side and then come upwind towards her.

We were closer to the shore that way and the Lillian stirred up the bottom with the force of her prop as he brought us around. I told The Owner that I thought the foot of the mast was a better tie-off point than the bow cleat, but he was quite insistent that the bow cleat would be plenty strong enough.

I got my flippers on, spit in my mask and swirled water in it, pulled the elastic strap back over my head and, clenching the snorkel in my teeth, grabbed one end of the hefty rope and jumped in.

The water was still icy cold and it got difficult to see just a few feet down. Tugging at the rope was useless against the strain. The guys on the boat weren't playing it out easily enough. I surfaced and clung to the gunnel of the Lillian and, gasping, pulled the snorkel from my mouth.

"If it's too hard then don't try it!" The Owner hollered.

"It's not that," I yelled back over the combined rumble of the engine and roar of the wind. "You're not giving me enough slack on the rope."

"What?"

"Gimme more slack!"

"How about," he said, "I'll just feed about thirty or forty feet out real fast. After that, if you want more, give it one hard pull. If you need us to pull you back, give it three pulls."

"Sounds good," I said, replacing my snorkel.

I took a deep breath, flipped over and, with my feet against the Lillian's hull, shoved off and kicked my way down the sunken boat's mast, pulling myself hand over hand along the sails and rigging.

I swam straight for the open hatch. The cold was quickly getting the better of me and I didn't want to have to do this dive again.

I tied the thick rope below the deck of the cabin, around the foot of the mast, in a sturdy bowline knot, then ran the slack forward and, just to make The Owner happy, fastened the line to the bow cleat in two wraps and a pair of hitches. It was time to kick and claw my way back to the surface.

I didn't think I'd gone down all that far, maybe twenty feet, surely no more. Yet, with each kick and reach of my arms, each time I thought "Now! Now I'll break out into the air! Now!"... I didn't.

And had to kick again.

And again, and reach.

And finally, lungs bursting, I broke through and the guys on the boat hauled me in.

"Did you get it?" he asked.

"Yu-yu-yu-yeah" I shivered. "Sh-sh-she's tied f-f-f-fast."

"Okay then," the skipper said, and eased the Lillian forward until the slack was pulled out of the line and then, ever so gently, eased the throttle up until, as I said she would, the sunken sailboat started to slide her way forward along the sandy bottom.

I laid down on the vinyl-covered engine compartment to soak up some heat from the motor while we chugged along slowly. At one point there was a sudden jolt to the line, like we'd just caught a really big fish, and I knew that it was the bow cleat ripping out of the forward deck. We were still solidly tied to the mast, though, and that knot held until we brought her all the way in to the shallows under the electric hoist.

I didn't have to go back in the water. A couple of club members figured out how to get heavy lines under her bow and stern and they made a sling, fastened it to the hoist and started lifting her until the gunnels broke water. Then they dropped in the electric pumps and she began, slowly, to rise.

I went into the men's shower room and stood under the hot spray for a good half-hour, warming up. The Owner brought me my ten dollars, along with a shot of brandy in a snifter glass with a warning not to let anyone know that he'd given the alcohol to me. As I raised the glass to my lips I silently thanked Bob and his little sacrificial wads of paper.

And, of course, Neptune.

Chapter 19
Salt Horse

Finally feeling warmed all the way through, I dried and dressed and left the clubhouse to see how she was doing. As I surveyed the scene, the keelboat was rising quite nicely as the last of the light of the sun left the sky. The excitement had calmed down and, with nothing more to see here but a pair of electric sump-pumps slowly emptying her out, most of the members still hanging around the club had returned to working on their own boats.

The Junior Club boats, Nordberg class, wooden hulls, adjacent to the small-boat hoist, still rested upside-down under tarps, their masts, booms and spars stored in the Junior Club sail shed. Most of the Yacht Club's boats were still sitting in their cradles, waiting patiently to be slid along the butter boards to the marine rail system where the donkey winch would slowly deliver them back into the water (a reverse of the process that had seen them hauled out last fall). The air was still, scarcely a ripple on the Bay, no remnant of the blast that had hit such a brief hour or so earlier.

The boat I had crewed on for three years was there, Stewball, and I briefly inspected her hull in the fading light.

Starchy's dad was known to the other QC members as the Chairman of the Junior Club Committee. To us, he was The Commodore. Any decision made by him in a race challenge was final. An assignment from The Commodore was unquestionable. What he decreed was law absolute.

He assigned each of us to a boat when we joined and, barring his overriding that decision, that was the boat we stayed with for as long as we were in the Junior Club. But we didn't sail her for the first week.

That first week we stripped her down, scraped, sanded and cleaned, prepared and then varnished. We mended sails and lines, made all necessary splices and whipped all lose rope-ends with marlin twine.

And woe be to any captain and crew who weren't ready to sail come the start of the second week.

I ran my hand down Stewball's keel and felt a stabbing sensation in my finger. A Splinter!

Her bottom was going to be glass smooth and splinter-free before she went anywhere near the water. We'd make certain of that.

Gliding my palm over the curve of the old Stewball's stern, I could hear again the music that The Commodore played over the old record player while we sanded and painted and spliced and stitched. Sea shanties and Calypso music. Sailing songs. Berl Ives and Harry Belafonte.

I walked quickly over the Algonquin Bridge singing Salt Horse and Matilda all the way home. The evening was a bit cool, but the wind had dropped. It felt like the weather was waiting.

The next morning, at the back of the bus on the way to school, I heard that the dive team from North York had shown up at the QC in the morning. The Owner of the keelboat had neglected to tell them not to bother coming. They were quite upset, having made a long and costly journey for nothing, but there wasn't anyone around to complain to. The Owner simply wasn't at the club. He was off sailing.

After the obligatory renditions of "Don't Laugh When You See A Hearse Go By" and "Great Green Gobs of Greasy Grimy Gopher Guts", I started up "Salt Horse", and everyone from the Junior Club joined in.

And, since Mr. Stark's well worn recording had skipped at that point, we sang:

"Salt Horse, Salt Horse, I'll have you know
That to the galley you / the galley you / the galley you..."
Until someone went "Click!"
"... / must go

"The cook, without a sign of grief / sign of grief / sign of grief (Click)
Will boil you down and call you beef."

That's the way The Commodore's record player played the song, so that's the way we sang it. Kids who didn't go to the Queen City Junior Club didn't get it.

Percy Saltzman had explained what weather I was seeing in the sky when I looked up, but he taught only rudimentary, fundamental things about wind and weather. I learned from Percy Saltzman what it might do tomorrow from the way the weather patterns looked on a map. But Starchy's dad, The Commodore, taught me how to know what it might do in the next ten minutes by observing the way the wind smelled and tasted and how it resounded in the ears.

I could smell heat, but was it really coming? The professional forecasters certainly weren't predicting it... But they didn't have the advantage that I did. They didn't have the ability to slip silently out of bed in the middle of the night and cross the wild-grass barrens over to the Eastern Gap. Out to the Southern tip of a concrete surface, a bit wider than a single-lane road. That concrete wall of the Eastern Gap has since been torn out and re-aligned to let ships take a different course out of the harbour. The old spot where I stood is maybe a hundred feet East of the tip of the pile of jagged broken rocks that currently line the channel.

To go now to the place where I stood then, you'd have to walk on water. Or, more accurately, about three feet above it.

Right there, at that spot, there used to be a tower made of steel girders, about ten feet high, with a big steel channel marker sign attached.

It seemed strange to me that it never got hit by lightening.

There was something odd, powerful, about that spot, and I wasn't the only one who sensed it.

Chapter 20
Wither the Weather?

I felt the huge air mass stall, stagger and start to back up. The systems were hesitating, waiting.

I studied the sky from the place out at the end of the Gap, and willed the warmth to come. It kinda felt like I was calling a dog to my side. I sensed within myself a lack of commitment. Was I sure this was what I wanted?

The whole of the weather patterns of the entire region seemed to halt. Weather forecasters called it stagnant air, and saw no significant changes to come.

School came and went, and another night saw me once again slipping the backdoor latch.

I didn't see Bob Mallory standing there, in the deep dark of the night, until I was already just about all the way out to the end of the Gap. By then he'd seen me, had been watching me walk along towards him. "Hi," I said tentatively, not sure who that was out there in the dark.

"Hi," he said back, not certain who I was in the pitch-blackness. There was a mutual flash of recognition, each of us knowing the other's voice. "Lorne?" he asked.

"Yeah. Is that you, Bob?" I was still a good ten paces away.

"He-ey. What brings you out here in the black of night?"

"Oh, I just couldn't sleep," I truthfully replied.

"Yeah, me neither. This is an interesting spot."

I agreed as I came up beside him. It might have been dangerous for anyone else to try strolling out here in the dark, the cold lake on each side and no guard rails, but I felt perfectly safe and confident in my ability to distinguish the ever-so-slight difference in the darkness of the water from the darkness of the concrete top of the Gap. I stopped about three feet from the end, right on the power spot, just to Bob's left.

"That glow in the sky, over that way, that's the lights of Buffalo," I said. "And way over there, that's Rochester."

"Really? That's Rochester?"

"Uh-huh." We stood and strained our eyes against the darkness in silence for a minute. I could sense the frontal edge of the weather pattern before me, like a great lumbering imbecile, just waiting for me to tell it which way to turn.

"This certainly is a phenomenal evening," Bob said.

"Yep, a night for phenomenon's and phantasmagoria."

"What does that mean?"

"Oh, just that it feels like one of those nights when almost anything might happen."

The weather was waiting for me, and, whether Bob was here or not, the hot days needed a nudge. It felt like they were asking me, "Should I come around like you asked?" I had to make a decision.

"Of course, it doesn't bother me, one way or the other," Bob said.

"What do you mean by that?"

"Oh, just that, whatever happens, I just want to be there to see how it turns out."

Did Bob know what I was thinking? Was he on my wavelength? I wasn't sure, but I was certain that I had had enough of winter, enough of being cold. I wanted heat. The hot blast of summer. I raised my arms and made a beckoning gesture. Bob probably couldn't see it in the dark, I thought, even though he was standing just a few steps away.

I made my beckoning gesture, then stepped back and felt the faint breeze follow. I stopped, the air continued to move, caressing my cheek.

"That's a pretty neat trick," Bob said, and for an instant I thought that he knew what I was doing, that he was referring to me calling the weather. Maybe he was, but he held something that glowed, and he could have been talking about that as well.

"What's that?" I asked.

"It's a crystal," he replied, holding the glowing object closer for me to see. "It's for detecting Ley Lines."

"What lines?"

"Ley lines. The Druids knew about them. They're lines of power that run all over the surface of the Earth. Sometimes they cross each other. You've heard of Stonehenge? It's built at a place where the Ley Lines converge, very powerful forces there."

"Okay," I said, trying not to sound too skeptical.

"I came out here following a faint line of power that seems to run down the length of the Gap, and it just sort of peters out right about here..." He scraped his shoe on the concrete. "But when you did that thing with your arms and stepped back, away from the center of the line, the crystal suddenly got quite a bit brighter."

"Is that so?" I was definitely intrigued now.

"Yeah. Would you mind doing that again?"

"What, that..."

"Yeah, just step up to, where were you now, right about there. Now, bring your arms up and back like that again."

And so, again, I beckoned to the clouds, tugging on the edge of the big High pressure system that I knew was hanging around right about, oh, just over... there.

And I stepped back and felt it move again, following. I looked at Bob's crystal and the glow was brighter for a few seconds, then began to dim again.

"Now isn't that something?" he said, stooping down and making a scratching noise with something on the cement. "I'm putting a chalk mark here so I can come back and study it during the day. Do you know what it means?"

"Well, not entirely, no."

"There are some places," he went on, "Where the Ley lines go roughly East and West, and others that run North-

South. Where they intersect are known places of great mystical power. There are a few spots, though, where the lines come straight up out of the Earth, running off into the sky. I think this is one of them."

"Really?"

"Well, either really or maybe. Either way, it looks like you've found one of that kind. What is that you were doing there, with your arms?"

"Oh, I was just hoping for good weather."

"No, really, what were you trying to..."

"Really, that's what I was doing, trying to bring on a heat wave. I want some hot, sunny days."

"Well in that case, I guess we'll have to wait and see if it comes to pass. By the way, how did that wish for ten dollars turn out?" As we walked back toward the lights of the houses on Ward's I told him about the gale that had sunk a sailboat off the QC, and how I'd managed to earn ten bucks getting her back up off the bottom.

"That sounds like it should be safe enough, since you earned it. You have to be very careful, though, if you just, say, had been walking down the street and found a ten dollar bill lying there."

"Why?"

"Well, like I told you before, sometimes you get your wish, but in a backwards, warped sort of way. It can be quite dangerous. Look at the Hell that Poseidon put Odysseus through."

I told him I didn't know that story, and he told me that Neptune, as Poseidon, likes to snatch things, reads the messages they carry, and sometimes takes a notion to torment you if he thinks you owe him something in return.

"Drop by tomorrow after school and I'll show you some of the legends," he said. "I've collected quite a lot of books on the subject."

"Okay, yeah, I guess I could do that."

"There's one thing, though, some of this stuff is intended for adults only. Are you sure it'll be okay with your folks?"

If The Teacher had given out a study assignment enforced by threats of expulsion and beatings I might have half-heartedly tried. But Bob telling me that he had books with knowledge that was for "adults only", well, of course, I couldn't be dissuaded from wanting to see everything. I could hardly wait.

"Where do you live?" I asked. Bob was going to walk on, continuing along Lakeshore as I turned the corner at Second.

"I'm staying with the Acorn's for a few nights, at 10 Second."

As I headed down Second for home I called out, "I'll be there."

The next day I dropped by after school, as promised, to see Bob's "research" books, and caught them all just leaving.

"It's poetry night on Thursday's," Gwen said. "At the Bohemian Embassy. We're just on our way out."

"Sorry about that," Bob said as Milt locked the door behind them.

"Okay, maybe another time." I said, turned and headed back for home. The weather was still cool, but in the morning the forecasters were calling for a warming trend to set in tomorrow.

Chapter 21
Stuck In The City

Friday was a stifling hot afternoon in class, and after school there was nobody home at the Acorn's, but I still had ten dollars burning a hole in my pocket. Even though it was so warm, I took my heavy blue topcoat along and stashed it in a locker at Union Station for later on, just in case.

Radio station CHUM put out the CHUM charts, crude paper pamphlets with jokes and riddles and prizes and such, along with the latest standings of favored pop stars on the chart that week. And they sponsored dances for teens, announcing them in the CHUM chart. Sock hops, they called them, and there was one tonight at a hall up near Yonge and St. Clair. There would be girls there, girls who weren't Island girls, that I could actually slow dance with and imagine perhaps asking out on a date.

A real date.

The music was all on 45's, vinyl disks about seven inches across, each with a huge hole in the centre, and the most popular dance craze at the time was a new thing called The Twist.

I had just barely learned how to Twist, but, when they played one of the older songs, I had a chance to show off, because I really knew how to do the Hucklebuck!

I tried to chat with girls, buying pop and snacks for any of them that would dance with me in an attempt to gain favour.

By the time the night had wound down to just a few stragglers standing around blinking in the bright lights that they turned on to make everyone go home, I was down to just ten cents left out of my ten dollars.

Ten cents, and about a half-hour to make the last boat.

It was miles to the docks, but at least it was mostly down-hill.

I ran and ran until my lungs hurt, then held my side and ran some more.

Down Yonge Street all the way to King. Across to Bay. Echoes of my feet bounced back from the concrete walls of the underpass. This stretch was completely flat. I was no longer getting the benefit of going down-hill. My lungs and legs were killing me. Then across Queens Quay and up to the turnstile on wobbly spaghetti-strand legs with just seconds to spare.

And the ticket-taker wouldn't let me on.

Too tall.

The ten-cent child's fare was only for those who were four foot eight and under. If I wanted to ride the boat, I'd have to pay the full adult fare of twenty-five cents.

But I didn't have twenty-five cents.

And that was just too bad for me.

The wicket closed, the boat sailed, and there I was, stuck on the city side.

It was chilly and I was soaked with sweat as I walked back up to Union Station to get my heavy blue topcoat out of the locker.

Chapter 22
Steam Pipe

"So what did you do? How did you get home?" Gwen asked in a soft voice, almost a whisper, as we sat at the table. Bob stirred slightly and rolled over on the folding army cot that was set up in the kitchen. Milton's snoring came in tortured bursts from the bedroom. The kettle was steadily crackling and popping on the burner, not yet at a boil.

"I went over to the foot of York Street and waited for the one o'clock water taxi," I said, quietly setting the Book of Tao on the table. "I owe John Durnan a dollar for the ride, so I was just sort of wondering, do you have any chores I might do around here, any work I could do, for pay?"

Her jacket was draped over the back of the chair she was sitting in. She put her hand into the pocket and took out a wallet, sort of like a man's wallet, but embroidered with red and yellow yarn to give it a feminine touch.

"Here," she said, offering me a dollar bill.

"No, no," I protested. "I'm not asking for a hand-out."

"It's not charity. It's payment for fixing our toilet. Please, do take it. What you did was worth that, at least. Please, I insist."

I reluctantly accepted the bill and put it in my pocket. She smiled as if I was the one who had just done her a great favour, and got up and put some loose tea into the cold pot. The kettle wasn't quite boiling yet, but she poured the hot water in anyway and set the pot on the counter to steep.

There was a pile of freshly typed pages all heaped by the typewriter. The overflowing pile of ash and butts in the ashtray, the scatter of books laying open at odd angles and stacks more with paper between the pages, told a story of hours of concentrated research and writing. I picked up and noticed the titles of a few: A History of Magic and

Experimental Science; The Dharma Bums; The Golden
Bough. She said that she hadn't slept at all last night. But
what an incredibly productive night she'd had. "It's
something in the wind, in the air at night. Have you smelled
it?"

"Actually, " I said, looking apologetically at the floor, "I
think I caused it."

Our eyes locked and I wondered for a split second if I
should tell her about the special relationship I felt with the
weather. I made a quick wafting motion with my hand
behind me, as if I had farted, and she hesitated just a bit
before she laughed. I wasn't sure if she had "read" me or
not.

"The boys didn't sleep either," she said. "They missed the
last boat too." The way she said "boys", it sounded like she
was referring to naughty children. "They went over to the
rail yards and spent all night trying to stay warm sitting on
the steam pipe."

I didn't know what the steam pipe was, and she told me
that she'd never seen it, but some hobos had told Milt about
it. The steam pipe was a fat steel pipe wrapped in a thick
layer of asbestos insulation, she explained, that ran
underground from the CN railway boilers all through
downtown, providing steam heat to many of the tall office
buildings of the city. There was a section of it, near the rail
yards, where it ran above ground, and the hobos curled up
on it for warmth against the cold night air.

Bob and Milt had gone there for the night, but there were
a lot of seedy characters around and they hadn't slept a
wink, worrying about someone slitting their throats just to
steal their shoes during the night.

"Now, there is something you can do for me," she smiled
as she poured. "You can leave a bit of tea and leaves in the
bottom of your cup this time."

That turned out to be easy to do. The leaves hadn't settled. They floated around on top of the tea, forcing me to strain it with my teeth as I sipped.

Wham!

There it was. Another one of those sudden moments.

Telepathy.

You know that the other person knows that you know what they're thinking, because, as you looked into their eyes, they just suddenly knew what you were thinking.

And, the same way she knew I didn't know the word Kismet, she now knew that I was holding the cup in my left hand, as I knew that I was holding the cup in my left hand, and she said, "They... she..."

And I knew that she saw what I was thinking, and she smiled and said, "finish the cup first."

She relaxed back in her chair and I downed another sip. Not very strong. Not warm enough, really. Kind of weak. The jasmine taste was there, but it wasn't rich. Not a heady aroma the way she had made it last time.

Not bad, mind.

But not great.

" 'Not' is a very powerful word," she said as I took the last swig. I swirled the cup a bit, making sure there was a good coating of leaves around the bottom.

"Now, slowly, pour the last drops into the saucer. Good. Keep the cup upside down like that and let it drip until the last drop falls."

I did as she directed and, after a few seconds, realized that I was counting the drops.

Six.

Seven.

"Eight," she said at the instant that I thought it.

I looked up into her eyes as she took the cup from my outstretched hand. She slowly turned it right side up, cradling it with both hands, looked at me, held the cup up toward the ceiling and looked up at it in her hands, then slowly lowered the cup. I imagined an image of an egg resting in the nest of her intertwined fingers.

She cast her vision upwards, around and down the way you would cast a fishing lure or crack a long whip: at me, down, around and up to the ceiling, then down.

Locked.

Staring into the abyss of my teacup.

"They made you use your right hand, didn't they?"

"Yes," I said, remembering...

"Remembering her... She..."

Yes, she had it right, that's exactly what I was remembering.

"She hit your left hand. Hit it with hers. Whenever you reached for anything. A spoon. A crayon."

I remembered the spoon. I remembered the hit.

"Left hand bad! Bad! Bad! Bad!"

She snapped her eyes up from the cup and water was collecting on her lower lids. "That really hurt, didn't it?"

"Yes." It was my turn to feel a tear forming. And I felt again the heat, the hot way the skin on the back of the hand stings. The way it feels right after it's been slapped. Gwen leaned forward and reached out, touching the spot on the back of my left hand where I'd been slapped. I felt the warmth of her hand gently caressing mine.

But the cup was still resting there in the nest of her intertwined fingers! She still had both hands on it!

Yet...

Yet I felt the warmth of her hand gently caressing mine, stroking the pain-spot the way you would pet a cat.

I looked down and there was no hand touching mine! Yet the feeling was still there, so real.

There was no hand touching mine.

But there also was no pain.

It was like a part of me had been hurting for so long that I had just gotten used to the pain.

But now there was no pain.

And the lack of it was startling!

I looked back at her, both hands still wrapped around the cup. She lifted her feet from the floor, put her arms over her knees and pulled them up to her chest, heels on the lip of the chair, and smiled an impish smile, knees to cheekbones. She seemed to dwindle into a smaller version of herself, a Pixie, a Gnome. She winked and said, "It feels odd not to hurt, doesn't it?"

Of course it did.

"Of course it does." She raised the cup up, slowly rotating it in her palms, clockwise, then she suddenly looked up into my eyes.

"You counted them, didn't you? You counted how many times you got hit for using the wrong hand."

I nodded.

"Let's see, there were..."

I knew the number.

"Twenty, uh, twenty three. Right?"

That was the right count, but it wasn't the number. Not really.

"Twenty, oh... fingers, toes, eyes and nose," she exclaimed.

That was the number: fingers, toes, eyes and nose! That was the number!

The only "numbers" that I knew were one, two, three, four and five. Everything above that I just counted in groups of five. I didn't know the number twenty three.

One hit, one finger. Two hits, two fingers. Three hits, three fingers, up to five. Then I had a hand, plus however many fingers of the other hand I needed. I kept count in fingers, and then in toes. Then eyes, ears and nose, another five. I counted lots of things that way before I learned anything about numbers. I did it so that I knew if, say, some of my marbles or crayons were missing.

Fingers, that was ten. Plus toes, another ten. Plus eyes, two, and nose, one. Total: twenty-three.

I didn't reach for things with my left hand after twenty three. The smacks were getting harder and harder each time. But the answer wasn't: "fingers, toes, eyes and an ear." No, it was: "fingers, toes, eyes and nose," because that rhymed.

"You liked to rhyme words right from as far back as you can remember, didn't you?"

She was right. But this wasn't a one-way transfer. "You did too, didn't you?"

It was her turn to be jolted just a little bit. She confirmed the truth with her smile, then cast her eyes back to the cup.

Chapter 23
Two Mothers

"This is odd," she said, a puzzled look on her face. She turned the cup around, then back again. "You have two mothers?"

Bob farted and rolled over in his bed.

"Well, yeah, I guess that's true." I replied in a soft voice. "I..."

"Shhh," She cut me off. "Not yet."

She lowered her feet to the floor and set the cup in the saucer, still wet with the last drops of tea. A sound similar to a needle scratching on the blank part at the end of a record emanated from the cup as she twirled it around with a finger.

Shhh-scrape...

Once around.

Shhh-scrape...

Two.

"You ate the flowers?" she asked.

"Well, yeah, I was..."

She cut me off again with: "not yet."

Three times around she turned the cup in its saucer, then stopped, stared, and slowly turned it three times back again. It seemed to me that she was turning it in time with Milt's snoring. She answered that thought out loud, saying: "I am, you know." And as she turned the cup she slowed down, and his breathing slowed, keeping pace. He turned over and the snoring stopped.

She raised the cup in both palms and her eyes once more met mine.

"Well, now," she said, somehow managing to sound as if she had just finished reading a table of contents. "Where to start?" She looked back into the cup and tilted it ever so slightly. "I see hard, starched linen and drowning, and two brothers, but now they're dead, or, no, not dead. Moved away or something.

"But there's a whole bunch, four or five, or maybe more, of other brothers, shadow brothers... and a sister who, let's see, turns into a different sister? And something called an 'ammy'.

"And, what's this? A rather rude stone carving?" She paused...

... and lowered the cup.

Her eyes said she was done, and she looked at me expectantly.

"Is it my turn?" I asked.

"Yes. How did I do?"

"You know you got them all right."

"I do, and I did," she said, putting the cup down on the table. As she removed her hands from it I felt as if someone had been hugging me and had just let go. "So, what does it all mean?" she asked.

I felt the same way I had when The Teacher caught me passing a note in class. I'd been apprehended, found out, and all I could do was own up to everything and hope for the best. But first I bought a few seconds by asking, "What does what mean?" She gestured broadly, indicating the whole thing. "What part of it?" I asked, a last ditch attempt at stalling, my last bit of resistance.

"How about the two mothers?" She pulled her knees up, arms around them, shrank back into being a cheerful Sprite, and I had to explain.

" 'Born on the wrong side of the bed' was the expression that someone used to describe me. From a distance, but I overheard it. I had heard of 'getting up on the wrong side of the bed', and thought for the longest time that it was important, literally, to get out of bed on the same side you got in each day or you'd be in a bad mood. But I hadn't heard of being *born* on the wrong side of the bed. When I asked my mother what it meant, she made a phone call and my sister came over and they sat down and explained it to me.

"I had only heard the word 'bastard' as a swear word before that, and didn't know that it had a real meaning. And, essentially, that I was that meaning. That is to say that I was, and am, a bastard. The woman I had known all my life as my mother was actually my grandmother, and the one I had always known as my sister was really the one who gave birth to me."

"How long ago was it that they told you?"

"Last year, right around my birthday, when I turned twelve. A little over a year ago. So yeah, I guess I have two mothers, sort of."

"Okay. Drowning?"

"I don't remember anything about drowning. Well, there was that time at Daytona Beach that I nearly got washed out in the surf, but... Oh wait! Yeah!

"That was the nightmare I had over and over... that some nurse with a starched board of a uniform was holding my head underwater in a tub, and only trying to make it look like she was washing me. In my nightmare I was a squirmy little baby and managed to slip out of her grasp, to fight my way back into the air no matter how she tried to hold me under.

"I woke up screaming with that nightmare until I was maybe seven or eight. I was sure she was trying to drown me."

"And the two brothers who died or moved away..."

"Are really my uncles, Jimmy and Barry. They're just not my brothers any more, now that I know who my real mother is. Jimmy has a wife and family down at 164 Lakeshore, and Barry and Flo have a daughter, my cousin, Karen. I live with them."

"And the shadow brothers?"

"Well, they told me that my father, my real father, was already married when I was born, and had kids. I don't know for sure, but I think of them as all boys. I like to think that somewhere, out there somewhere, I've got brothers who wouldn't know me if they bumped into me on the street. But they could be almost anybody. So that means that pretty much every man I meet could be my brother. Sort of makes me feel good to think that I might have family ties with anyone. So I like to watch TV or movies and just pretend that any guy on the screen might be my brother, so I'm just as good as him."

"Okay. And what's this about eating the flowers?"

"Oh, that was my sister's... I mean my mother's wedding. The reception was held in the big Island Canoe Club hall. It used to be down at Centre, behind the fire hall, right next to the Island Canoe Club bleachers. I was six when my mother, who I knew as my sister, got married. They, the waiters, brought plates of food down the table from the right to the left, and from the left end towards the right. I was at a seat in the middle, at the centre of the table, and the waiters ran out of plates at the person on each side of me. I waited and waited, and they served everyone else at the other tables, but I didn't get any dinner. Everyone else around me in the reception hall finished their food, and they cleared the tables away to make room for dancing, but I just sat there, hungry. So I went out back and ate the flowers that had been in the vases on the tables."

"Roses?"

"No, carnations. I liked the dark ones best."

"That really happened?"

"Yes," I said sadly.

"And the sister who changed into a different sister?"

"After my sister/mother married she had a daughter, who is actually my half sister."

"I see. And this thing called an 'ammy' ?"

"I don't know."

She stood and brought the cup up in front of me. She turned it ever so slightly and my view of the random splatter of tea leaves stuck to the bottom shifted ever so slightly and, there it was, "ami", and I knew what it meant.

"That's from when I was four or five," I said, surprised to remember it. "Arthur Godfrey had a TV show, and used to open up with, 'Welcome to the beautiful Fountain Blue Hotel here in Miami.' But I didn't know that he was saying the name of the city he was in, Miami. I thought he was saying "...welcome to *my ami*". I thought an ami was a big amusement park, like the CNE or Disneyland, and he had a hotel on his. I remember my father/grandfather telling me 'We're going to Miami,' and I thought that he had an ami too. I remember asking him if his ami was as big as Arthur Godfrey's ami, and not understanding why everyone thought that was so funny."

"Well," she said turning the cup one last time, "The only thing left here is this rude stone carving."

She held the cup for me to see.

"Oh, that!" I exclaimed. "That's a picture I saw in a magazine last week!"

She studied the leaves, then, surprised, said, "Of course it is. I recognize it now. It's the temple carvings of Muria. That's in India."

I didn't care where it was. I was just embarrassed that she knew I'd been looking at dirty pictures.

"But something I don't see, here, is your father. What do you know about him?"

"Well, I thought my Grandfather was my father. He and my Grandmother have a house over on Algonquin now, on Nottawa."

"But your real father?"

"I don't know anything about him, really. I've asked my mother, but she just says it's none of my damned business."

"That's not right. Who's business would it be but yours?"

"I just know she gets really angry if I ask anything about it, and she can get very violent when she's mad. So I don't ask any more."

"And her husband?"

"Ken. He's told me flat out that I'm not his son and he doesn't want anything to do with me that way. I know him as a friend and neighbour, and that's enough."

"Really?"

"Yeah, really. I respect Ken, because he's always been straight up and honest with me. That's a lot more than I can say about a lot of people I've met..." I paused, then added, "...and family too."

Yes, that was it. That was all.

She had read my tea leaves.

And I had to admit that she was right: she really could do it.

But she had shown me the cup, and I appreciated that there was one image in there that she hadn't brought up.

I saw it.

And I knew she had seen it.

But she pretended it wasn't there, and so did I.

We both knew it, and knowing that it was something that wasn't said was enough.

Nicknames just sort of "catch", like a firecracker going off or a static spark when you walk on a rug and then reach for a doorknob. And, no matter how hard you wanted to shake it, you couldn't lose your nickname. But sometimes they'd get replaced, old ones forgotten, when you got a new one.

And sometimes a bad nickname was a good thing. Like when my old nickname had been booger-breath. I got teased with that nickname in grade one until I broke that awful habit.

On the inside, I thanked her for her discretion, her tact, in not bringing it up.

On the outside, I thanked her and rose to leave.

As I stood up I pointed out that the Book of Tao was back on the table, and she noticed my eyes upon the very large stack of books on the writing desk. She picked out a blue hardcover one with: "The Dharma Bums" embossed in gold on the spine. "Would you like to read it?" she asked.

She handed me the book, a yellow envelope pasted inside with an Island Public School library card sticking up. It hadn't been checked out. Along with the circulation card, there was a note inside the envelope, saying: "I think this material is quite too obscene for circulation at the grade school level. I strongly urge you to review it and consider it for discard." The note was signed by The Secretary.

Would I like to read it? Of course I would.

Slips of various coloured paper protruded from between the pages with notes and comments. Gwen's research, she informed me.

"But you need this, don't you?" I asked.

"Yes. But you can get it back to me after school."

"Sure, yeah," I said thumbing through the pages, wondering how long it might take to read.

"By this time next year," she beamed, gesturing toward the newly typed pages beside the typewriter, "I'm going to be a published novelist!" She was so thrilled as she said the word: "novelist" that she actually wiggled in her seat. Milt began once again to snore.

Chapter 24
Grey Paint

My heat wave was coming on strong and was welcomed with open windows and doors. No bugs were out yet. A perfect Saturday for starting to work early on your tan in the hot beach sand. A perfect Saturday for checking out babes in bikinis. A perfect Saturday for cycling down to Centre or Hanlan's. A perfect Saturday for doing a lot of things.

Barry got a spectacular bargain. A gallon of super high quality floor paint, battle ship grey. "No Fumes" it said on the label. "Dries in 1 hour."

A perfect Saturday for painting my bedroom floor, as it turned out.

We got every bit of furniture out of my room and piled in the living room, just for an hour, maybe two, tops.

He opened the can and, with a length of coat hanger wire fitted into the chuck of the electric drill, started to stir.

The thick, oily, golden amber coloured top portion of the contents of the can slowly turned a light, pale looking grey. Then it slowly got darker, the stripes and lines of different colours blended, blurred, and vanished into sameness.

Grey.

Battleship grey.

Removing the coat hanger found it dripping a thick viscosity of paint resembling soft-serve ice cream.

Barry was concerned that, since it was such fast setting paint, we'd have to get it all done in one quick coat or else we'd have overlaps. Slathering this slime on the floor resulted in a texture akin to what you might get with white school glue and a trowel.

By the time we were half done it was obvious that we'd have to work faster in order to finish before we passed out.

We didn't quite make it and resorted to borrowing an electric fan from a neighbour and putting it in the doorway to give ourselves enough fresh air to breathe so that we could cover it all in just one coat.

We gasped for breath in our shorts in the front yard, sipping iced lemonade through straws, with an hour or so to kill.

Barry wondered if it would need a second coat after all. If one was sufficient, he'd have enough left over to do the middle bedroom too. We threw a softball back and forth in the front yard. He had just bought a new mitt that needed breaking in and let me use his old one.

Hank Hanger rode up on his bike and asked if we were coming to the park. Barry wanted to stick around, but said I could use his old glove, so I took off.

There were four teams: the Osoeze, the Ottazel, the Dingbats and the Brownies. It was still way too early for league play, but we roughly fell into groups that had been the remnants of last years Dingbats and Brownies, with long, tall Tommy English pitching. Then Jim Socket pitched for a while. We didn't keep score, just took turns up at bat and in field, and even I took a turn pitching.

After a couple of hours of playing mostly second base and right field, my rumbling stomach called me home and I headed back through the path beside Bradley's.

Barry had the barbecue out on the front lawn and the aroma of sizzling burgers hurried my step. Frank Sullivan was nursing a beer while, with one hand, helping Barry set up a table before going off to his own place up Second. Flo carried utensils and napkins out the back door. I hurried in to wash up.

There are times in life when something happens, something takes you so totally by surprise that you're doubly shocked. You get the initial impact of what happens, and then you have a moment to think about it, and the impact hits you again, from a different direction, through another sense.

And Wham!

There it was.

That moment.

That impact moment.

That moment when I went: "Wow! That smells bad!" To understand how bad, just imagine a mixture of gasoline and vomit, with a hint of rotting garbage.

And then there was that echo moment, when the impact of it hit me again from a different direction, and I went: "Wow! I can't breathe!"

And I fell backwards out the door.

Literally.

Tripped over the threshold, going backwards, ass-first onto the ground.

They say that laughter has the power to heal, to mend. And, yeah, they all laughed at me. It took me a moment to become aware of it, but the way Flo laughed, she just seemed to be in need of a larger dose of that medicine.

And so we dined outside that Saturday afternoon.

Chapter 25
Hercules Switchblade

Sunday and the floor paint wasn't dry, the small house was crowded, and Flo was in a snuggly mood. Barry gave me some money and asked me to make myself scarce for a while.

Whether or not they were in contravention of the Lord's Day act, the Hercules was open on Sunday.

Bins of gas masks for a dollar. I'd seen them before. But there was always something new at the Hercules. Bashed and bent army helmets, fifty cents each. They weren't there the last time I came in. I headed up the wide set of worn wooden steps, rolled aside the racks of heavy dark blue overcoats and started going through the bamboo poles, picking out five perfectly straight green ones and wondering if I could possibly manage to carry six. Five had nearly crushed my shoulder the last time, so I decided to go with the ones I had.

While waiting in line to check out, where they would tie the bundle together with butcher's twine for me, I noticed a counter offering other trinkets for sale. There were several green painted metal ammunition boxes containing a heap of something marked "Novelty Switchblades."

I leaned over and peered into the box at a bunch of tiny imitations of the de-sprung full sized ex-switchblades that filled a bin on the other side of the floor. I picked one out and the plastic side of it fell off. Dangling from an inch of chain, a key ring on the other end.
Cheap pieces of junk.

But they were spring loaded and actually worked. They were only two inches long. I picked out another, not broken, and pressed the button.

Snick! The blade flipped out and locked in place. I folded it closed and pressed the button again.

Snick!

For twenty-five cents? Even with the blade out it was only about as long as my baby finger, not much more than a metal toothpick. Still...

A quarter?

I couldn't resist it.

I picked up a sleek chrome penlight about the size of a slim cigar from another bin. And my poles. Paid up and started walking, all the way to the docks.

When I got my poles home Barry and Flo still had their bedroom door closed. I changed quietly and headed right back to the City

It was still a fairly warm day, but there was a sniff of rain in the air and it was likely to be cold later. I brought my heavy blue topcoat and again stored it in a locker at Union Station. I put the funny shaped locker key with the fat, red plastic knob in my pocket and headed back up Yonge Street.

Yonge Street.

Another huge movie theatre used to have its entrance on Yonge Street, the Imperial. The Imperial Theatre wasn't on Yonge Street, but its entrance was. The Imperial was far too big to be on Yonge Street. The huge auditorium part of it was East by a half block. The ticket booth part of it was just a narrow storefront on Yonge Street. From the entranceway, where you bought your ticket, you had to go up a long flight of stairs, then across what I later found out was a second floor walkway built over the alley, and then into the cavernous theatre itself.

The Imperial was an old opera or vaudeville house style of showplace. It had an immense wrap-around balcony and an enormous screen that, back when Cinemascope came in, made use of three projectors simultaneously beaming the movie onto a screen somewhere in the football-field range of size.

A year ago, when "Windjammer" came out, it was advertised as the first really big deal in entertainment since talkies. Windjammer started with an image of a square-rigged sailing ship in the bottom half of the centre screen. A typed caption read: "This is normal, the projection size you have been used to, until now..."

Then these weird swirling purple paisley shapes appeared covering the rest of the screen to the left, right, and top half of this image. Barry leaned over and hoarsely whispered to Flo "This Cinemascope stuff is a load of crap."

Then the caption read: "THIS IS CINEMASCOPE" and that square-rigged ship just expanded until our heads were uncomfortably craned back, trying to take in the whole enormous majesty of the film. Before the movie was over several people had actually become seasick.

There were more movies in Cinemascope, and other formats. Sailing movies and jet planes and racecars and such.

This particular Sunday evening I bought my ticket and took my seat up in the balcony, the section they called the smoking loges, for "State Fair" starring Pat Boone. It was in full Cinemascope.

The balcony seats were almost completely filled, and the usher showed me to a seat all the way around at the right-hand front corner of the balcony, almost parallel to the screen. The lack of ability to see much more than an elongated view of Bobby Darin's right eyebrow from this point was compensated for, however, by the ease with which I could see down the blouses of some girls down in the floor seats when bright outdoor scenes on the screen lit up the darkness.

State Fair was probably a pretty good movie. I'd like to see it some time. That first time doesn't count because I wasn't really paying attention.

The next "greatest thing" to come out of that huge screen, even bigger than Cinemascope, was Todd-AO, projected on a screen so large that, from the front row and corner balcony seats all you could see was a vertical blur. And, from a good seat, the most forceful thing that ever loomed out of that flickering darkness was the head of John Wayne. John Wayne was leading "The Horse Soldiers", on to "The Alamo", and "The Comancheros" where coming. By the end of each John Wayne film I knew that the world had just been made a better place by the good guys.

That was so much better than that tortured soul crap, that James Dean "I'm so hurting inside" stuff.

James Dean had been an influence on me, I'll give him that. I saw "Rebel Without a Cause" at a drive-in theatre in Florida when I was six. On the way home, with my Grandmother at the wheel, I remember thinking that switchblade knives were cool; and that that was a pretty neat trick, opening the door and rolling out of a moving car like they did in the movie.

I figured, if you got yourself spinning fast enough before you hit the ground, you could probably do it without hurting yourself at all. In fact, it might actually be fun, sort of like rolling down a hill. Rolling down a hill was easy because it was downhill. With the car moving along at just the right speed, it should be enough to help you roll, sort of like going downhill, for a few seconds anyway. Then you'd probably just slow down and it would become more like just rolling around on the ground.

But, for the first bit, it should be sort of easy, I thought.

At six.

In the passenger seat.

Going along Biscayne Boulevard at about thirty miles an hour.

That seemed a bit too fast.

I waited, looked around behind us. We slowed to about twenty. I pulled the door handle back and started rolling before I hit the pavement.

Just right!

I did it just right!

I really couldn't understand why my Grandmother was so upset. To me it seemed perfectly natural to try to do what I'd seen in the movie. Not the James Dean tortured soul stuff. That was just boring.

But rolling out of moving cars seemed neat. And so, in a way, I was kind of influenced by James Dean. But nowhere near as much as I was impressed by that giant image of John Wayne shooting bad guys and making the world feel like a better place.

Unfortunately for Pat Boone and Bobby Darin's elongated right ear, John Wayne wasn't in the movie showing this Sunday evening. Besides, like I said, I wasn't really paying attention anyway.

Chapter 26
Forbidden Fruit

Barry kept my bedroom door closed for another night, with the fan set up in the window to blow the fumes out. Most of the stuff from my room got shifted from the living room into the middle bedroom, piled on top of the piles of stuff already piled there, making a tight stack right to the ceiling. At least the lumpy old couch was clear in the living room now.

The last thing I did at night... after supper and shower and teeth and pajamas and under covers... the last thing before turning out the light, I read.

Sometimes I read too much.

Yes, it is possible to read *too* much, and, sometimes, I did. Ray Bradbury, Robert Heinlein and Isaac Asimov had just replaced Superman, Batman, and the Fantastic Four on my night table. There had been many Monday mornings that found me bleary-eyed from having read right through until it was time to get up for school.

I sat up at the end of the couch, turned the table lamp on behind me, opened the book I'd gotten from Gwen and read:

"Jack Kerouac.

The Dharma Bums.

Copyright ©Jack Kerouac, 1958."

I opened it at one of Gwen's bookmarks.

"...I'm the old mother of earth. I'm a Bodhisattva."

I thumbed through, looking for the naughty parts.

"...I distrust any kind of Buddhism or any kind of philosophy or social system that puts down sex..."

"...Princess was stark naked, her skin white as snow when the red sun hits it at dusk..."

If I'd been given a book this thick as a reading assignment it could have taken me a year to get through it.

But this felt like forbidden knowledge, the stuff I wasn't supposed to know.

I might even learn something the Teacher didn't know.

If I could catch the Teacher in a mistake. I'd like that, I thought, as I drifted off to sleep... Catching the Teacher in a mistake... I would like to do that...

I woke up about two, turned out the light and went back to sleep.

Karen was up and out of her crib in Barry and Flo's bedroom first thing in the morning and enjoying riding around in circles in the centre of the living room.

She'd get up enough speed, take her feet off the pedals of her red and white tricycle and coast into the wall. Then the door. Then the end of the couch. With a mighty thump and a big laugh and grin.

First thing in the morning.

Right beside my head seemed to give her the greatest joy. I had read late and then barely slept due to all the lumps in the couch, and staying awake at school was going to be pretty much impossible.

Flo tried to call me but I didn't get up. I figured I needed about, maybe, five more minutes, with Flo clattering stuff in the kitchen and Barry gulping toast and coffee. So after five, twelve, maybe seventeen or nineteen minutes, I felt a slap on my foot and Barry said, "Gotta go, pal!" before he dashed off to catch the ferry, all London Fog topcoat, Old Spice and briefcase.

I crawled off the couch to the bathroom.

Cereal, teeth, gotta run or gonna be late now and...

On the bus and remembering that The Dharma Bums was still on the coffee table beside the couch, and the last thing I'd been reading was something about, about how Princess was stark naked, and something about orgies.

I worried all day that Flo would find the book and throw it out. Couldn't concentrate on a thing. Didn't even pay attention to the Teacher writing "book report" among the upcoming assignments on the chalkboard.

At the end of the day I was off the bus and tearing off for home at a flat-out run, a stiff wind from the East trying to push me back the other way.

In the back door, quite out of breath, slowing down only to ease the door shut so it wouldn't slam.

And Flo yelling: "DON'T SLAM THE DAMN! Oh, you didn't..." as I turned and bounced into the living room in a hop and two steps.

And it was still there! Face down between the newspaper and my pillow, which was still rolled in the sheets I'd left at that end of the couch when I went to school. It probably hadn't even been touched.

The other end of the coffee table had an overflowing ashtray and Flo's Book of Lucky Green Stamps.

I flipped The Dharma Bums open and read. Sort of.

I skimmed through the first page, looking for smut, found something about hopping freights. So the "Dharma Bums" weren't female bottoms, they were hobos.

A few more pages: more bums and freights.

I skipped and thumbed, skipped and thumbed, looking for the sexy parts. The Secretary's note said, "I think this material is quite too obscene..." So far I couldn't find any dirty parts at all.

I'd gotten up to where the hero was on a ferry boat, listening to the "...Mark Twain talk of the skipper and the wheelman..." when I heard Cliff Hadrall outside, talking loud to someone as he went up Second. If Barry was on the same boat with him, then, to avoid getting stuck with any chores, I only had seconds to get out the back door and up the street unseen.

Chapter 27
A Bastard's Story

And so, in seconds, I was out the back door and up the street, unseen, though not completely dry. The clouds were starting to open up, working their way toward a deluge.

"You finished it already?" Gwen asked. "You read the whole thing?"

"Well, yeah... I... um..." I held the book out to her. "I thought you needed it back."

"I said you could bring it by when school's over."

"Well, school's over."

"I meant for the year. In June. When school's *over*."

"Oh," I said, feeling stupid. "I thought you wanted me to bring it back after school, like, after school today."

"That's what she said," Milt boomed from the green corduroy armchair. 'As long as you can get it back to me after school.' "

Gwen said: " 'As long as you can get it back to me when school's *over*.' I'm sure I said 'as long as you can get it back to me when school's *over*.' "

"Nope. Heard it clear as day," Milt gloated, going back to reading a book.

"Actually," Bob said from back in the kitchen, "I believe the exact phrase was '...Yes. But you can get it back to me after school,' spoken in answer to the question: 'But you need this, don't you?' "

"Hey wait a minute!" I protested. "You guys were asleep!"

"Well, I was trying to sleep." Milt galumphed, the way you might expect Mr. Wilson, the guy who lives next door to Dennis The Menace, to galumph. "And now I'm trying to read."

"And I'm an extraordinarily light sleeper," Bob smiled. "Care for some tea?"

"So you guys were listening the whole time?" I sat at the table, "You heard everything?"

"Well not everything," Milt confessed. "I heard you coming in, then drifted off again. Until, that is, Gwenny started grinding that cup and saucer."

It was Gwen's turn to be on the defensive. With her eyes she pleaded guilty to the offense, was very repentant and promised not to misbehave again and, with his eyes, Milt was accepting of her apology and forgave and thanked her for her gift. Not a word was spoken, but I understood.

And I knew that the gift wasn't her submission, or admission, or whatever that was.

There was something more.

"I hope you don't mind," Milt said to me. "But a damned good poem is a damned good poem, wherever you find it." He passed me a typed page.

I read.

I read: A BASTARD'S STORY

And he was right. It was a damned good poem.

"But it wasn't cold water," I protested.

"Makes a better image," he said. "And..." he continued, anticipating my next argument, " 'an old man with beautiful hands' sounds like admiration for a life well-lived. Young man with beautiful hands sounds, well..."

"Queer," Bob said.

"Yeah, sort of faggy. Not what I want to convey."

I had to agree, it was a pretty damned good poem, and asked if I could have it, if he'd sign it for me?

"Can't," he said. "That's the only copy I've got right now. Next time Gwenny can get some copies made I'll give you one, okay?"

Gwen smacked him on the head with the book.

"What?" he asked, ducking and covering his head.

"I told you not to call me that!"

"What? Gwenny? Gwenny! Gwenny! Gwenny! Gwenny! Gwenny!"

He was up and out of his seat, laughing as she, laughing, chased him into the kitchen and back, catching him beside the table and, with mock pummeling fists, drove him down into a pulverized heap in the armchair.

He lay there, not breathing, feigning absolute motionless death.

"Say, what's that?" I got up and touched a curved-bladed sheath knife that I hadn't seen before, hanging from a hook on the wall.

"Careful of that," Bob said. "That knife has a spell on it. Once drawn, it has to have blood before it can rest again in its sheath."

I examined the black leather handle and sheath wound with shiny wire. "I saw a bunch like this at the Hercules store," I said. "Two bucks each."

"There are many knives that look exactly alike," Bob answered. "But each one has its own history, and each its own individual future, as do we all."

Bob brought the pot to the table and Milt jolted back from his frozen state, proclaiming, "Tea's ready!"

After the right amount of time to sweeten, stir and relax into the cup of tea, Gwen asked: "What would happen if a bunch of people got together and just picked a guy, the way the kids in the schoolyard play tag, but instead of saying 'you're it' they said: 'you're god' and then they bullied him for being god?"

"Good question," Milt answered. Then, to me, said: "Just as a point of interest, if someone else declared that *you* were divine, either A god or The god, how could you prove that you weren't?"

I had no idea how to answer that. "How can you possibly bully god?" I asked.

"Happens all the time," Bob said. "People are always praying, somewhere, all the time. Poor guy doesn't get a second of relief from it."

"Poor guy, or *girl*," Gwen pouted, then went on, "Could a person stay sane, if they had divinity forced upon them? If they had to hear everybody's prayers all the time? If they were assaulted with hideous worship that just never relents?"

"Oh, yeah," Milt said, "I remember that line, 'hideous worship'. Good turn of phrase."

Bob waved his hands up and down, bowing to an imaginary, invisible being somewhere at the centre of the table, and said, "I'm going to worship you until you give me what I want! Now answer my prayers, dammit!"

"They'd martyr you so fast," Gwen said. "They're going to cast the yoke of adulation on my shoulders!" she wailed in mock misery. "How do you escape that?" She had stopped mocking and there was just the slightest edge of true fear in her tone.

"I suppose," I said, "it'd be kind of like how those girls ripped up the old Shea Theatre trying to get at Elvis when he was here."

"Exactly!" Bob said with a snap of his fingers. "If they decide Elvis is god, then there just isn't anything he can do to prevent it."

"But the guy's got more money than Fort Knox," Milt said. "So at least he can hire a bunch of body guards."

"So the prisoner has to hire the guards for his own prison," Gwen said matter-of-factly.

"More than that," Bob said, adding to her point, "the prisoner has to be his own warden, buy his own prison, pay taxes on it, *and* hire his own prison guards."

There was a pause, a sip of tea, and it was another one of those moments when, well... there are some times when there's a natural opening in a conversation, and they usually pass, and the conversation goes normally on. This seemed like it was going to be one of those times.

But it wasn't.

We thought.

Sipped...

Nothing needed to be said, so nothing was, for several seconds.

It sounds strange, but it was enough just to be. It was one of those telepathic moments of communication, but the thought was: "Nothing needs to be communicated at the moment." I have rarely felt times of such contentment anywhere since, and know now how to recognize and cherish them when they occur.

And then, after what seemed like a very long time and it began to feel a bit awkward, I felt that something ought to be said. The words just rolled out of my mouth: "But what if there's more than one prisoner?"

I hadn't thought about the words, it just seemed like something to say. But then I did begin to think about what I'd said, and Gwen's eyes shone with the thought, and then Bob and Milt caught it.

"If there are two gods..." Milt began.

"They could watch each other's backs..." Bob continued. "And three..."

"Four!" Gwen cut in, looking around the room. There were four of us.

"Right," Milt said. "Four prisoner/gods could stand square, facing outward, back-to-back..." His thought trailed off.

"Add in some hired guards and you've got a defendable position," Bob said, lifting the chessboard and setting it in the center of the table. He placed four pawns in the center of the board. "But hardly enough flexibility to have normal movement and interaction with the world. You're still marked, hunted by the adulators."

"If you've got one Elvis/king plus twelve disciple/guards... " Gwen suggested.

"Too obvious," Milt said, while the wind made the front door groan as if to emphasize his point.

"Still, there is something about the numbers twelve and thirteen," Bob said, sounding like what he was saying carried much more gravity of meaning than I could possibly understand.

"Then again, if everybody's a prisoner," he continued, "then there can be no guards. Indeed, there is no need for them. Guards become obsolete."

"And omnipresent," Gwen said, looking at the floor. "If no-ones a guard, then everyone is. It's a locked system."

"That's right," Bob said. "Freedom becomes the ultimate imprisonment."

The hour was getting late and it had been a long day. The bright flash of a bolt of lightening jolted our attention to the windows. I yawned as I waited, silently counting.

A deep rumble shook the house as I got up to fifteen.

"Hmm," I thought to myself, "About a mile and a half away."

"About a mile and three-eighths," Milt said, as if correcting me.

"Oh, I make it four-ninths," Bob said. I wasn't sure whether he was serious or not.

There was another, much brighter flash and an almost instantaneous "KA-BOOM!"

"That was a lot closer," I said.

It poured much more heavily after that last thunderclap, then I could hear the rain easing off. There was a gap in the downpour. I figured I had just a few seconds before it was going to start hammering down again.

"So," I said, "I'll see those books another time, okay? I'm going to head out."

"Okay," Bob replied. "Oh, that's right. I was going to show you some of the history I've collected. I've got a lot of books I'd like to show you, when you've got time."

"Sure," I said, opening the door, "maybe another time."

"Oh, and take this with you until after *school's out*" Gwen said, handing me The Dharma Bums.

Milt said to Bob, "You wanna play chess?" He started setting up the chess pieces,

Gwen rolled a fresh sheet of paper into the Remington and started typing.

When I got home I took the drawing of Gwen with her eyes in the back of her head from between the pages of my Atlas. I used it as a bookmark as I read my way through The Dharma Bums, and continued to use that drawing as a bookmark for years, until the paper finally cracked, crumbled and totally disintegrated with age.

Chapter 28
Week of Wetness

Tuesday, and no library period. We went back out into the recess yard instead and lined up at various spots to try out for the Track and Field events. The inter-mural track meets were coming up in a few weeks. Hundred Yard Dash, High Jump, Pole Vault. Running Broad Jump brought about snickers and elbowings. Standing Broad Jump even more.

We were allowed to participate in up to three events and our names went into a ledger book beside the sports in which we were going to compete, if we qualified.

I got home from school and wanted to check the paint, but Flo was worried that Sam would run in there and get his paws all sticky with the stuff, so I plunked down on the couch, reading The Dharma Bums while The Living Strings played Ebb Tide on the console stereo.

After dinner Barry told me that phone calls had been placed. Decisions would have to be made. If the paint on the floor still wasn't dry, we'd come up with a solution.

If the paint still wasn't dry.

We opened the door again.

"You could sleep a night, maybe two, if necessary..." Barry began to say as I put a finger to the floor, pressed hard, and pulled up a finger-print wad of sticky goo. Sam came up beside me to see what was going on in here.

"Don't let him get in!" Flo shouted.

Sam sprang for the empty room.

I made a grab for Sam as Barry shut the door, slamming it into the poor cat's face as he was in mid-leap.

Wham!

Just like that! I spun around and caught an armful of rebounding feline!

It would have been a great save if we'd been playing hockey and Sam was a puck. A bunted baseball caught mid-torso? Would have been a real easy catch. But, of course, we weren't playing hockey. Or baseball. Once you hit a puck with a stick, then catch it, it stops moving. Same with a ball.

But there is a subtle difference between hitting a ball with a bat or a cat with a door.

Unlike the cat, the ball doesn't continue to move.

Unlike the ball, the cat does.

The fully understandable movement that the cat makes, of course, is toward the nearest exit. Which exit, from the cat's point of view, I am blocking.

When you catch a ball or a puck, it doesn't try to take the shortest route to the other side of you by climbing over you the way the Swiss climb mountains, with grappling hooks.

A cat, however, does.

And Sam did.

My tee-shirt wasn't much protection. If anything, it probably helped facilitate his claw-holds, so he got over me a trifle faster, so I may have gotten a few less bleeding claw-marks because of it. But, in just the blink of an eye, I had quite an impressive number of cat-claw punctures up the front of me, over my left shoulder and down my back. The back screen door proved no more resistance to him and actually fared worse. At least he went over me, not through.

Flo got the Hydrogen Peroxide from the medicine cabinet.

As I got cleansed and bandaged, Barry said again that phone calls had been placed. Decisions had been made.

The paint still wasn't dry.

"You could sleep a night, maybe two, if necessary..." And the choices were... I was welcome on Jimmy's couch, if I wanted, or...

"Well, the Old Man says you could take the back bedroom for now, if you want."

That seemed like probably the best idea.

There are so many things I have forgotten.

My mother broke up with Ken Sinclair in a big nasty brawl.

Again.

I don't remember if this was the time they split up that he used a hot frying pan to fight her off with her butcher knife.

Or the time they split up that she cracked his head open with a rum bottle and he knocked one of her front teeth loose.

Or the time they split up that...

As I said, there are so many things I have forgotten, and I'd just as soon keep it that way. Suffice it to say that a bed under their roof wasn't an option.

But if it was okay with my Grandfather, then taking up residence in the back bedroom of my grandparent's home at 12 Nottawa really was the best plan all the way around. My Grandfather was working security, nights, at the QCYC. I'd planned to move in there in a few weeks anyway, to be closer to the QC once school was out and Junior Club started.

So, after a truly fine meal of crispy chicken and corn nibblets, mashed potatoes and gravy, followed by lemon meringue pie for dessert, I packed a bag and headed for Algonquin.

And, yes, it really was a dark and stormy night.

The rest of the house was warmer with their back bedroom door closed. When my Grandmother opened that door a pool of cold, dry, stale air cascaded to the floor, visible in the swirl of cigarette smoke that otherwise filled the living room and kitchen. The living room walls got incrementally more brown toward the ceiling, the layers-of-tar-coated windows a leaden hue.

"He's still sleeping," she whispered as I tiptoed into the back bedroom. I could hear him snoring in the front bedroom.

I put my bag on the bed and came back out, leaving the door ajar so the room could warm up and air out while we went to the kitchen.

We chatted about, "How's school?" and "How are your friends?" kind of stuff, but I knew I was just a distraction. I said that I should probably do some homework and she said, "Oh, of course. And maybe I'll just make myself some tea and watch a little TV while you do."

And she did. Made tea and watched a little TV. That is to say, the TV wasn't very large. But, man, she certainly did watch it a lot.

I stretched out on the bed and opened The Dharma Bums. Heat from the oil burning space-heater in the living room soon had my bedroom warmed up.

She made fresh tea, smoked and watched Dr. Kildaire, "That Raymond Massey is from the Massey family of Toronto, you know..." Garry Moore, "You see that, when Carol Burnett pulls her ear like that? That's a signal. I read it right here..." and Red Skelton, "He's so brilliant. He ad-libs most of his show. You know what that means, don't you? Ad-lib?" All the while stirring her tea. I joked that she was trying to wear a hole through the bottom of the cup and she stopped stirring, briefly.

If someone were to pose the question, "How much television can one person watch?" the answer, in my Grandmother's case, would have been "all of it." Or at least as much as is humanly possible. From Car 54 Where Are You to The Naked City, Perry Como to Ernie Kovacs, she watched it all.

My Grandfather would wake around eleven to go to work, then she'd watch TV until there was nothing more to watch.

Once every anthem had been sung and every test pattern placed on the screen, once every last channel had shut off for the night, then and only then, she would push the knob in, reducing the blue glow to a single dot in the centre of the screen that would slowly diminish in brightness, fading, fading...

As I fell off to sleep I remembered that I still had to get my new poles from Barry's.

In the morning I got up and left early, ran over to Ward's, got my bike and poles and headed off for school just ahead of the bus. They passed me on the road, the strains of, "Found a Peanut" bursting from the open windows of the first bus, "The North Atlantic Squadron" echoing away from the second as it roared down the road before me.

At least I wasn't late for school, and that was something.

The rest of the day sucked.

It was sunny and windy while we sat in class, then drizzled cold rain during recess. I shivered as I gripped the pole and couldn't get a good jump at all. The same thing at lunch, but I did feel better about my technique. I was using a slightly skinnier pole, so it had a better chance of breaking, but I was getting some real spring out of it. I could feel the difference. It was just my timing I had to get right.

The afternoon sun poured in on my shoulder as I hunched over my desk. I felt it was mocking me.

Then of course, just before the bell rang to go home, it poured.

We weren't supposed to leave our bikes in the rack overnight, but I just didn't want to struggle home on it in that weather. I got on the steamed-up bus and headed for home, on Algonquin now.

My Grandfather had just gone to bed, so I had to be very, very quiet.

I told my Grandmother I was going to the rope swing at the end of the street, promising to come back for supper when the streetlights came on.

It was rainy and windy and there was nobody else outdoors to hang around with. I headed for Ward's. Barry and Flo were both out. I let myself in and made a peanut butter sandwich, checked the state of the paint - still not dry - and headed off up the street.

There was nobody around at the Acorn's. I kept on going up Second.

Left on Lakeshore and out to the Gap.

As I said, the old Gap has been ripped out, re-aligned and re-built. Now it's a breakwater composed of a line of jumbled boulders in a pile. But it used to be a solid concrete structure, running roughly North-South. Lakeshore Avenue had the same brushed-concrete surface, and service trucks could (and occasionally did) drive to the Gap. They would rarely turn right or left to drive out toward either the Lake or the Bay. A row of iron bollards for tying up ships ran down the centre of the Gap, leaving little or no room for even a narrow car, much less a truck.

There were three steps built into the concrete gap wall at that point, down to a lower level, designed so that small craft could dock. And, right there, at the place where Lakeshore Avenue ended, there used to be an old shelter, with a roof made of steel, above this docking spot. A rusty steel roof on rusty steel supports, with peeling black paint and very ornate wrought iron scroll-work that probably dated back to sometime in the late eighteen-hundreds.

In the summer months we would come down here in our trunks and climb up to the top of that roof, then leap hard to get into the water past the railing and the lower steps. That plunge was refreshing for most, and fatal for a few. The authorities would chase us away if they caught us diving there. That, of course, made it all that much more fun.

This particular day, though, it wasn't much fun at all.

I stood shivering in the shelter, rain clattering on the steel roof overhead and splashing back up from the numerous little bulls-eye ripples it caused in the slowly undulating water of the Gap. I gazed out, across, toward the mirror image of this concrete wall on the City side, and lit a smoke.

As I smoked I cupped my hands around the glowing end of the cigarette, trying to capture a wee bit of warmth from it. I contemplated walking out to the end, to see if I could feel it, the weather, but I was already so miserably cold that I just headed back to Algonquin and actually spent the rest of the night catching up on my homework.

All day I had hoped and prayed for sunshine, and all day it rained. Morning and afternoon recess, trying to grip a slippery, wet bamboo pole, trying to get that bounce, that spring, just right.

A thicker pole was less flexible, but would last longer. The skinnier poles were treacherous. I landed hard time and time again on top of a splintered pole, but sometimes it would all come together, I'd get the spring I wanted. I did it!

I just knew that I could do more, I could clear eight feet. Dink and Gronk had each made eight foot, one inch. By now they both had Fiberglass poles.

Homework done, or at least mostly done, I drew a picture of a stick-man figure holding onto a curved pole, erased it and started again, finally crumpled it and tossed it in the trashcan before turning off my light for the night.

My Grandmother didn't do mornings well, if at all. The interesting TV shows didn't start until noon, and neither did she. There was cereal in the cupboard and milk in the fridge.

My Grandfather, Jimmy Jones senior, Gord to my grandmother, came home Thursday morning just before I left for the schoolbus.

"So, how are things?" I asked.

"Fine, just fine," he answered as he took off his raincoat and went into the kitchen, opened his lunch box and rinsed out the empty thermos under the kitchen tap.

"You're okay with my staying here for a day or two?"

"Why shore, you know you're always welcome." He replied. I knew it wasn't true.

"Okay then, I gotta go. Maybe see you tonight?"

"Maybe," he said, taking a seat in the kitchen and opening a beer. I noticed, in his lunch box, some sheets of writing paper with rows of three numbers, printed in pencil.

"23-8-12,

"23-8-13,

"23-8-14..." Row after row of them, page after page.

Chapter 29
Mighty Fishy

Row after row, page after page. Writing paper with rows of three numbers printed in pencil.

"16-13-32,

"16-13-33,

"16-13-34..."

They were in the garbage, wrapped inside a roll of newspapers, all encasing a big kitchen-waste tortilla in the garbage can. I was out on the back porch trying to slide those older bundles apart so that I could squeeze the new roll of the night's after-supper garbage in between them. Rain was splashing off the roof and down my neck. Some drops were starting to darken the paper, washing the pencil numbers away. I jammed the newest garbage roll in the can, locked the lid back on and went in out of the weather. Something was on TV. Something was always on TV.

There were no remote controls, no way to change channels or adjust the sound without getting up, going over to it and turning a knob. There was no mute button. Commercials had to be listened to. Thus sayeth The Tube.

But my Grandmother wouldn't let me smoke, thought I was too young to be starting such a filthy habit.

I didn't have much choice. Either go for a cold, wet walk to get a drag, or?

"I've got homework to do," I said, and retired to my room, closed the door and, pulling out The Dharma Bums, lit up a smoke. I didn't think there'd be much chance that she'd smell it.

I woke up and had to pee sometime around one-thirty, maybe quarter to two. My Grandmother was happily stirring her tea to the rhythm of Fred Astaire's feet in some old-time movie on the TV screen.

As I came out of the bathroom the phone rang.

"Hello?" I said, picking it up, as my Grandmother said, "Oh no! Don't!" and my Grandfather's voice on the other end of the line screamed, "What the hell do you think you're doing!" in my ear.

Okay, I was wrong.

It wasn't the first time.

"Just let me talk to him," my Grandmother said, getting up and coming over to take the phone.

"I'm sorry, I forgot," I tried to say as I handed the phone over. I could hear, coming through the heavy black Bakelite receiver, my Grandfather ranting about the damn dime he'd just lost.

It was his code. His angle. His way to beat the system. If the phone rings once, just once, then call him back. The number was written on the wall. The payphone will ring and he'll pick it up, keeping the dime to use over and over. Unless somebody stupid, like me, picks it up on the first ring.

I set my alarm a quarter-hour earlier so that I could be gone to school before he got home in the morning. I left a shiny, new silver dime on the table and a note that said, "Your old one was getting worn out anyway". If he laughed at that, everything would be fine, otherwise...

I hoped he'd laugh.

I made a mental note to find something else to do after school, coming home well after he would have gone to bed.

Friday we had some "project" time and were allowed to talk among ourselves, within reason. I was looking up a word from the Dharma Bums in the dictionary when Dink stuck his nose over my shoulder. "Or - jee?" he laughed.

Dooly took a glance. "It's pronounced org - ee, isn't it?"

Debate broke out around the dictionary until Peno, squinting at the phonetic symbols, declared that it was or-jee, with a soft "g", even though it came from the root org-asm, with a hard "g". We jostled for shoulder room to read the definition of orgasm, then guiltily disbursed, fearing that we might catch The Teacher's attention.

I read on.

In the afternoon we were introduced to the way in which decimals could be converted to fractions, and vice-versa. My brain developed a new ache.

At least the weather had turned fair. I hung around the pole vault run until both buses had gone. Then, as the last one to leave, I put the standards, crossbar and my poles away for the night.

It was a beautiful evening to ride my bike home and, as a pleasant surprise, even though it had been locked in the bicycle rack over the previous night, the tires weren't flat, the chain wasn't off, and the lock wasn't busted. My legs were glad it was still there.

I thumped and bumped among the pothole-puddles in the pressed cinder road near the school at a snail's pace, trying to keep from splashing oily mud from the road into my face. It was too nice a day to be in a rush anyway, I thought, and swung myself back down from the seat. I walked along in the scrub grass and sand at the side of the road, pushing the bike all the way to the end of the Filtration plant. There the road turned back to concrete pavement and I re-mounted and sped up as fast as I could, then relaxed back to a comfortable cruising speed past Centre and along to Hooper.

I didn't turn at Hooper, the road only changed back to cinder path with its potholes and puddles that way. I carried on straight for the Boardwalk.

The Boardwalk was still the front view for a long string of mansions all the way to Ward's, and a few folks in enormous picture-windowed living rooms on my left waved back to my smile and nod as I road by. The enormous rolling expanse of Lake Ontario undulated all the way to the horizon on my right.

The pleasant, familiar thumpity-thump vibration of riding along on the cross-planked surface, plus a gentle but steady tail wind made riding easy, but I didn't want to hurry anyway. Maybe that's why I cruised right by the turn to Algonquin and just sort of automatically kept going towards Ward's. I was past the end of the boardwalk and back on the concrete road surface before I remembered that I was supposed to go to Algonquin tonight. I could see someone standing out at the end of the Gap and, well, I figured that I'd rather ride on out and see who that was first anyway, and kept on going.

It turned out to be a couple of city folks, a guy and a girl who looked like they were newly fallen in love. I circled around them at the white tower at the end of the Gap, smiled and nodded "hello," and headed back again.

Back slowly along Lakeshore and then turned on Second.

That was odd. A couple of guys were walking along Channel, at the far end of Second, carrying what looked like a smelt pole and net. I stopped and turned the bike around, peddled back to Lakeshore, then turned down First. There they were, just turning from Channel at the far corner.

I peddled up fast and recognized Billy Morrison and Kim Scott-wood. Kim was about a year younger and a head shorter than me and had the pole on his shoulder, the net swinging back and forth behind. Billy was about a year older and far taller than Kim. He carried a galvanized steel bucket.

"Hey!" I shouted as I jumped on the brake, skidding the back wheel out in front as I stepped off. The result of this maneuver was that, as I stepped to the ground, the bike was flung forward and, in that one smooth move, it was turned facing the other way as I hung onto the handlebars .

"So," I said to Kim, "your family's opened up the house already?" Scott-wood's house was a summer cottage that had been boarded up for the winter, like quite a few Island houses at the time.

"Naw," he said, shifting the weight of the pole back further on his shoulder, "We're just here for the weekend. Daddy Frank wants to make sure the place got through the winter okay. Randy's back there with him checking the plumbing, and I'm just hanging out with Billy, um, smelt fishing."

"Are the smelts running? It still seems a little early to me,"

"Well, Daddy Frank figures there's a chance that the bit of heat we had last weekend might have started them running early," Kim said, "so we're going down to see. You wanna come along?"

"It's gotta be way too early, isn't it?" I said, walking along with them.

"Maybe it is, maybe it isn't," Billy said. "But we won't know until we try."

"Well, maybe so," I said, looking at the bright sky, "But it's not nearly dark enough. Won't be for hours. And we don't usually see them until closer to Victoria Day."

"Oh, shit!" Billy stopped and dropped the bucket into the sand at the side of the street, "that reminds me... crap!" He was quickly running his hands through his coat and pants pockets. "Did you...?"

"Bring some matches?" Kim said. "No, I thought you were going to get some, from your Mom's, you said."

"WELL I FORGOT!" Billy yelled.

I felt in my pocket. "Here, I've got some matches, if you..."

"Hey, great!" Billy said, taking the matches from me, followed by: "Hey, there's not many left."

"That's all I've got," I said. "I can get more from Barry's and bring them out to you later, maybe."

"Ah, that might be enough," Kim said. "I've got some punk."

Punk? Okay, now I knew what was really up.

"What've you got, four-inchers?" I asked as if I knew all along.

Billy looked suspiciously at me, wondering if I really had figured out what they were up to, ready to deny it, if...

"Naw, nobody can get four-inchers anymore" Kim said. "But we got a bunch of wizz-bangs and some wickedly powerful two inchers." He opened the brown paper bag in the bucket and showed me several packages of Hand brand firecrackers, and another brand wrapped in blue that I'd never seen before. There was a small bundle of Roman candles and assorted cone-shaped fireworks too.

"Just as soon as it's dark..." Kim said.

"It's still a long time until dark," I replied, looking longingly at the tempting bag of artillery.

"Oh, there it is!" Billy exclaimed. He reached into in the bag, pulled a shiny lighter out with a flourish and pronounced: "Ta-Da! I told you I didn't lose it in the store!"

"Well you must have dropped it in the store," Kim said, looking at the shiny chrome Ronsinol lighter as Billy flipped it open and lit a huge flame from it's wick. "I mean, when else could it have fallen into the bag?"

"I dropped it in the bag!" Billy responded as he snapped the lid closed and slid the lighter into his pocket.

"Okay, you dropped it into the bag, but you dropped it in the bag inside the store!"

"But I didn't *lose* it in the store."

Kim was leaning over to heft the pole back up to his shoulder. Billy stooping to take the bucket handles, said, "I mean, it wasn't..."

Cla-thunk!

A hip-flask slid out of Billy's jacket into the sand. An eight ounce "Mickey" bottle of Beefeater gin!

"Well, I guess that would keep you warm until sunset," I said.

"Yeah," Billy replied, turning to look straight at me. "It will keep US warm until sunset." His meaning was pretty clear: I wasn't invited. They headed on up the street towards Lakeshore and I went down First the other way.

Chapter 30
Bob's Home

Bob Mallory was just coming up Second, and I sped up to meet him.

"Hi," I called in friendly greeting. "I haven't seen you in a while."

"Oh, hi. Yeah, I guess it has been a few days," he said as he turned the key in the lock at number 10. "Anything new happening?"

"Not much. How about you?"

"Oh, about the same, I guess. I was going to show you something about Neptune, wasn't I? Would you like to come in? Gwen and Milt aren't here just now, but I can make you some tea, if you'd like."

"Yeah, sure," I said. "Just let me put my bike away."

I wheeled the bike over to Barry and Flo's and stood it in the rack in back. The kitchen light was on, but I didn't stick my head in to see if anyone was home.

"Sorry," Bob said, peering into the kitchen cupboards. "It looks like we're out of tea."
He reached over to turn the heat off under the kettle he had put on the burner.

"No, leave it on," I said, heading back out the door. "I can get some tea."

"Okay," he called after me. "Oh, and maybe some sugar too?"

There turned out to be no one in at Barry and Flo's after all, though there was a pot on the stove, turned down to simmer. I knew better than to lift the lid.

If the rice hadn't yet cooked, and the stroller was gone, then Flo would be back with Karen by the time it had cooked for twenty minutes. I grabbed a small bunch of tea bags, found a clean, empty glass jar in the cupboard and filled it with sugar. I phoned my Grandmother and told her that I was going to be doing some studying with a friend, and I'd leave here when the streetlights came on.

I grabbed a handful of cookies and some slices of bread and a small jar of some Scottish marmalade that had been opened once, tasted and then left at the back of the fridge since Christmas.

"Hey, that's a real feast," Bob declared when he saw what I'd gotten.

"Yeah, well, it's enough for an after-school snack, anyway," I said. Bob found a plate and a butter knife.

"So," he said as we shoved piled books aside, setting down plates of unbuttered white bread spread with an astringently tart marmalade with a super-concentrated citrus peel flavour, and cups of sweetened Salada tea, no milk.

"So," I replied.

"Um... Ah, yes. Neptune..." He took another sip. "Well, he's one of the gods. They're sort of an interesting lot, but where to start?"

"Isn't Neptune the same guy as Posiedon?" I asked.

"Ah, you're familiar with Posiedon? Tell me what you know of him."

"Well, that's the god the Greeks called Posiedon, and the Romans called him Neptune? Isn't that right?"

"Ah, yes, that is correct."

"That's part of the sea and sailing stuff that the Commodore told us, for understanding the wind, some stuff about Posiedon. Like, if you picture a big mouth blowing winds from big puffed-up cheeks, that's what he'd call a Posiedon. So if we could recognize that pattern when we saw it, we could figure where the best winds would be."

"The Commodore?"

"Oh, he's like, you know, how Scouts have a troop leader. Well, I go to junior sailing club in the summer, and he's our fleet leader."

"Well, the Romans did have a god, Neptune, and most of the history of Posiedon was rolled into his story, so he was sort of Posiedon turning into Neptune. But the Neptune of the Romans was a composite that also included an older Etruscan god, Nethuns."

"So somebody just decided that they could take these two gods and mash them together?"

"Well, more than that, actually. Pretty much all gods are like dirty snowballs from other, older religions mish-mashed together. The Celtic god Nechtan was also added to the Neptune mix."

"What did he do? I mean, was this guy, Nechtan, was he like Poseidon too?"

"No. And it's important to remember that we shouldn't really be addressing them in the past tense." He opened his eyes bug-eyed wide and looked suspiciously over his shoulder. "They don't like to be reminded that they're dead."

I laughed and he laughed and we had another bite and a sip.

"No, seriously," he went on, the laughter down to just a chuckle, "A god is like an imaginary friend, a hallucination. He's only as real as you imagine him to be. And the scary thing is that, if enough people imagine the same god, they can actually make him manifest."

"Huh?"

"Well, not corporeal, in the flesh, but they can all see him, or her, or it... or even them. There is, you see, a capacity of the human mind that can allow people to link up, like batteries in a circuit, and make them all see the same hallucination together. And for them it's real. They will all really see the same thing, the thing that they are all imagining, together. They can all make the same imaginary friend appear, and show him off to others who have joined them."

"So, like, would it be possible for a line of people to all hallucinate that they are walking down the road, when they're actually walking off the end of a pier?"

"Well, yeah, I suppose..."

"Yeah, I read that in a comic book, once."

"Okay, so you've got the picture? A god exists if people believe it does. And man creates gods in his own image, that is to say, in his own imagination."

"I thought it was the other way around, that we were created by god?"

"Think about it. There have been creatures, that is to say, living things that were created, a lot longer than there have been humans to make up imaginary friends."

"And that's how gods are made?"

"That's the only way gods can be made. Within the human imagination."

"So all gods are imaginary?"

"In so much as that is where they are created, yes. But, once imagined, they are capable of being whatever we want them to be, to some extent. We give them the power to perform the deeds we want them to by the act of worship.

"And there are ways, chemicals and herbs and such, that can be used to enhance and magnify the visions."

"Okay, so Neptune is a god, and people once imagined him into existence."

"Now you're getting it."

"And when they worshipped him, they gave him power?"

"Right."

"They took some other, older imaginary friends and put them together to make a newer one, with a new name."

"Right. Posiedon, Nethuns and Nechtan became Neptune. Plus a few other gods. They all link back to Nepot, whose name means 'relative of the waters.' He rules 'the fiery waters which grant wisdom.' Alcohol, actually. Like I said, there are herbs and chemicals that can be used to enhance the vision. That's why booze is referred to as spirits. It helps make the believers see the gods and spirits.

"To the Greeks Poseidon was the god of only the sea, but was equal to his brothers, Zeus and Hades. So, in a way that makes Neptune an ultra-powerful god. Nethuns was the Etruscan god of more than the sea, he was god of all water, including wells, lakes, rivers and springs. The Celtic god Nechtan owned the hill upon which stood the Holy Well of All Knowledge. They're all water related, but they all add certain aspects to Neptune's personality.

"There are a lot of gods that have little or nothing to do with water. Other herbs, like mandrake or belladonna, are used by devotees to enhance their vision of the darkest of them. Certain mushrooms help people see others. But those herbs are really, really dangerous."

"So that makes you a, what, a Neptuner? Neptunite?"

"What? No, no, I'm not one of his followers. He follows me. I just use his power, the way I use all the gods. They're just lapdogs that I have fetch my slippers."

"There you go with that god is dog thing again," I laughed as he slapped his thigh and snapped his fingers.

"Here god, here god. Come on, that's a good little goddy," He chuckled as he mimed calling an invisible dog to his side. "I did tell you that I'm a magician," he said.

"So, I'm guessing that you're talking about something more than just tricks like pulling rabbits out of hats, right?"

"Oh yeah. I live in two worlds at the same time. What I try to do is use the other world as a source of power, like a lever, on this world.

"There are seekers, people who look for a divine reality, a god, and they believe that the other world is the real one. They are the devotees, the ones who would be Neptunians or Neptunailians or whatever. Even though they believe in the same god, they're sort of the opposite of magicians.

"I can see and exist in that other shadow world just as easily and comfortably as they do, but the main difference is that they are universally trying to escape a bitter existence, so they invent a sweet place, a heaven. That comes along with a myriad of trappings and entanglements in order to support that argument, and they all eventually go totally mad."

"But you're not like that?"

"No, no, the magician's way is to recognize all the gods that the devotees have created, and to pick and choose whichever ones we can draw on to fulfill our needs."

"And how do you do that, if you don't fully believe in him, or her, or it?"

"Well, that's the thing, you see. The only way to use the power of a god is to actually, fully believe in him, or her, or it, as you say. You have to open your heart and accept that they are real, and they then become real to you. It's as easy as that, and as dangerous." He paused to drain his cup. "You see, there is a very difficult process that you have to go through to get rid of a god once you've accepted them. And it takes a circle of anywhere upwards of six trained magicians about a month to do it. Can't be done alone, on your own."

"Okay," I said, taking another bite, "why Neptune?"

"Well, think about it. All the modern gods, Christ and Allah and Buddha and such, have people praying to them all the time, bombarding them with pleas for this, that, the other thing. Those gods are constantly being drained. But Neptune was pretty darned big, and was for a good long time. His worship has been paid, so there's still a lot of charge left in him. So a prayer to a big, powerful god with very few true believers left is like striking an oil well. You're rich. Rich with all the power to make that imaginary friend appear and perform miracles."

"You can make Neptune appear?"

He looked like he was thinking seriously about that statement and, with a straight face, said, "You know, I have so many times, it's become almost too easy. He's not my favorite god, mind, and it's sometimes awkward to have to ask him to leave." He let that statement hang as long as he could, then a twitch at the corner of his mouth broke the moment and he started laughing again. I did too. Neither one of us could take this all that seriously.

"Neptune also has another branch of followers entirely. See this?" He opened a book to a photograph of a statue. The caption said it was in Florence, Italy. Neptune, naked, standing on something like a tabletop, and that on top of four wild looking horses. "And this," he said, showing me a different picture in another book. "Neptune Calming the Tempest" was the name of that one, and it showed a muscular long-haired old Neptune with a white beard gesturing to the sea from his chariot, a team of wild-eyed horses in front. "Notice the horses," Bob said. "Neptune also had a cult of followers among horse lovers. Still does, among the horse-racing crowd, to some extent."

Bob needed to take a pee break and left me to thumb through the fantastic full-colour illustrations. I flipped open a large book from the table, The Secret Teachings of All Ages by Manly P. Hall.

There was a rattle of keys at the door and Gwen stepped in, bent over, struggling with two Loblaw's shopping bags. She looked shocked to see me there.

"B-b-b-Bob's home," I stuttered. I hadn't stuttered for years.

"You probably haven't stuttered like that for years," she said as I lifted one bag from her arm and helped make room for them on the table. There were red blotches like clown make-up on her cheeks and tears in her eyes. It wasn't that chilly or windy out. She must have sat on the exposed upper deck all the way home, I thought.

"Sorry," I said, "it's just, well the look on your face. You scared me."

"I scared you?" she said. "I almost pissed myself. Which..."

"Oh, hi," Bob said, coming out of the bathroom.

"I'll be right with you," Gwen said, hurriedly shoving past him into the small bathroom.

"So," Bob said, "we were talking about...?"

"Well, you'd just told me about the horse worshippers..."

"Yes, a rather peculiar lot, but..."

"Would you mind just backing up a bit? That part about needing six magicians to help you get rid of a god?"

"Oh, at least! Plus a month's time! But it can be done. Opening your heart to a god and letting them in is an act of faith that anyone can do alone, or, more easily, with a little help. 'Faith is believing something you know isn't true.' Mark Twain said that. Some folks, priests and such, make it their mission in life to help, that is, convert as many people as they can to their belief. Salesmen, peddling their god door to door.

"There are some afflicted people who recognize that they have a problem, and a magician sometimes gets asked to intervene, to cure someone that has gone mad with belief."

"And you can do that?"

There was a low moan from the bathroom.

"Um, well, not alone, but I can," Bob said. "It does take a very long time, though," he continued as we both tried to be polite and pretend that we didn't hear a quiet but distinct cry and a gasp from the bathroom. It sounded like Gwen was sucking in her breath while biting a knuckle.

"An unwanted god isn't the only thing a magician can help with, though," he continued. "There are herbs, like rue, for example, that can be used to get rid of fleas and lice."

"You need a magician to get rid of fleas?"

"Well, not really. But a magician, or a good one, anyway, should know how to properly use herbs like rue to get rid of problems like that. Ordinary folk in old England might have swept their house out with a broom of rue branches, but a magician knows that a specific cure for a specific problem takes a certain, very exact amount, and just the right length of time."

There was another low moan and whimper from the bathroom.

"It doesn't take as long to boil up a fresh pot of tea, though," he said, rising and turning on the tap.

"Yeah," I said, just a tad too loudly. "That's that Salada tea that I mentioned before. It's okay, I guess, but I really like that Jasmine tea."

The kettle started to make crackling noises on the burner.

"Ah, well," Bob said, looking in the cupboards, "I don't see any here."

"So what's with that thing about throwing your pictures into the Bay?"

"Oh, offerings" he said. "All the gods require offerings, acts of sacrifice, and some gods are more needy than others. But Neptune is quite happy with my work, so far. I make my art as fine, as high quality as I possibly can, and then offer them up to him upon his watery alter. Not all of them, of course, but most. That's how I stay on his good side. That reminds me, that heat-wave request of yours? I know that we got a few record-breaking days last weekend, but did that turn out the way you wanted?"

"Well, yeah, we did get some warm weather, but it's turned pretty lousy now."

"And you didn't have any misfortunes, any string of inexplicable bad luck?"

"Nothing really out of the ordinary," I lied.

"It's not so bad right now," he said, looking out a window.

"No, tonight's all right, but it's been lousy weather all week. And it's going to be another cold one next week too."

"You sound pretty sure of that."

"We might even get more snow."

"What? Really? Here? I haven't heard anything about that," he said as the kettle started to boil and he rinsed out the empty pot with scalding water.

"No, they're calling for a warming trend, but that's not going to happen. There's a cold flow of arctic air that's going to come pouring straight down out of James Bay, and it's going to last..."

The bathroom door swung open and Gwen stepped gingerly out, slightly bent over, showing a friendly smile that was just a bit too big to be real.

"I'm just making some fresh tea, m'dear," Bob said.

"Oh, that would be nice," she said. Then, to me, "Would you mind..."

"Um, I think maybe I'll just go now," I said.

"Yes, would you? You don't mind?"

"No, no, not at all. I'll see you later."

By the time I got to my Grandparent's home the streetlights had been on for about a quarter of an hour. My Grandmother had fried liver and onions ready for me, along with pan fried potatoes and canned peas. I sat beside her at a collapsible TV table to eat, being quiet so as not to interrupt Route 66. Buz was desperately trying to rescue a woman whose foot was stuck between some boulders at the sea shore while the tide was coming in, threatening her life. My Grandfather's steady snoring emanated from behind the front bedroom door.

Chapter 31
Bottoming

Barry told me to bring everything from the shelves beside the back door, so I did. Wire brushes, scrapers, tri-sodium phosphate, and even the can of grey floor paint went into the cardboard box that fit neatly into the big carrier on my bike.

Over the winter long, fine threads of green algae hanging from the launches hull when she was hauled out in the fall had become sheets of dead brown matting. She was up on cribbing of criss-crossed timbers, three feet of room between her keel and the ground. And, since I was the shortest, scrubbing her lowest extremities with a stiff brush on a long handle was my chore while Jimmy and Barry scrubbed and scoured her sides and decks.

It took us the full morning to get her scraped, washed down, rinsed off and sanded. She had sat all winter under a big old willow tree in Jimmy's back yard and droplets of willow sap had made tiny black polka-dot blemishes all over her mahogany decks. Barry had brought the Magic Wood and had just finished applying it to small cracks and crevices around her transom when Fram Ward rode up on his bike to admire and give advice on our workmanship. Somewhere in the conversation I interjected that we'd probably better not use the grey paint that was on my bedroom floor, still not dry.

We laughed and Fram said that some anti-fouling paints were designed to do exactly that, to never fully dry. Jimmy wasn't sure that he believed that, but Fram insisted that, yes, some paints are formulated that way. If the paint never fully dries, he said, then the theory is that algae can't grow on it.

"You can't buy it anymore, but the best stuff for keeping the algae off had a blend of high concentration DDT, arsenic and lead in it."

"Really?"

"Yep, though straight arsenic works almost as good. What kind of paint is that?"

"This, oh, let's see, it's copper, I think…" Barry said, lifting the unopened can of bottom paint and reading the label.

"No, not that stuff. The paint that you said won't dry."

"Oh," Barry said, "I think we brought that can with us." he began searching through the box of assorted cans of paint and cleaners. "It's, um… Lorne, do you remember what that said on the label?"

"I just remember 'FLOOR PAINT', in big letters, all capitals."

"Like, right around the can?" Fram made a circular motion across the label of an imaginary paint can.

"No, one above the other."

"Black letters on a light grey background?"

"Uh-huh."

"I remember that stuff. Real popular before the war. I haven't seen it around for ages."

"Well," Barry said, hauling the can in question from the box "I can show you some now."

"Seems to me," Fram said, studying the label, "that there was some sort of problem with this stuff."

"Yeah, like it never dries," I said.

"No, it wasn't that. It was supposed to be odor free. But, if it sat around any length of time, like a year or more, it took on this real sour smell."

"Boy, you sure got that right," Barry said. "But how do you get it to dry?"

"Oh, it dries just fine," Fram said, turning the can around, studying what he could of the label. "Only takes about an hour. Nice and hard, too, once it sets up. But you gotta use it in the summer. Won't harden up at all unless it's over, what was it, seventy-five or eighty degrees I think. Or was it seventy? It should say somewhere here on the can."

The paint that had run down the outside of the can was now about the consistency of chewing gum. Trying to pull it off to read the label just resulted in the paper tearing.

"If you've got it on the floor now you might be able to get it to harden up with heaters, or heat lamps. I remember, though, that it was real flammable, so don't use any torches or anything like that."

That sounded like such good advice that Barry offered him a beer. There wasn't much else that could be done at the moment and, since the Magic Wood was going to need to cure overnight...

And, as the afternoon was getting late anyway...

And, since the beer was out...

Well, that ended up being all the work that got done on the old launch that day.

Jimmy headed up the stairs to his apartment on the second floor to put the tools away, promising to come back down with a few more brew.

I had a Coke while the guys sipped away at their stubby brown beer bottles.

Fram peddled on ahead while Barry and I loaded up the box on my carrier with whatever wasn't going to be needed for further work on the boat, then back to home for a late lunch.

Flo set out a platter of ham and cheese sandwiches, quartered into perfect little triangles. Just as Barry bit into one, the phone rang.

"Hello?" I said, picking it up.

"Hello," a male voice said as Flo asked, "Who is it?"

"Yes?"

"Yes, is this um, let me see, EMpire 4-7525?"

"Yes it is," I said. Barry wasn't finished chewing yet.

"I've got your phone number from a note posted at the shelter at the ferry docks at Ward's Island. Is this the place that does septic tank clean-out service?"

"Oh, yes it is. Just a moment, please." I turned the phone over to Barry. "Septic tank," was all I said.

"Right," he replied, swallowing quickly, pulling a pen and a pad of paper from the counter as I handed him the receiver. He took the phone over to the far corner of the living room to talk business.

Karen plunked her plastic Mickey Mouse on the table with the statement, "Mickey eat too!"

"That's right, dear, Mickey eats a sandwich too," Flo encouraged as she held one of the perfect little triangles to Mickey's mouth and went, "Mm-mm. Nummy-nummy good. Now you have some."

Karen took her turn, alternately chomping on the bit of food as Flo held it for her, then giggling happily as Flo put the sandwich to Mickey's painted-on mouth for a pretend bite.

"Well, there's a nice little plum that just fell into our laps," Barry said, dialing the phone as he returned to the table. He crooked the receiver to his ear with his shoulder as he reached for a sandwich.

"Hey, guess what I've got," he said into the phone while looking back and forth at Flo and me. I was sitting close enough to him that I could just ever so faintly hear Jimmy saying, "Whatever it is, I'm sure they can cure it with penicillin."

Barry laughed back that, no it was even better than that. "We're on for a tank job. No, tomorrow. It's... yes, we'll have time for that too. It's just up the street. And get this, the guy already called the pumper truck and they can't come until the first of next month. He's in a bind, with a renter moving in on the fifteenth...

"Yeah...

"Yeah...

"Yeah, that's just it. He's paying the full pop. Yeah, no kidding. Well, I guess we could, but I'd rather get it done this weekend."

Then, putting the phone down away from his mouth, he said to me, "You're okay for tomorrow aren't you?"

I nodded.

"Yeah, Lorne's good. Yeah, it's just at the corner of Second and Lakeshore. Yeah, the place is closed up for the winter right now, shuttered and all, but he'll meet us there tomorrow at ten. Yep, ten. Okay then, see you there."

Barry hung the phone up and looked very content. He had every right to be. The "full pop" on a septic tank clean-out was fifty dollars. That's what the company with the tank truck charged. Of course, the way they did it was legal.

The way we did it, well, maybe not so much. We followed that infamous old "if you don't ask, then you don't have to know" philosophy. And we undercut the competition. They charged fifty bucks. Our going rate was thirty.

Usually.

This client hadn't asked, he'd just assumed that our rate was the same as those other guys, whom he had called first.

But the problem was that they only came to the Island when they had at least six customers lined up, so they could justify the extra expense of coming over on the truck ferry that only ran to Hanlan's.

No, the only concern for this fellow was that the tank got emptied before his new tenant moved in. And, since we could get it done on time, we got the job.

The track and field competitions were coming up next week and I was going to be able to afford new poles! Life was good.

After lunch we dug out the old electric heater and tried to get the grey paint to dry by placing it in the doorway of my bedroom, but the radiant coil aimed the heat up, not down. Then Barry had a bright idea, literally. He had an eight-millimeter film camera that, like all the home movie equipment of that era, needed a lot of light to produce a decent image indoors. That meant using a device called a light bar which fastened to the camera, basically a three foot long aluminum bar with a long power cord and four light sockets into which four incredibly bright flood-lamp bulbs were screwed. On its own, though, and held about a foot above and aimed down at the floor, it produced a lot of heat.

A lot.

In about twenty seconds the paint started to bubble and turn brown and smoke. Since the bulbs were quite expensive and were only supposed to last for about four hours anyway, we figured that this wasn't going to be the solution. We were just going to have to wait for warmer weather.

And, like I said, I had a pretty strong notion that we had a very cold week ahead of us.

Chapter 32
Honeydipping Again

We brought our shovels and pump and The Owner of the house, 6 Lakeshore, met us at ten in the morning as promised. Seemed like a nice guy, but he didn't have any idea where the septic tank was, pointing out the sink in the kitchen and the direction the pipe took from there.

"No," Barry said, "That goes into the soap-run. Same with the bathtub. What we need to see is the location of the toilet."

He led us through the big empty barn of a house, dark behind the wooden shutters clamped shut on all the windows.

"Ah, here we are," Barry said from the bathroom, lifting the toilet seat and shining a flashlight down the hole. "The tank goes, let's see... Oh! It goes out to the South from here."

"Are you sure?" The Owner asked. "I would have thought that it would go out to the West, that's the nearest wall to it."

"Nope," Barry said, "You can see here how it projects back that way. Lorne, go around and see if you can find the outside lid."

"Right," I said, winding my way back through the dark maze of unfamiliar rooms to the back door.

The houses over on Algonquin had much larger yards and newer plumbing, so they had proper septic tanks with distribution fields that allowed the sewage, after fermenting in double-chamber tanks, to percolate down through the sand. Those houses had been barged in from Hanlan's Point just a few decades ago.

But here on Ward's the houses were older and much too close together to permit the building of distribution fields. Most of the houses here had holding tanks, around four-hundred gallon capacity, and they just plain filled up and then had to be emptied.

I went around the house and traced the outline of the bathroom wall. I would have suspected that the tank ran out to the West, but dug around at the South side of the foundation and, sure enough, there it was. I cleared the lid off and pried it up, calling down the hole to Barry that I had found it. I could here him call back that he could see daylight showing in the tank from his side. Then I could hear him and Jimmy chatting with The Owner, but couldn't make out what they were saying.

They were talking loudly enough, and the passageway through the half-full tank was large enough, but I couldn't distinguish their words against the background sound of CHUM radio scratchily playing from the piping.

CHUM had done something to increase their broadcast signal a few years ago and, due to some sort of an electrical ground error, random oil stoves, eavestroughs, washing machines and other assorted appliances had become receivers. At certain times of the day it was almost impossible to hear conversations over the phone as a result of this problem. Even the bell buoy in the Bay marking the channel to the Eastern Gap played all the hits, audible from the shore hundreds of yards away.

Here, at 6 Lakeshore, the volume of this errant signal was steadily rising and falling in waves and, though I could recognize the melody of Cliff Richards singing The Young Ones, it was impossible to make out what the Disc Jockey was saying between songs.

I dug out around the lid, making a flat surface we could stand on once we started pumping. Barry, Jimmy and The Owner of the house came around to see what things looked like out here.

Barry determined where the best place to dig our drainage pool would be while the homeowner looked into the tank, noting that it was only just over half full. I was a little worried that he might decide to call the job off, but he was still of a mind that the tank should be completely empty before his tenant moved in.

"Maybe you know her," he said, "Lorraine Sinclair, know that name?"

Jimmy froze in the midst of tossing a shovelful of sand as Barry said, very casually, "I think I've heard the name around before."

So, my mother was going to be moving into 6 Lakeshore on the fifteenth of the month. Jimmy followed Barry's lead and acted like she may have been just a casual acquaintance while we continued to try to enlarge the hole. Of all the spots to dig on the Island, though, I couldn't imagine finding a place with a greater tangle of thick roots. We were going to need the axe, and I got sent down the street to fetch it.

Going down Second, past number 10, I heard hammering and sawing coming from somewhere inside.

Sam wondered what was going on and followed along, trotting beside me like a dog. On my way back up Second, axe in hand, I could hear more hammering coming from the Acorn's, then Milt shouting "AH! GOD DAMMIT!" Then I heard what sounded like a plate smashing against a wall.

There were big roots, lots and lots of big roots, and each time we scraped the dirt away from one it was my chore to jump into the hole and chop it off at both ends. Then Jimmy or Barry would go back to the easier chore of digging and, while I caught my breath, the homeowner talked constantly about the way that the radio station's engineers should have foreseen this ground-fault problem. And wasn't it turning out to be a chilly day? And would it be a good idea to check the state of the soap box as well? And every other topic under the sun.

Jimmy truly hated this type of customer, one who wanted to watch your every move and keep you engaged in conversation while you tried to work. Barry usually came up with some excuse for increasing the bill if the customer wanted to irritate us like that (we privately called it an impertinence tax), but this guy was already paying the top price we could possibly charge.

The prospect of working on the soap run as well as the septic tank was the best chance we had of getting more money for this job, and so Barry went off around the corner of the house to investigate while Jimmy and I continued to dig.

"It's a lot easier to work without that warm breeze blowing in your face, isn't it?" Jimmy asked. It took me a second to realize that he was referring to the homeowner's breath, his constant chatter. "You getting along okay with the Old Man?"

"I'm, um, just trying to stay out of his way."

"Yeah, that's probably best. Just don't do anything to get him going, okay?"

Sam inspected the hole and, apparently satisfied that our work was acceptable, sauntered off for home.

By the time we finished up we had pumped out the septic tank, rinsing it repeatedly with clean water from the garden hose, dug up and cleaned out the soap run, and checked the vent pipe from the toilet for drafts.

The place had been closed up all winter and needed to warm up. Barry got the key to the back door with the promise that he would check daily to see that the forced air furnace, which the homeowner had just started up for the first time this year, was working properly. The total for the job had inflated quite nicely beyond the original fifty-dollar quote.

The homeowner paid up with a cheque, but Barry had enough cash at home to settle up my share. I still didn't have anywhere near enough money to buy a fiberglass pole, but I certainly could make a run to the Hercules after school tomorrow and get enough brand new bamboo poles to have a fair chance at the track and field games coming up later in the week.

The job took quite a bit longer than we had anticipated, and there simply wasn't enough daylight left to get back to work on the launch.

I showered up, then had supper with Barry and Flo. By the time I got to my grandparent's house, the Toast of the Town was just ending. Ed Sullivan thanked Bobby Darrin for being his guest tonight and signed off and, since I was still on my feet, taking my jacket off, I went over and changed the channel before Ronald Reagan could introduce the G.E. Theater. My Grandmother didn't want to miss a second of Bonanza.

Adam got caught between a lynch mob and a crooked sheriff's deputy. I saw the show through to the end, then got myself hurriedly off to bed well before my Grandfather would wake up and get his breakfast.

Chapter 33
Time Trials

Monday mornings usually found me running bleary-eyed for the bus, but this particular Monday I wasn't just bleary-eyed, I was puffing steam and watchful of slippery patches where white strips of frost had formed on the planks of the Algonquin bridge. The sky was clear, the wind cold out of the North. My nose was running and my ears were numb by the time the first bus showed up with a crowd of Ward's Island kids already fogging up the windows.

With just days to go until our big Sports day, The Teacher had suddenly become interested in our athletic pursuits. Monday afternoon was usually Art, but The Teacher informed us that there would be time trials for the hundred yard dash, since so many had signed up for that. Some hopefuls were going to have to choose another event.

I made the cut for the sprint, then qualified for the standing broad jump. There was only Dink and me in my age group for the pole vault. I easily cleared the six-foot bar to qualify for that event with the last decent pole that I had left at school.

I caught the early bus home and dashed to drop off my school stuff and get changed before catching the ferry to the city. My Grandfather was reading the paper on the sofa in the living room and I tried to only say "Hi" on my whirlwind way through the house, but he wanted to show me something. "I gotta catch the boat," I protested as he passed me a page of the Globe and Mail newspaper. I glanced at the page and froze.

"I saw that in the paper last week and thought you might like to read it," he said.

"Um, yeah, thanks," I replied, studying the picture. The caption read: "**Leaves Launching Pad**---Marine Lieut.

Dave Tork demonstrates catapult action of glass vaulting poles."

And the picture!

His back toward the ground, feet swinging skyward, and what a bend to that pole!
Dave Tork, the article said, was the world record holder, having cleared sixteen feet, two inches.

"Yeah, I'll, um, I'll take this with me, thanks."

"Shore thing," my Grandfather said. "Just thought you might like to see that."

"Yeah, yeah, thanks again."

"Just remember one thing," he went on as I was trying to leave. "To succeed at anything, you've got to be focused."

"Right," I said, pulling the door shut behind me, "I'll remember that."

I was cutting it pretty close, but then I was always cutting it pretty close when I ran for the boat. I just had to pump my legs a little harder, run a little faster, and... I made it! The captain whistled off, and the deckhands started pulling the ropes to raise the gangplank right under my feet as I raced, full speed, onto the boat.

Gasping for air, heart pounding, I dashed straight up the stairs to the second deck and sank to a sitting position on a bench on the starboard side, sprawled out to let the headwind dry my sweat.

It was too chilly to stay out there very long, though, and I headed for shelter downstairs once I'd caught my breath. I pulled out that page of last Thursday's Globe and studied the picture.

I could feel it.

The strain on the arms.

The whip-like snap that the pole would be delivering at the exact moment that the photo was taken.

The weight of his feet as Tork struggled against the force of gravity, compounded by fighting foreword momentum, converting it into upward movement.

This was the time of day for working folk to be coming home from the city. The boat was nearly empty going this way, with maybe a dozen or so passengers on board going towards the city, but I didn't notice. All I could think of was getting some bamboo poles that would give me that kind of spring for at least a couple of jumps.

I studied that picture, felt that moment so intensely that I even knew how it smelled to be there, in that moment of soaring towards the bar.

All the way up on the streetcar and subway, that's all I could think of. What size, what colour of pole would deliver the best results? By the time I got to the Hercules store I knew exactly what the perfect pole would look and feel like. But could I find it?

Bins of gas masks that I'd seen many times before.

Bashed and bent army helmets, fifty cents each.

I bounded up the wide set of worn wooden steps, shoved my way between the horse-stall sized rack of oily smelling tents and the stack of army-green metal boxes, past the heavy dark blue overcoats and... the bamboo poles! They weren't there!

I saw a teen-aged store clerk on the other side of the shelves of parachutes and asked him where the bamboo poles were.

"Oh, they're, ah, where did they put them? Right! There they are, over there."

I wound my way through the various displays and found a few brown, split and scraggly looking poles lying on top of a long wooden crate.

"Is that all you've got?" I asked him.

"I guess so. I mean, if we've got it, it's out on the floor. There isn't any stock room to check or anything like that."

I looked at the pathetic selection. A bunch of rejects that no one in their right mind would ever want to use even for garden stakes. There wasn't a good pole in the bunch. I turned around and sat, dejected, on the crate upon which these few remaining poles were loosely stacked. What was I going to do now?

There had been some vendors at the St. Lawrence market who sold bamboo poles last year, but they wouldn't be open until early tomorrow morning. Then there was the shop in Chinatown that I had bought poles from before I discovered the Hercules.

I was wracking my brain, trying to remember where else I might find what I needed, staring blankly off into the distance, over there, past the rack of heavy dark blue overcoats. Heavy, dark blue overcoats, which people would try on before buying.

For some strange reason my Grandfather's words came back to me, "To succeed at anything, you've got to be focused." I thought about it again, "...be focused."

I brought my eyes into focus.

Heavy overcoats, which people would try on before buying. And so, beside that display, there was a full length mirror. And in that mirror...

I jumped up and turned around like I'd been stung by a bee!

Scraggly looking bamboo poles lying on top of a long wooden crate. A long wooden crate with large black lettering on the side that I hadn't been able to read upside-down, standing so close to it. But, for some strange reason, upside down and backwards, in the mirror on the far side of the sales floor, I was able to read: "Bamboo Poles, ten feet and over."

The top of the crate was nailed tight, and the clerk wasn't sure if he should try to open it or not. I wasn't about to be dissuaded and got him to fetch his boss.

The manager came wheezing up the stairs to tell me that they weren't going to open the crate until morning. But I was persuasive, promising to buy five, if they were decent quality, and so the clerk was told to get a crowbar from behind the counter and pry the top off.

A crate of emeralds wouldn't have looked as attractive to me as that array of beautiful, smooth, rich green poles. Straight and strong.

By far the best spring I'd ever felt in my hands.

I thought again about my Grandfather's words, "...you've got to be focused." Yes, these were the best poles I'd ever seen, they were all great. And yet, some may have been greater than others. A line from the Book of Tao came back to me, "When living, all animals and plants are soft and pliant; when dead, they are withered and brittle ...being flexible and yielding is part of living."

Okay, there was a whole crate of nearly perfect bamboo poles in front of me, but some of them would be more nearly perfect than others. Some of them might have been harvested in the morning, some were cut later that same day. Some of them would have just a little more of the life force left in them than others, even though they all looked the same.

I began taking them out, flexing them against the floor, judging which ones felt better, more alive than others. And I found that there was a subtle difference, a more springy "feel" to a few that made them stand out, just ever so slightly, from the rest. I took my time and went through the entire crate, carefully setting the rejects aside and then stacking them neatly back in their box.

It took me quite a while, and the store was close to closing by the time I carried my selections down to the cash register, but the manager didn't mind because I ended up buying six.

The weight of the bundle nearly killed my shoulders, but I couldn't have been happier, even when I missed the ferry. The whistle blew and the boat pulled out just as I was crossing the wide expanse of Queen's Quay.

I had nearly an hour to wait for the next boat, but Mike's Diner was still open. I stashed the bundle of poles in back, in the space between the garbage cans and the skirting around the bottom of the Diner.

Mike's Diner was a converted streetcar that had been serving coffee and meals to local workers and Islanders waiting for their boats for as long as I could remember. Stools at a counter that ran the most of the length of the place faced the narrow kitchen area and I sat at one of them and ordered. The place was essentially a lunch counter, with less business in the evenings. Mike and Abe only worked until around four, then Nick came on until closing time.

Mike's was famous, among Islanders at least, for the burgers and fish and chips, but they also served the best grilled-cheese sandwich. It started with a slice of cheese between two slices of bread, with a light brushing of melted butter from a rectangular stainless-steel pan beside the grill. That was the start. The thing that set Mike's grilled items a cut above all others was an appliance that sat back behind the grill, a two-plate toaster griddle. This device had two iron heating plates, top and bottom, and it was always on, always hot. Nick pushed the handle that pried the top plate up and placed the prepared sandwich between them, letting the weight of the top plate squish down on it with a sizzling sound. In just a minute the whole thing had heated through and toasted a golden brown. But something about the amount of weight from the top plate, plus the subtle taste of the thousands of other items that had been cooked in that griddle over the years, had changed the texture, changed the flavour, into something completely new and different.

I had fries with it and ordered another, then a toasted Danish for dessert.

Cut in half cross-wise and cooked the same way, with the cut and buttered surfaces out and the sugary parts pressed together in the centre, the common Danish Pastry benefited equally from the odd alchemy of that wonderful two-plate griddle. A toasted Danish enhanced with hints of cheese and bacon and onion and a myriad of other flavours.

If I could time-travel, there might be a whole host of treasures and riches that I'd go after: the standard list of lottery ticket winnings and horse races that I could bet on and become phenomenally rich. But, if I really could go back in time, the taste of one of those toasted Danish pastries from Mike's Diner would be among the first things that I'd want to experience again.

Chapter 34
Sports Day

I began my run with a little hop, twice on my right foot. Not too fast at first, making sure to get the spacing of my steps correct.

Then I poured on that surge of speed, lowered the tip of the pole, aimed at the stop-chock and hurled my body with all my might. I was throwing my weight at that invisible place just about a quarter of the way between the ground and the bar, making the pole bend as it absorbed the force.

Converting forward momentum into upward movement as that force came back from the pole, I twisted my body, legs toward the sky, and made it! Eight Feet! I had set a new personal best!

Dink was already clearing eight-four, but that didn't bother me, I was a serious contender, and that was good enough for now. Once the inter-school competition was on, anything could happen, and we all knew it.

But for now, all I could think about was getting back into my sweatshirt and pants in order to stay warm until my next jump. It had gotten colder through the day, and a few white flakes were mixed into the intermittent drizzle.

Tuesday afternoon, and again no library in lieu of track and field time.

The same on Wednesday afternoon, with the wind from the North picking up sand from the playing area and throwing it in our faces as we tried to perfect our athletic abilities.

I cleared eight feet a second time, and felt fairly confident that I could do better under pressure, if the weather improved by the day of the track meet.

Thursday morning was chilly, but not quite as cold. The wind was still coming from the North, but had died down to a light breeze. I had taken four poles to school, keeping the best two at home for this day.

We didn't catch the bus to school, assembling instead at the Ward's Island ferry dock, where The Teachers and some other school staff met us and took attendance. Then we all got on the boat and headed for the city.

We had to wait at the curb at Queens Quay for the charter bus to arrive and, during that wait, Dink's dad showed up with a car to take him and his long fiberglass pole to the sports field.

A few minutes after they left two specially chartered buses showed up for the trip to the Christie Pits athletic field, and that's where I ran into an insurmountable obstacle. The front door of both buses were constructed with a steel panel in front of the front passenger seat. To board, we had to go straight up the narrow steps, towards the driver, then turn around this barrier to go down the aisle to our seats. My poles simply would not go in and around that panel from the front door. The bus had no back door, and the windows didn't open. Try as I might, there simply wasn't any way that I could get those ten-foot poles onto the bus.

There was a taxicab coming along Queen's Quay and I hailed it, but the driver wouldn't let me hold those long poles, with my arm around them, on the outside of his vehicle.

Everyone was waiting. I argued that I could walk all the way up to the sports field, but The Teacher wouldn't let me leave the group. He told me not to worry about it, he held a school board notice that stated that poles would be provided at the meet, so I should be fine. And so I had to make the hard decision and leave my two best poles stashed at the back of Mike's Diner and get on the bus.

I sat at the front of the bus, feeling depressed about the loss of my poles, while kids at the back started singing back-of-the-bus songs (the cleaner ones, since there were teachers on board).

We got to the field and took up residence on the East side grassy slope facing the field. Dink's dad had already dropped him off, his cherished fiberglass pole resting on the grass close to his side.

I couldn't find out what type of poles the school board had for us since the pole vault equipment wasn't out yet, but I had other things on my mind. There were girls here from other schools!

A tinny sounding set of loudspeakers made inaudible announcements at irregular intervals, and a charming brunette in baggy blue sweat pants from a city school asked if I knew where the Hop Skip and Jump was being held. She couldn't make out what they were saying over the PA system either.

I walked with her, over to the printed schedule of events posted on a clipboard hanging from the chain-link backstop of the baseball diamond at one end of the field, and scrolled my finger down to the line where the time and location for her event was posted. She thanked me with such a sweet, pleasant smile that I felt like I was melting inside. I told her that I was entered in the pole vault and looked it up to show her when I'd be competing. There was only one set of landing pads, and the schedule was set up so that the pads were used for high-jump in the morning. Pole vault wasn't going to happen until the afternoon so they could use those same pads.

I had two events in the afternoon, the hundred-yard dash at one PM and pole vault at two, the same time as her Hop Skip and Jump event. In the morning's competition I was signed up for the goofiest event in the history of track and field.

The Standing Broad Jump cannot be performed in any way that looks athletic or cool.

You start by placing both feet on a plank anchored in the ground, then squat down and rise, usually two or three times, pumping your legs, getting the feel of how you're going to jump.

Then, without getting your toes over the edge into the sand at the edge of the plank, you leap like a frog as far forward as you possibly can, swinging your legs out in front, landing with, hopefully, just enough forward momentum to not fall backward. The judges then pull out their tapes and measure the distance from the plank to the nearest mark made in the sand, then rake it all clean of your imprint in preparation for the next contestant.

I got a third place ribbon.

At least, I thought, even if I can't make a decent showing at the Pole Vault, I've already got a third, and still have a really good chance at a ribbon in the sprint.

I walked around to the various other events, enthusiastically cheering on the other Islanders.

Christie Pits park is literally a pit, an old gravel pit, I was told, that had been gouged and shaped and groomed into an athletic field after the gravel had been exhausted. Steep grassy banks rise on three sides from the flat central playing area. I went up on the Eastern hill to join some classmates and eat my lunch while scanning the various groups for that cute girl in the baggy blue sweat pants. Her name was Joan, and she was much more interesting than anything that the officials might have to announce over that scratchy sound system.

I finished one sandwich and was just starting the second, along with a sip of hot chicken soup from my thermos, when Dooly leaned over and asked me if I was dropping out of the hundred-yard dash.

"No, why?"

"Well, it's starting right now."

"But it's not scheduled until after lunch, at 1:00 PM," I protested.

"They moved it up. They've been announcing it for the past half hour, didn't you hear it?"

I ran down off the hill, around the chain-link cage, still chewing, and up to the starting line just in time to hear, "On your marks. Get set." I was just barely able to get in line as the judge fired his starter's pistol into the air.

Suffice it to say that I certainly didn't win, but I did come in fifth. Out of a starting line-up of ten kids in my age group, that was pretty good, all things considered.

I wished that I hadn't just eaten, though, and just made it into the bathroom to vomit.

After that I rested on the grassy hillside in the afternoon sun, regaining my strength for the Pole Vault.

One of the judges came up the hill. She'd been looking for me, after the race, to present me with my "participant" ribbon.

I reluctantly accepted it and stashed it in my lunch bag, along with the unfinished half of my second sandwich and the "third place" ribbon that I'd gotten for the standing broad jump.

The high jump was over, and the landing pads were pulled across the grass to the two cinder tracks that led up to the stop-chocks for the pole vault. The officials brought out the sets of pole vault standards and took their time getting them anchored with heavy sand-bags. They checked with both a bubble level and a plumb bob, then measured and re-measured, ascertaining with great exactitude that they were the required distance apart, and the cross-bar height and level were as exact as they could get them. Then the officials brought out the pole vaulting poles that, many years ago, had been purchased by the Board of Education.

Aluminum, about two inches in diameter at the grip end, and tapered like an overgrown chopstick. Hockey-stick tape wrapped around the grip area. About as flexible as a telephone pole, and just about as heavy.

There turned out to be only four of us signed up for this event in my age group, Dink, myself, and two other grade-sixer's from other schools. The majority of kids entered in the pole vault, including Gronk, were older, and Gronk had a fiberglass pole too. I had no idea how he had gotten it to the field.

Dink and I both waved off the six foot setting, opting to wait until they put it up to seven, which was fine with the judges. One of the other kids, using an aluminum pole, made six feet, the other took his three tries but couldn't clear that height and was eliminated.

Dink went next and easily cleared seven feet, then it was my turn.

I began my run with a little hop, twice on my right foot. Not too fast at first, trying to get the spacing of my steps correct.

Then that surge of speed, but lowering the tip of the heavy pole too quickly.

I pulled up, trying to place the tip in the stop-chock… and missed it entirely!

I speared the landing pads and went hurtling face first into the dirt, sliding like a baseball runner stealing third. I thrust my arms out in front of me, and my forward momentum became upward movement just as my face grazed the wooden end of the stop-chock.

I was dirty and a bit shook-up, but mostly embarrassed as I quickly bounced back to my feet, brushing the dust off.

Two of the officials rushed up and checked that I didn't have a nosebleed or any scrapes or gashes but, besides a lot of dust on my face, I was okay.

I took my second run, starting with a little hop, twice on my right foot. Again, not too fast at first, making sure to get the spacing of my steps correct.

Then that surge of speed, lowered the tip of the pole, placed the tip in the stop-chock and, hurling my body with all my might at that invisible place just about a quarter of the way between the ground and the bar, swung up from the ground. But the pole wouldn't bend! All that force came back up the pole, ripping the skin from my palms as I clung, swinging up, then stopped!

I didn't make it over the bar. Didn't even get close.

My forward momentum ceased, along with any upward movement, about two feet short of the crossbar. I started to fall backward, away from the bar. Slowly at first, then I landed on my back on the grass at one side of the cinder track with a mighty "thump" that knocked the wind out of me.

One of the officials explained to me that, since I had made two tries at this height, if I made a third attempt and missed, I would be eliminated.

If, however, I wanted to go back and try the six foot qualifying height again, I could have three more tries at it. If I made it, I could keep on going up, of course.

The kid who had cleared six feet with the aluminum pole made it up through six-one, two and three, then missed six-four three times and was out.

By this time I had regained my composure and tried, unsuccessfully, three attempts at the six foot qualifying height.

Dink was the winner for our age group, and went on to compete against the older contestants in an attempt to set a new record.

Since there wasn't any third-place finisher in our category, the other kid who failed to qualify and I were both given one more chance to make it over the six-foot mark.

My hands were raw, my back sore, but I wanted so badly to get in at least a qualifying jump of six feet.

But it wasn't to be.

My only consolation was that the other kid didn't make it either.

I was going home with just two ribbons. Without qualifying, I didn't even get a "participant" award for the pole vault.

I got back to my spot on the grassy hillside and looked in my lunch bag, at my meager winnings, one third place and one participant ribbon. Plus the remnants of my remaining half-eaten sandwich. I made a conscious decision that, in future, I would avoid any sports that required packing around a ten-foot pole.

Chapter 35
The Best Sports Day Ever

"How'd you do?" a girl's voice at my shoulder asked.

I jumped to my feet, closing the bag, then showed Joan, the girl in blue sweats that I'd met earlier, the two lousy ribbons I'd won.

"You got a third for pole vault?" she asked, sounding impressed.

"No, um, that was for…"

"I got two firsts and a third," she said, proudly holding out her ribbons for me to admire. "I knocked down two of the hurdles and only got a third for that, but I got a first for Hop Skip and Jump, and another first in High Jump. I'm done all my events now. Are you still waiting to compete in anything?"

"No, I'm through for the…"

"Well, I'm going home to change. I just live a couple of blocks over that way. What school are you from?"

"Uh, I'm here," I indicated the few Islanders who were still stretched out on the grass around us, "from the Island School. We came up on buses from…"

"The Island? Oh, we stayed there for a week! The whole class! It was great! Is that where you are this week?"

"No, that's our regular school."

"What, you mean you live there? On the Island?" I nodded. "What's it like to live there?" I started to open my mouth to answer but she went on too quickly for me. "It must be wonderful in the summer, having the beach right there all the time? You're probably a wonderful swimmer, aren't you? I just love to swim."

I smiled and nodded, which was about all the input I had in the conversation, as we walked along. I didn't mind. This was a girl, and she was talking to me!

"Our home is just up this way. Would you like to come along with me? My mother made some cupcakes. You just have to try one! My mother makes the best cupcakes. My dad says that it's because she uses real rum in the batter, but I've helped her make them and I've never seen her put rum in them. Ever. But that's where my dad thinks the rum goes, when the level in the bottle is lower than he thinks it should be. My sister and I know where it really goes, though," she winked at me in a conspiratorial way.

I didn't know if she meant that she and her sister drank it, or her mother. I just didn't get it, but I smiled as if I did as we continued up a street on the North side of the playing field and then between some houses and up a back alley. She talked so continually that I found myself waiting, listening for her to take a breath so I could reply.

"Here's where I live," she said, opening a gate off the alley and leading me up the back steps of a house with brown siding that looked very much like most of the other three-story houses around the neighbourhood.

There was a clay flowerpot on the landing at the top of the stairs, the withered stems of a dead plant sticking out of its dry, cracked soil. She tilted the pot and slid the key out from under it, unlocked the back door and replaced the key, then lead me into the kitchen.

I picked up mixed aromas of garlic, onion and cabbage, plus something else, something exotic to my nose... Strange girls!

"Joan, is that you?" a man's voice called from the front of the house.

"Oh, hi Daddy," she called back, obviously surprised that he was here. "I'm just here to get changed, then I've got to get back to the track meet."

"Ah," he replied, a sound denoting understanding as we went into the living room. "And how did you... Oh! Who's this?"

"Ah, Daddy, this is..."

"Lorne, sir," I said, reaching to shake his hand.

"Lorne, is it?" he said standing up, towering over me and giving my hand a squeeze that I'm sure Superman would have been proud to use to turn coal into diamonds.

"Yes, sir." He still hadn't let go of my hand.

"Lorne what?"

"Um, Jones, sir. Lorne Jones."

"Jones," he said, flatly, letting go his grip. "A Welshman, are you?"

"Well, I suppose that's where the family name came from, at one time. I only know that we've been in Toronto for, I don't know, a lot of generations."

"I'm going to get changed," Joan said. "Be nice, now," she said to her father. I didn't know what that meant, but had a quick image of him not being nice otherwise and wondered just how un-nice that might have been.

He sat in an overstuffed armchair, a newspaper and briar pipe in an ashtray at his elbow. He motioned for me to sit on the couch, pointing to a bowl of mints, telling me to help myself.

"So, Lorne, what do you do?" he asked as he lit his pipe.

"Do, sir? I'm in school. I do homework." I replied popping a rock-hard white mint into my mouth.

"I presumed that," he said, shaking the wooden match to extinguish the flame. "I mean, it's sports day, what do you do? What's your sport?"

"Oh, um, I'm, ah, well, the hundred yard dash, and, um, the standing…" I suddenly knew that this wasn't going to come out sounding right, "…the standing broad jump." He raised an eyebrow. It might have been the smoke. "And, well, the pole vault."

"Pole vault, eh?" he said, pipe clenched in his teeth. "That was my sport, in college. How did you do?"

"Well," I said, looking at the floor, "rather badly, I'm afraid."

"Really? How so?"

And so I went on to explain about how I'd been practicing with bamboo poles, but couldn't bring them along on the bus. He nodded as I told him how the aluminum poles had no bend to them at all, and the hockey-stick tape had ripped my palms. I showed him the blisters and he told me that I should soak them in salt water. From upstairs, I could hear a shower running, then being shut off and doors opening and closing.

They had mostly used stout hardwood poles in his day, he said, but he and a couple of other fellows had tried bamboo as well.

"Trouble was," he said, "when they broke they splintered so badly that there was concern that someone could get impaled."

I went on to explain about the green poles being better, and how wrapping the joints with a bit of hockey-stick tape would increase the life of the pole. He puffed away and thought about that.

He then asked me who I liked in the National elections next month. I answered without hesitation that I'd vote Liberal, if I could.

He didn't seem to like that answer and asked me why. There was something in his tone that indicated that what he meant was more like, "Why on earth would someone in their right mind vote for the Liberals?"

"Well, sir," I replied, "Red Kelly is running for the Liberals. I really don't know much about politics. But, if the Liberals are the ones that Kelly likes, that's good enough for me."

He puffed thoughtfully on his pipe for a long moment, then said, "You just might have something there. It might be the wrong party, at the wrong time. But I'm afraid that a lot of voters might agree with you."

"Daddy!" Joan admonished, coming down the stairs in a knee-length dark blue skirt and matching sweater. "Are you talking politics?"

"Guilty, Jo-Jo," he replied, sheepishly, as she walked over to where he sat.

"Well, see that it doesn't happen again!" she teased, planting a big kiss on his cheek.

"Well, I can't promise," he replied, opening the newspaper, "but I'll try."

"Just you see that you do," she said back with a pout, shaking her finger in his face.

"We've got to get back before they take attendance," she said, leading me back into the kitchen. "I promised Lorne one of Mom's cupcakes," she called to the living room. "Would you like me to get one out for you?"

"Not right now, dear," he called back through the doorway to us.

She asked me to get a couple of small plates from the cupboard as she lifted the top of a round cake tray, revealing a small pyramid of cupcakes topped with pink icing.

"Oh, not those plates," she said, taking my hand and leading me to another set of cupboards beside the fridge, out of view from the living room. "Those ones up..." she came closer and stretched her hand toward a higher shelf, pressing right up against me, "...up there."

I swallowed what was left of the hard mint candy.

I stretched my left arm up to the stack of plates she was pointing to, while my right arm went around her waist.

I was pretty sure that I was supposed to kiss her at this point.

I did.

She took my right hand in hers. I thought she was going to pull it away. Instead, she pulled it up under her sweater. I almost dropped the two plates.

"Everything okay out there, kids?" her father called from the living room.

"Just fine, Daddy," she said. "Just getting the plates down from the top shelf."

The cupcakes tasted...

I have absolutely no recollection how the cupcakes tasted, or how we got back to the park. Nor do I recall anything about the bus ride back to the docks.

I'm pretty sure that Dink got three firsts that day, and Gronk and the rest of the guys did pretty well too. In fact, I think the Island placed first among all the trophies awarded that day. But I can't be sure. I wasn't really paying attention to anything at all.

We were at the ferry docks by the time it occurred to me that I didn't get Joan's last name, or phone number, and couldn't for the life of me remember exactly how to find my way back to her house.

I only had one third-place and one participant ribbon in my lunch bag to take home and pin on the wall, but for me this was the best sports day ever. I GOT TO FONDLE A BOOB!

Chapter 36
Holding Up The Ferry

The William Inglis, smallest ferry in the fleet, would have been crowded anyway, what with all the folks coming home to the Island after work, plus those rare mid-week passengers who intended to get off at Centre, her next stop. But, with all of us school kids on our way home from the track meet, well, it was just plain jammed on board, both upstairs and downstairs.

I crowded together with the guys from school at the rail on the upper deck, despite the chill in the evening air. The Teacher and the rest of the authority figures from School had seen that we got on the ferry and then, determining that their obligation of duty to us was fulfilled at that point, headed off for home before the boat sailed.

I lit up a smoke.

The wind carried the ash back into my face, but the crowd was too tight for me to turn around. I let the breeze blow the smoke back at me as I savoured the warm, glowing feeling of having won a wonderful prize. I got to fondle a boob today!

If I had a crystal ball, if I had any idea how much time would pass before I'd next get to feel a girl's breast, I wouldn't have been so happy.

But I didn't.

So I was.

The ferry pulled into the slip at Ward's, the forward deckhands threw the massive hawser ropes over the dockside bollards to winch her in tight to the dock. The Inglis was small in the berth, but tightening the hawser pulled her Starboard side in close to the bumpers. We weren't about to struggle our way down the stairs and off the boat through that tight throng. About a dozen of us climbed over the rail from the upper deck, down onto the dock, and strolled away before the gangplank was even lowered.

"Well, that's a neat trick," a woman's voice called out from among the people waiting their chance to board.

"Oh, hi, Gwen, ah, Mrs. Acorn," I was still in school mode. "Um Gwen?"

"Gwen's fine," she said. "You're just getting home?"

"Yeah, sports day today."

"Oh, how did you do?"

"Oh, sort of, well, less than okay, I guess." I smiled, unable to suppress my glee.

"I bet you're just being modest," she said as the gangplank came down and the boat started to empty.

"No, no. I really didn't do well at all. So, you're off to the city?"

"Yes. It's poetry night at the Bohemian Embassy. Milt's up there already, waiting for me. You should come along, and bring some of your poetry."

"Aw, I've got school tomorrow."

We stepped back a bit to make more room for the crowd exiting the boat. "Well, if you ever get a Friday off school, you really should check it out. Thursday nights."

"Yeah, well, maybe when school's out. In the summer."

"That would probably be best," she said. "The place does go pretty late into the night."

"Yeah? And you're feeling better now?"

"Better?"

"You looked like you were feeling kind of, well, in pain. The last time I saw you. When you came home and found me and Bob there?"

"Oh, that. Just a... well... a lady thing."

The crowd leaving the boat was thinning out. They'd be letting people on board soon. Her continuing silence was enough. I'd obviously raised an awkward topic.

"So," I said, trying to think of something else to say. "I heard some pounding coming from your place last weekend. Sunday, I think it was."

"Oh, Yeah, Milt was fixing the wall, that hole in the kitchen."

"I see."

"Yes. He, um, knocked some dishes off the counter in the process. Made quite a mess."

Somehow it didn't sound like she was telling the truth. People were starting to board the boat.

"Well," I said, "I hope you have fun at the poetry reading tonight."

"Oh, I'm sure I will," she said, starting toward the gangplank. I could see, across the field, someone coming from the end of Channel Avenue, running flat out.

"You know," I said, taking her elbow, "if we walk slowly, that guy might have a chance of catching this boat."

She looked up and, with a twinkle in her eye, said, "Just how slowly?" as she stepped onto the end of the gangplank. The deckhands weren't too thrilled with our antics, and one of them barked at her to hurry up and get on board.

"Oh, am I holding things up?" she asked demurely without moving. I could see now that it was Danny Cox, red faced and pounding the dust up in little clouds from the path for all he was worth. "Well," she said to me, turning slowly, "I'll just have to say goodbye now then, won't I?"

She gave me a big hug, her feet on the tip of the gangplank, mine on the dockside, and just held it for the extra couple of seconds that it took for Danny to go flying on to the boat.

She strode on into the ferry, an impish smile on her face, and called back to me, "Why don't you drop by tomorrow after school? Maybe have a cup of tea with us?"

"Sure," I yelled back as the deckhands pulled the gangplank up by its ropes and released the hawsers from the dock. "Tomorrow it is then! After school!"

The ferry slid out from the dock and cruised on over towards Centre.

I hit the road around to the Algonquin Bridge, then over it and back to Nottawa.

Chapter 37
May The World

I could tell something was wrong from three doors away.
The front door was wide open and, from the front bedroom,
I could hear my Grandfather singing "There is a tavern in
the town, IN THE TOWN!"

I could smell stove oil and soot as I dashed up the front
steps.

My Grandmother was on the couch, crying, and the oil
stove was lying on its side, oil dripping onto the floor from
the kinked and broken copper pipe at the back of it. The
fire was out, but there was soot from the disconnected
stovepipe all over the place.

I could presume, with fair accuracy, that it happened
something like this:

It started, I suppose, with his job of night watchman for
the winter months at the yacht club. Long nights with not
much to do but walk around and punch a time card at
various punch device locations around the property. That
would confirm that he was doing his rounds. And that, for
him, would have been his advantage, his edge.

Knowing that his punch cards were all in order, he would
look completely innocent.

And those sheets of paper that I found in the garbage,
with regular rows of numbers, were combinations that he
had tried on the lock to the club's liquor locker. The bar
had been shut down all winter, wouldn't be open again for
another month. If, once they opened the locker in June,
they found that it had been emptied, the theft could have
happened anytime after it was sealed up in the Fall. In fact,
how could anyone even prove that there had been anything
in it from ten hours after it was locked? The theft could
have taken place at any time. And my Grandfather's

faithful punching of his time cards would have put him above suspicion.

As far as he was concerned, his ship had come in!

The problem, of course, was that when he brought the first case of booze home my Grandmother simply wouldn't have any part of his crazy scheme.

Maybe he told her about his grand plan. Maybe she accidentally caught him hauling the case in the back door. I don't know.

The result was that, with a whole case of Seagram's 83 in the house, he simply couldn't resist opening a bottle and taking a swig. He probably spun the cap off "flying saucer" style. I'd seen him do that too many times before. With a swipe of his palm he could remove a cap, sending it spinning across the room followed by the proud proclamation: "We won't be needing that anymore!"

Maybe he just sat and poured himself a single shot thinking that, after one, he'd just put the bottle away and get on with other things.

When he put his mind to it, my Grandfather was capable of doing some amazing things. But putting a bottle of whiskey down was not among his talents.

By the time he'd gotten a few shots under his belt, my Grandmother would have turned into a person who couldn't do anything right. Even if he sneezed and she said, "bless you," he would have found some way to take offense at the remark.

There would have been shouting, and swearing. At some point he threw her across the room into the side of the oil heater, knocking it over. Fortunately, the fire went out. Now he was barricaded in the bedroom with a full case, twelve one-quart bottles, *three gallons* of his favorite brand. The dresser was against the door, and he was singing contentedly away to an imaginary audience.

"I'll hang my ha-at on a weeping willow tree. And may the world..." he stopped and I could hear the gurgle of the bottle as he took another swig, "And may the world go well with thee. WELL WITH THEE!"

I went out back and turned off the valve at the oil tank. I couldn't fix the oil stove without any tools, so I called Barry.

I tried to sound casual over the phone, like there was just a minor repair to make to the feed line, but he suspected something more was wrong than that when I couldn't explain in detail why the line needed fixing. He wanted to talk to my Grandmother.

She tried her best to disguise the fact that her hip was so badly bruised, but he deduced from her tone that there had been another blow-up. He came rushing over, dropping his bike in the front yard and charging up the stairs three at a time.

At first he wanted to kick the bedroom door down and beat the Old Man senseless, but my Grandmother got him calmed down and convinced him that the best course was to just let him sleep it off, fix the stove, and handle my Grandfather once he sobered up. After all, he was already out of his senses.

She phoned somebody on the yacht club executive to let them know that my Grandfather was sick and wouldn't be in to work tonight.

Barry examined the stove and determined that the quarter-inch copper feed line was busted beyond repair. There was a small tank built into the back of the stove, but that had been disconnected when the feed line from the big tank out back was hooked up.

We used sponges and newspaper to mop up the spilled oil from the floor, stood the stove back up and reconnected the stovepipes through the ceiling. The house was getting very cold with nightfall coming on, and Barry wondered if it wouldn't be better for my Grandmother and me to squeeze in at his place, somehow, and just let the Old Man freeze.

My grandmother wouldn't hear of it, though, and so I went on a scavenger hunt through boxes in the attic for the short length of copper connecting pipe that had come with the stove and would make it possible to use the tank on the back again.

My Grandfather's singing became quieter, then erratic, then stopped. In a few minutes his snoring began, then became louder than the singing had been.

I finally found the tank connector pipe and Barry fastened it tight to the tank at one end and the carburetor at the other. I filled the old oilcan from the big tank out back, brought it in and topped up the small tank built in to the back of the stove. Then Barry turned the flow back on and tossed a lit Kleenex inside.

A lot of oil had sloshed up the inside of the stove when the fire went out, so when it was re-lit it smoked terribly for about five minutes. Then the flame slowly changed from a dirty orange ball, settling down to a steady blue ring, the flapper valve on the side of the vent pipe balancing back and forth to compensate for minor variations in the wind outside.

It was getting close to midnight, and I had school in the morning. My Grandmother said that she could sleep on the couch, but I insisted that she take my bed. The couch was fine with me, I said, and got out the sheets and blankets to make it up.

She didn't show Barry the long blue bruise that I'd seen, from her hip to her knee, and she was trying to not walk much so as not to let him see how she was limping.

He got back on his bike and headed for home, promising to phone before he left for work in the morning to see how things were going.

While my Grandfather snored away in the front bedroom, my Grandmother took a couple of the powerful pills she had for arthritis and was soon snoring from the back bedroom as well, though more softly.

My aching stomach reminded me that I hadn't had any supper, but I didn't feel much like fixing anything. I put a half-dozen slices of white bread on a plate and sat at the kitchen table, washing down chunks of bread with a glass of milk.

Chapter 38
Debts Unpaid

It had been a long day, but I just couldn't get to sleep.

I thought back on all the things that I had done, all the lessons I had learned in life, all the things I had seen.

I remembered something.

Something that I'd come across while looking for the tank-connector pipe in the attic.

I climbed back up, flashlight in hand, and went through the boxes, the collected memorabilia, assorted things that were too important to throw away, but too insignificant to keep handy.

There, in a large brown cardboard box full of odds and ends, I located the small case with its shiny, chrome-plated contents. There was no need to be extra quiet climbing back down and pulling my coat on as I left the house. Neither of my grandparents was likely to hear me.

I got on my bike and rode, over the bridge, along Lakeshore to the Gap, then out to that special place at its Southern tip.

With just the softest of chilly breezes teasing around me, the water slowly undulating on three sides and, somewhere out in the darkness, a single seagull calling a mournful complaint, I slipped the contents of the case from my pocket.

I lifted it to my lips, took a breath, and, tasting the cold chrome of the old Hohner, I softly blew a long, steady note.

The really nice thing about a harmonica, compared to other wind instruments, is that you don't have to stop playing to take a breath. There are notes that you can play while breathing in as well as out.

I didn't play any particular song, just played.

At some point I realized that the melody was starting to sound suspiciously like There Is A Tavern In The town and made a deliberate change to Suwanee River, then went back to just randomly playing, and allowed myself to cry.

Blocking the centre of the instrument with my tongue, playing two low notes and one high one together at the same time, then switching around, hitting lots of bad notes but not caring. I just wanted to let it out, the hurt.

I sat and played until the sky began to get light in the East, then stood and stared at the sky.

"You owe me!" I yelled.

"I asked for a heat wave, and all I got was one lousy day! I paid the price! You want me to suffer? Okay! I've given you your damned sacrifice! NOW DELIVER!

"I WANT A HEAT WAVE. SOMETHING TO MAKE IT ALL WORTH WHILE!"

I'd never really thought about gods in the clouds before. To me the weather systems had been like broken up ice flows in the Bay, big heavy unthinking objects that we could jump on and push around like rafts when the pack ice was breaking up in the Spring. They were as dangerous playthings for children as abandoned refrigerators that you could get locked in and suffocate. We were courting disaster. Still, some of us just couldn't resist the winter fun of running out on those heavy, crumbling ice flows with rubber boots, smelt poles in hand, and riding them around in the shallows.

That was how I felt about pulling those heavy, dumb weather systems around in the sky.

I didn't know if I really believed that stuff Bob Mallory had said about Neptune or not.

Maybe it was all just a pile of crap.

But, if there was anything to what he said, then I wanted Neptune to know that he wasn't pulling his weight, wasn't keeping up his end of the bargain.

I raised my arms and pulled on the wind, pulled the clouds and high-pressure systems my way.

There hadn't been anything on the television or in the papers to indicate that there was even the smallest chance that a system of warm air was out there to call, but I made the effort, and felt confident, and somehow better for it.

The sun broke spectacularly over the Eastern end of the Lake, the heat of it evaporating away the remnants of a thin layer of cloud. I rode my bike home and got changed and showered and gulped down a bowl of cereal, then threw a slice of baloney between two slices of bread, put it into a bag and left in time to catch the schoolbus.

Chapter 39
Sunny and Warm

It was sunny and warm. I fell asleep at my desk, The Teacher coming over and shaking me awake to the laughs of the rest of the class. Apparently I'd been snoring face-down in a textbook.

I overheard someone asking if they knew who it was that shot him. Shot who? I wondered.

"Liberty Valance. The movie's out. Has anyone seen it? Who's the man who shot Liberty Valance?"

Nobody knew.

The song had been on the charts for weeks, but the movie had just hit the theatres, and now the answer was finally available. But nobody at school had seen it yet.

I had enough money to go to the show, but I'd promised to drop by and see Gwen after school.

"Maybe tomorrow," I thought.

Meanwhile, I had a whole school day to try to get through.

I staggered around at recess, fell asleep in a sunny corner of the playground during lunch, and vaguely remember, at the end of the day, The Teacher saying something about assignments due, before catching the bus home.

I missed the Algonquin Bridge stop, the bus driver shaking me awake to get off at Ward's.

I didn't really want to go to my grandparent's anyway, even though the small tank on the back of the oil stove would probably need to be re-filled by now. I didn't feel any need to hurry, it was a warm afternoon. The fire could wait for a couple of hours. I decided to walk over to Barry and Flo's.

The back door was locked, Sam prowling back and forth in hopes that I'd open it. I got the key out from under the mat and let him in, calling "hello" into the kitchen, but there was nobody home.

As I walked up Second I could see Milt hammering away at his typewriter through the open door.

"Hey, come on in," he bellowed in friendly greeting. "Gwen said you were going to drop by after school. She'll probably be on the late bus, said something about a staff meeting. Have a seat."

I dropped my schoolbooks to the floor and sank into the green corduroy armchair.

"I've been thinking about that poem of yours," he said, turning from the typewriter. " 'Vulnerable nestlings an everpresent possibility' is good and strong, and expressions like flyswim, sharkhawk and pikeduck are actually quite good. But do you know what it's missing?"

It didn't seem like a rhetorical question, he was actually waiting for me to answer. I couldn't think of what it was missing. I could hardly even remember the poem. How was he able to recall it in such detail?

"Um, I don't know."

"People like to hear poetry about people," he answered, very seriously. "They might think a baby duck is cute, but put that baby duck in a person's hands, and now they're intrigued. Is it someone who loves the duck, or someone who means it harm? They'll wonder about things like that, what the person is going to do. Do you see what I mean?"

"I guess."

"For poetry to be strong, to have impact, it has to have a human element. Without that, all you've got is textbook prose."

"Okay."

"I'm not saying there's anything wrong with your poem. In fact, there's quite a bit of good, strong imagery there. All I'm suggesting is that, in future, you add in a little sprinkle of something that people can relate to. Something that includes them in, gives them some emotional investment. Give them a part in the story, no matter how small."

"I'll keep that in mind," I said.

He re-lit his cigar and turned back to typing, saying, without slowing the speed of the hammer strokes, "You don't mind if I keep working, do you? I've got a lot to catch up on."

"No, no. That's fine, I'll just rest here for a bit."

The chair's arms were rounded enough to rest my head, and the seat wide enough, the shape comfortable enough that, within minutes, I had curled up and drifted off to sleep.

Dreams came to me in waves, dreams of Hanlan's Point, the big house at 604 Lakeshore, where we had lived from when I was born until I was six years old.

Most of my dreams took place in that house, one of the first to get demolished in the war of total devastation that the Metro Toronto Parks Department waged against the Island homes.

When I was born there were over fifteen thousand homes on the Island. Big and small, rooming houses and apartment buildings. There had been a movie theatre and a bowling alley, several hotels, the Crystal ballroom dance pavilion, an amusement park, and still plenty of room for many more thousands of city visitors than have ever made day trips to the Island in all the years since the expropriations began.

Gone.

All gone except for about three hundred houses still standing on Algonquin, Ward's and along the Boardwalk down to Hooper.

The Parks Department had made it absolutely clear that the remaining houses would all be gone within six years.

The rest of the Island had already been bulldozed and sanitized of all trace of homes and businesses. Replaced by acres and acres of lawn grass, plus a regimentally regular array of rectangular concrete flower beds that were constantly in need of fertilizing and re-planting by Parks Department employees. No wilted or brown vegetation was allowed to be seen by those few hearty souls who still ventured over to Centre. A place devoid of the human element. A place stripped by bulldozers and wrecking crews of its poetry.

I dreamed of Hanlan's, of the time when there were sidewalks full of kids on tricycles and people with fishing rods lining the lagoons. I dreamed of playing tag and racing tricycles and of marbles and slingshots. Dreams of rowboat races and BB guns and learning to ride a two-wheeled bike on concrete pavement that seldom saw cars or trucks.

Dreams of things long gone.

Chapter 40
My Own Bed Again

Milt woke me up, shaking my shoulder, trying to pull me back from a deep dream of baby ducks crowding around as I tossed bread crumbs to them from a rowboat.

"Lorne! Hey Lorne! Come on, wakey wakey. Someone's calling you."

Then he hollered to someone out on the street, "He's in here!"

As I swayed to unsteady legs I saw Barry in silhouette in the doorway. Corduroy imprints lined my cheek as I rubbed my face, wiping away a bit of drool. How long had I been asleep?

The sun had swung around, no longer pouring straight in the front door, and the house had become chilly.

"Come on," Barry said to me, "we've got stuff to do." Then, to Milt, he said, "thanks for minding him."

"That's fine," Milt said, going back to his writing. He had a heavy plaid shirt on and didn't seem to be aware of the cold.

Barry, as usual, had found a solution. Phone calls had been placed, decisions made. He had talked to The Owner of 6 Lakeshore. His new tenant, Lorraine Sinclair, wanted to put a few things into the outside storage room there early, before the fifteenth, Barry said, and The Owner gave his okay.

We moved around several times over the intervening years after leaving 604 Lakeshore, living at various places in the city as well as back on the Island. My first home, 604, was one of the first to be obliterated from Hanlan's Point, and we were in 610 until it was bulldozed along with the last of the properties to be erased from existence at that end of the Island. That's when we moved to Ward's, leaving Hanlan's for the last time.

At 3 Channel there was an overflow of stuff from all those moves stored in the attic. Boxes, lamps, rugs, anything small enough to go up through the hatch, did. Anything solid enough to survive the elements: smelt pole, fishing rods, extra shovels, had been stashed under the house.

Everything else: bed frames, mattresses, extra couch and matching armchairs, was stored in the middle bedroom, along with all the furniture from my room (where the paint was still not dry).

It was this last trove of treasured belongings that we were about to tackle.

But first we had to go up the street and inspect the storage room at the back of 6 Lakeshore. It turned out that the skeleton key that Barry had for the back door also fit the storage room.

It was a small but dry room with a door that opened onto the lane. There was a big old push-cart inside, painted the same rusty brown as the house. It looked so dusty that we figured it must have been stored in there for years. We had to take the wheels off and turn it on its side to get it out.

Its two wooden-spoked wheels were about three feet around, with metal rims, and one of the legs on the front end was broken. We repaired that leg with a piece of two-by-two, greased the hubs, and had an ideal means of transport for all the heavy furniture that needed to be shifted.

First, all the stuff from my bedroom got stacked up in the living room, taking them out very carefully in order to not cause an avalanche. Then the rest went outside, onto the big-wheeled wagon. Load by load we hauled the contents of the middle bedroom up to the house at the other end of Second, building a compact stack of things not immediately needed but too precious to discard.

Gwen came home on the late bus and I chatted with her briefly about how things were, what do you think of the weather, that sort of thing, but I didn't really have time to stop in and visit, promising to get together with them another time.

Flo had gone around to Algonquin to see that my Grandmother was okay, returning to inform us that the Old Man was still on his bender. The stove-oil had been topped up and everything else seemed fine enough. She made no mention of my Grandmother's bruised hip, and I didn't ask.

Moving all that stuff was quite a chore, and I was still very tired, but happy. Once we got everything that had to go neatly stacked up at 6 Lakeshore and the door shut tight and locked, we shifted my bed and dresser and such into the middle bedroom from the living room. I was going to get to sleep in my own bed again!

I woke up early Saturday morning to the aroma of pancakes, and Barry asked me what I'd like to do today. I still had a bit of my own money left, and told him that, what I'd really like to do, was see the Saturday morning cartoons in colour!

Chapter 41
Liberty Valance at the Imperial

There had been a fire at Leow's Uptown and the place was closed for renovations.

With the loss of their weekly gathering place there were a lot of kids who wanted another Saturday Morning venue. The Imperial tried running a pre-matinee program as an experiment, putting on the old cheap-seat menu of cartoons, Three Stooges and Western serials that the Uptown had offered, and we'd gladly pay to watch what we could see for free on TV, because they were in full colour! Available to any kid with a quarter!

The Imperial didn't open till nine, but they did have people from radio stations giving away stuff.

I tried, at the cavernous old Imperial, to chat with girls here, there, and got shot down mostly. Okay, not mostly, completely. "Picking up girls" was a skill I didn't have. But I tried.

There was an occasional fight. I tried to avoid those.

There were thousands of us and, though the ushers were plentiful, they couldn't be everywhere.

The stairwell to the left of the screen, the one that went up to the far left side of the balcony, had a few kids going up ahead of me, a few coming down, a stairway wide enough for a crowd to walk up ten abreast. There was a flat landing in the middle, then more stairs. As good a place as any, I thought, to stop and have a smoke. I lit up and slumped my back against the wall, trying to look Cary Grant cool.

Another kid was coming down, lighting up, trying to look Robert Mitchum cool. Three guys in black shirts were coming up the stairs, saw Robert Mitchum, and the biggest of them confronted him.

"You wanna go me?" he challenged in Mitchum's face. His buddies spread out to each side. I took a couple of steps up and looked back. I kept going, slowly, interested, but definitely wanting to get a good head start away from there, just in case.

Mitchum took a slow drag and, exhaling smoke, said, "You *wanna* fight me?" There was just the slightest emphasis on the word: "wanna."

"Yeah, I *wanna* fight you," the big kid answered, moving a half step closer.

"How much you got in your wallet?"

"Huh?" Big Kid's buddies stopped moving closer.

"You wanna go *me*," this time Mitchum's emphasis was on the word *me*, "...then you gotta make it worth it. You got ten?"

Big kid was confused.

"Look, you even got five on you?" Big kid was backing up ever so slightly. "If I fight you," Mitchum said, staring unblinking as he spoke, "then I'm gonna clean your wallet out when I'm done. You up for that?"

Actions moved at the speed of thought, and Big Kid's thought process was obviously slow, but it was there. I swear, as I watched, Big Kid actually shrunk about six inches. Go for wallets? That's what they did in Regent Park. And they really played for keeps. Knives, brass knuckles, the whole works.

"Ah, nuts!" Big Kid said, and he and his buddies headed off back down the stairs. Mitchum hadn't moved from his spot. He finished his cigarette, crushed it under his foot and slowly strolled on down.

I went up and tried, in a completely innocent and off-hand manner, to ask a pair of pretty girls in matching yellow dresses how they liked the movie. They laughed and told me I was crazy. I laughed and told them I was and rolled my eyes in different directions. They both went

"Eeuw!" and headed off to the bathroom together. I went to
the concession stand and bought some more popcorn.

Saturday morning and any kid with a quarter could get in.
The Imperial always oversold tickets beyond the number of
seats because not every kid watched every movie. There
were shorts and serials and cartoons and usually two
features.

Three Stooges and Porky Pig.

Roy Rogers and Betty Boop.

We cheered Hoppalong Cassidy like we were all ten
years old again and booed when the ancient Popeye film
broke, then started up again, a big chunk of the story (…He
liveth at the corner of Chow and Main) missing. We just sat
down anywhere for the ones we wanted to watch and
milled around the lobby the rest of the time, buying
popcorn and chocolates. I was mostly trying to figure out
why this was supposed to be a fun time. That's what the
ads said we'd have, lots of fun, so I guess we were.

Previews of coming attractions burst onto the screen and I
noticed something missing. Liberty Valance wasn't among
them.

That had been the big question: who shot Liberty
Valance?

But "The Man Who Shot Liberty Valance" was no longer
a coming attraction.

It was here, tonight!

The feature presentation!

And I was dying to know: who was it? Who shot Liberty
Valance? And I thought of a clever way to find out.

On Saturday morning any kid with a quarter could get in
to the Imperial, and by eleven-thirty the place was empty
and swept out, ready to re-open for the early feature show
at noon.

Empty by eleven-thirty, that was the way it was supposed
to be. The ushers checked the stairways, went across the

balcony, back down to the lobby. A group of them came up to me, waiting outside the women's washroom.

"I'm just waiting for..." I motioned towards the door. They nodded and the three of them went into the North entrance to the men's room. They came out again through the South entrance to the men's as I slipped in through the North door.

I stood on a toilet, door slightly ajar, feet on the rim, and waited.

And waited.

The theatre became quiet, then sounds of vacuum cleaners went by in the hall. Someone came in and started cleaning toilets. I waited and counted until they had done three stalls, then tiptoed behind them and took up my position again, this time in one of the stalls they had already done.

Quiet descended once again, and then the sound of the crowd for the noon show coming in. I joined them and took a seat in the back row.

James Stewart was the man who came to town, "...a law book in his hand," from the song.

Lee Marvin was Liberty Valance, a cold-blooded killer. A bully and brute. But what was John Wayne doing? His character wasn't in the song.

I thought I knew what was going to happen, that John Wayne would be the man who shot Liberty Valance, and wondered how he'd do it. And I really never saw it coming. When it did, I couldn't believe it. How could a sniper be "The bravest of them all?"

How could he gun down Liberty Valance with a rifle, from the shadows, like that?

That was John Wayne up there. John Wayne was one of the good guys. And the good guys came at the bad guys face to face in the bright blazing sun at high noon. They didn't lurk in the shadows and gun you down when you weren't looking. That's what the bad guys did.

Roy Rogers would not have handled it that way.

I couldn't believe it.

The movie ended and the crowd took to their feet, stretching and yawning and filing out. No enthusiasm. This had not been a good movie. It certainly wasn't the movie I'd been expecting.

Maybe I had missed something. Maybe I got it wrong. I headed back to the bathroom and waited out another emptying and filling up of the theatre, and the lights went down and "The Man Who Shot Liberty Valance" started all over again.

I studied it, looking for subtleties, nuances, something that would convince me that the world had just been made a better place by the good guys.

But, once again, John Wayne failed to do the right thing.

The movie ended and a few people rushed out to avoid standing to attention for "God Save The Queen." The house lights came on and the crowd took to their feet, stretching and yawning and filing out, through the exits, out to Yonge Street.

That's all I wanted to do, file out through the exit, across and down to Yonge street and out.

Unfortunately, that's not what the head usher wanted me to do.

A small army of burgundy jackets surrounded me, blocking escape. The head usher, the one with a bit of gold braid stitched to his shoulder, made it quite clear that watching the main feature, twice, was going to cost me. After all, even the air conditioning was worth…

"How much you got?"

I was forced to empty my pockets. It turned out that the cost to me would be two "premium" tickets, at three dollars and twenty-five cents each.

Cash.

Now.

I didn't have a lot of choice.

I did have six dollars and sixty cents when the movie ended, but only a dime for boat fare by the time I got back out into the crush of humanity on Yonge Street.

Chapter 42
Three Little Words

Large willow trees throw a lot of root growth. Roots, which have a tendency to clog up a soap run. That means a lot of digging and chopping.

Flo had taken a phone message.

Unfortunately for Donna Russell's Dad, we were about to earn a bit of extra cash.

I did most of the digging while Barry went over to my grandparents to make the repairs necessary to hook the oil stove back up to the big tank.

On the bus, on the way to school, on a Monday morning so foggy that the bus crept along at a snail's pace, Donna called me "septic boy." After spending Sunday afternoon digging up muck in their back yard, I guess it was to be expected.

Fortunately for me, that nickname didn't catch on.

"Don't forget," The Teacher said, tapping the notice posted on the blackboard. The note had been up for at least a week, but I hadn't really paid any attention to it. How could I forget something I'd never bothered to know?

But I knew it now, and it had been drilled home often enough that everyone else in school, everyone on the whole Island, knew what had to be done that Monday afternoon.

When we lived at Hanlan's, at 604 Lakeshore, there had been a Red Cross facility at Gibraltar Point. It was built, we were told, to help the many victims of polio. Polio was the Great Fear, the tragedy that could hit anyone. The cause wasn't known, but stagnant water and mosquitoes were suspected. Tanker trucks spewing a thick fog of DDT had gone down many miles of country roads spraying for mosquitoes in an attempt to fight the dreaded polio disease.

Now the cause was known, and a cure had been found. Well, not a cure, but a certifiable prevention.

"Don't forget," The Teacher said, tapping the notice that told us to all go to the Algonquin Island Association hall to get our oral vaccine after school. The fear of polio loomed so greatly over our lives that there was little chance of anyone forgetting to attend the clinic.

After school, just before leaving Barry and Flo's on my bike, I had a thought.

I pulled up the flap that led to the crawl space under the house and found a can full of fuzzy old paintbrushes caked with rainbow layers of hardened paint crust. They had been placed there last Fall, soaking in turpentine that had long since turned to varnish.

Perfect.

Next I searched the plywood shelves beside the back door and hauled out the can of battleship grey floor paint that refused to dry.

It was a beautiful afternoon to ride over to the AIA clubhouse, not just warm, but actually hot. The whole rest of the Island population was either already there or on their way, forming a long lineup, moving slowly but steadily, with much exchange of gossip and pleasantries on all sides.

I finally got my turn, identified myself to the Public Health nurse who crossed my name off the list, then gave me my measuring-spoon dose of pink, cherry flavoured, strangely sweet vaccine.

When I was done I got my bike from its resting place against the railing at the front steps of the clubhouse, the can of paint and cruddy old brush still waiting for me in the carrier. I rode and walked my bike through the soft sand out to the West end of Algonquin.

Algonquin Island used to have a sandy shore on the side facing the city, but sometime in the fifties a steel breakwater had been installed to cut down on wave erosion. That rusty steel wall ended short of the channel we called The Cut, at the West end of Algonquin, and there was a stretch of it at that end where you could jump down and stand on a narrow strip of sand at its base, which is what I did.

There, standing on that wee bit of a sandbar, the water of the Bay lapping near my heals, I painted "Save Island Homes" in large letters on the steel breakwater wall, on the side facing the City.

Three little words, in large letters, slathered on with a thick coat of The Paint That Wouldn't Dry.

Nobody could see it from the shore, and it couldn't possibly be read from the city side, even with a powerful telescope.

Still, I felt I had to do something. The Parks Department was adamant that all the remaining Island houses would be demolished within six years. As far as defending the Island went, this insignificant little act of graffiti vandalism was all I could think of. Sort of like imagining that I could make the warm weather come up from thousands of miles away to the South by the miniscule gesture of waving my arms at the end of the Gap. It wasn't much. But it was something.

That night, for the first time all year, it was too hot to sleep under a full set of covers. I kicked most of my blankets onto the floor.

Chapter 43
Off Guard

While we were waiting for the morning bus at Ward's, Mickey got one of the Snoopies to write a note for him in her best hand, and asked me to read it over. It looked good to me, like an adult could have written it. Not too much information, which was the usual mistake with this type of forgery.

He handed it in to The Teacher and left for home on the noon bus, supposedly for a dental appointment. I wished I'd thought of that. It was too hot and humid for sitting in a stuffy classroom.

I sold hockey pool tickets during the winter months and helped Barry and Jimmy clean septic tanks in warmer weather. Mickey had his own sources of income. Among them, he occasionally helped Ken Sinclair in his freight delivery business.

It was Tuesday afternoon and we had an ordinary library session, with Mrs. Perdue and a couple of other volunteer parents in attendance. In-class poetry wasn't an option. I remember vaguely wondering where Mrs. Acorn was.

Ken Sinclair and my Mother had split up, again, and they never did have a friendly parting. But she needed help to get all her stuff hauled to her new house, and he had the only delivery business on the Island. When I came home after school I could see his big Chevrolet flat-deck truck, fire engine red, at the end of the street. I put my school books away, got out my nearly empty pack of smokes and went up the street to see what was going on.

Mickey was carefully wheeling a dolly down the ramp, unloading a large stack of boxes while Bullet, who had come along for the ride, lounged in the shade under a tree. It was a hot day, and hard work. Mickey had his shirt off and, as I got closer, I could see that his shorts, socks and even his runners were soaked with sweat. Whatever Ken was paying him, he certainly was earning every dollar of it.

I wasn't the only fan of matinee heroes like Roy Rogers. Roy had a horse named Trigger and a German Shepherd dog named Bullet, and that's what Ken named his German Shepherd too: Bullet. If he'd owned a horse, I'm sure its name would have been Trigger.

Bullet was an established Island legend. The tale had been often repeated of the time, when Bullet was at just the right age for training, that Ken had sent him off for lessons at a prestigious dog training facility in the city. After weeks of obedience and guard-dog training were over, Ken had to take a course as well in order to learn the commands that Bullet now knew. He showed up in his best going-to-the-city suit and diligently followed the instructor's lead, giving Bullet the commands and seeing his perfect response. Bullet was a very intelligent dog. And more thoroughly trained, it turned out, than Ken knew.

Ken brought him back to the Island, put him up on one of the barges moored at the dock of his compound beside the Clandeboye bridge, and gave him the command to guard the place. Then, confident that the barge would be secure from scoundrels until his return, Ken went home and got changed back into his work clothes, ready to get on with the rest of his day.

Bullet, however, had been told to guard the barge by Ken in his good suit. When Ken returned in oily coveralls, Bullet didn't recognize his scent. He was on the barge and, as Ken came across the ramp onto it, Bullet, with snapping jaws and fierce barking, made it clear that access was most definitely denied. None of the stand-down commands Ken had learned would work.

There was only one thing to do. Admitting defeat, he went home, got back into his suit and returned to find Bullet wagging his tail, excitedly trying to inform Ken that he'd fended off some trespassing ne'er-do-well.

It didn't take long, of course, for Bullet to recognize Ken's voice and whistle, whatever clothing he wore. And, once Bullet was given the guard command, he would protect whatever territory he was assigned until Ken, and only Ken, gave him the stand-down order.

Bullet hadn't been given the guard command though, as Mickey unloaded the truck. If he had been put up on the truck and given that command, then nothing, and I mean absolutely *nothing*, would have gotten him down again until Ken ordered him off.

But Bullet wasn't on duty, he was just lounging in the shade under a tree.

I came up the street and asked Mickey how it was going. He smiled and said hi, but didn't slow the pace of his work. Ken was inside, making sure that nothing was broken and that everything was going into the correct rooms, but he was not in a good mood. My Mother was checking all the boxes, apparently in an attempt to find fault. I didn't want to stick around.

As I came out the back door I saw Bullet rise and shake himself, the hairs down his back standing on end, his nose twitching about in the very slight breeze. Then he took off like a shot! Straight for the beach! Ears flat back and running like his life depended on it!

Then he slowed, sniffed about, and chased a black figure out of the scrub brush growing out there between Lakeshore Avenue and the shore of the Lake. John McLarty's Tina was in heat.

Round and round they went, first him chasing her, then she'd turn around and chase him back again.

The work of unloading the truck went on while, somewhere out in the distance, on that hot Tuesday afternoon, Bullet and Tina were beginning the blood lines of what was to become many generations of a canine Island dynasty.

Chapter 44
I Am Kali

I strolled up to the open front door at number 10 Second. Gwen had her back to me, typed sheets of paper in her hand, saying, "I am Lilith! I am Cybil! I am Kali, goddess of death!

"I will not bear your children, I will devour them!

"I will not wage your war! I will devour you!"

"Knock knock," I said. "Am I interrupting?"

She jolted and turned towards me.

"Oh, hi. No, not at all. I was just rehearsing."

"I don't want to be a bother, if you've got some, um, rehearsing to do."

"No, that's okay," she said, putting the sheets of paper down. "I need to take a break anyway. Really. Come on in."

"Is that a new poem you're working on?" I asked, sliding into a chair at the table.

"Not a poem, no." she said, heading for the kitchen. "It's a segue, a transition piece. Something to bridge the gap from one poem to another. Tea?"

"Ah, that'd be, um, it's kinda warm for tea."

"I don't have any pop or juice or anything," she said, opening the fridge.

"Actually, um, just a glass of water would be nice."

"Water it is, then," she said, running the tap a few seconds before filling two glasses. As she brought them to the table she said, "You sure do say "ah" and "um" a lot in your speech."

"Yeah, I, ah, I'll try to do something about that."

"It's just that, well, it makes it hard to listen to what you have to say. It distracts from your meaning."

I was self-conscious now and didn't reply.

"Sorry," she said. "I didn't mean to embarrass you."

"No, that's all right. I know I've got to break that habit anyway, somehow."

"Well, if it helps, I have noticed that you don't do it in class when you're reciting something from memory." She took a sip of her water, then lit up a cigarette.

"That reminds me," I said, "How come you weren't in school today?"

"Oh, we had a, um, parting of the ways. An amicable separation. There just wasn't room left in the budget for my position. I was just filling in for a few weeks anyway, putting things in order. The parent volunteer committee can handle things now. Mind you, it was fun while it lasted."

"Yeah, it really was fun having you come into class and teach us about poetry." I was speaking very slowly and distinctly now, trying not to um and ah. "Who were those people you were talking about?"

"What people?"

When I came in. Lilith and Civil was it?"

"Civil? No, you heard that wrong. It's Cybil. Cybil was a Greek soothsayer, a visionary, someone who could predict the future. Lilith was Adam's first wife, before Eve."

"I've never heard of her."

"But you've gone to church? Learned something about the bible?"

"Well, yeah."

"So you know who Eve was?"

"I think so."

"Okay, well, Adam had a wife before her, Lilith. But Lilith wouldn't do as she was told, so she had to go. The moral of that story is that a woman is supposed to be an obedient little mouse and do what her husband commands, or else he can toss her off and find another. That's actually the basis of most religions. That women should just shut up and do as they're told." There was something quite bitter in her tone. I pulled out the crumpled pack I had in my hip pocket and lit up.

"Do you really want to hear this?" she asked.

"Yeah, of course," I answered. There was so much about the poetry she had introduced us to in class that went right over my head, and I thought that it was because I was ignorant. As if the stuff in those poems was common knowledge to everyone else but me, and I wanted in on it too, wanted to know what it was that I had been missing.

"Okay then," she said, stubbing out her cigarette and lighting another. "The first thing you've got to know is that none of it is real. It's all been made up. Can you grasp that concept?"

"Sure," I replied off-handedly. "Bob told me about how all the gods are imaginary."

"He told you that, did he? Well, it's true, they are. But just because they're not real, doesn't mean that they're not *real*."

"Huh?"

"Look, is a country real?"

"Well, yeah. That is, I think so."

"But if you went up in a space ship and looked down on the world, you could see land and water, but could you see any countries? Could you see where one country ends and another begins?"

"Um, well, I guess not."

"No, of course you couldn't. They don't physically exist. We just imagine them into existence. But, once enough people believe that a country exists, they'll fight wars to prove that it does. Same with a god."

"Oka-ay…"

"So, just like a country, a god doesn't really exist, but a lot of people invest their time and energy into making their god real. History is full of people who killed anyone who didn't believe in the same god as them, and that makes all those gods that aren't real plenty real enough to kill and die for."

"And that means that a good woman should just be a mouse, how?"

"When you go back far enough, almost all of the great religions of the world started off with a goddess, a super woman figure. And she scared the hell out of the men. They had no control over her. She was the one who had mysterious power, the power to bring new life forth into the world. Men can't do that, they can't give birth.

"So ancient priests made strong, independent women into demons. That's what priests do. In culture after culture, religion after religion, they made up stories of some ancient Eve or Lilith type who made some great, horrendous mistake. And all women have to pay for that mistake right on down to the present day. They call it original sin."

"I've heard that, but never knew what it meant."

"What it means is that women are born bad, a womb is dirty, and women have a monthly period as punishment for a crime they never committed."

She took a moment to stub out her cigarette and let this information sink in.

"They tell you that you're guilty from the moment you're born," she went on, "so that they can sell you some voodoo cure they call salvation. Without it, they'll tell you, you're automatically condemned to eternal damnation. But, of course, like any good snake-oil salesman, they can save you from this eternal horror… for a price."

She paused to light up another smoke, so I asked, "What's the price?"

"It varies from religion to religion, but it always involves you having to pay some sort of fee to the priests over and over again. Quite a scam, actually. But…" Again she paused, making certain that I was following her logic. "…I'm going to change all that."

She sat back in her seat and waited for me to ask, "How will you do that?"

"There are certain times when you can just sort of feel that the time is right, you just sort of sense that this is one of those moments when the stars are all aligned, and mysterious, powerful things can happen. People are lost right now, looking for a new savior in the face of impending nuclear disaster. They are thinking of each moment as potentially their last. Or at least that it's going to be a marking point. A sort of a 'Do you remember where you were when the bomb went off?' kind of moment.

"They're marking moments in their lives that way. I just have to get them to take the time to read Julian, and, like snapping my fingers, they'll wake up.

"The time is right. People want something more than what the traditional religions can offer, and I know why. I've discovered the weak point, the place where the lies of the major religions can be undone with just a small push, like a tiny pin bursting a big, over-inflated bubble.

"All those great big, self-important religions argue with each other, fight endlessly about which one has the True Faith, but they all agree on one thing. They all use the same boogieman to frighten people. They have all created the same devil. They survive by propping themselves up against him in an endless struggle that they can never win. Because, if they ever did, their religion would fall apart.

"But I have a mythology which can sustain without need of the existence of their precious devil. Once I get that rolling, then all of them, the Christians and Muslims and all the rest, they all fall down."

This was a pretty lofty statement, and I didn't say anything, just sat and thought about it until she continued.

"I'm going to Israel this summer. That's where I'll strike. I've learned Hebrew, I know how to quote the bible in its original text. Once I get there, I'm going to be recognized as the deliverer of freedom from Messiahs, the deliverer of a New Truth. That's what my poetry is all about. I'm going to free humanity from the tyranny of the priests' religions.

I'm going to expose faith for what it really is, mental illness."

She stubbed her cigarette out into the ashtray with a violent downward thrust and ground it back and forth in the pile of butts already threatening to overflow onto the table. Somehow it felt like it wasn't really the cigarette she was trying to extinguish.

I thought of the line of Mark Twain's that Bob had quoted, "Faith is believing something you know isn't true." I said, "When Bob told me that Neptune and the rest of the gods were dirty snowballs, mixtures of more ancient gods, I thought he was just referring to those old Greek myths. But you're talking about Christianity like it's the same as those."

"It is," she said, lighting up yet another cigarette. "Christianity is the dirtiest snowball of them all. It was slapped together from a bunch of cults that were popular towards the end of the Roman Empire. Jesus is a composite of Prometheus, Apollo, Bacchus, Mithra, Orpheus, Osiris, and maybe a dozen more. It would take me a month just to list all the bits and pieces and where they came from. How much detail do you want?"

"Well, as much as you want to tell me," I said, getting up and taking my glass into the kitchen for a refill.

"Well, first of all, there never was anybody named Jesus Christ," she said matter-of-factly. "That's a name the Greeks tagged him with. It's like hearing about a Frenchman named Pierre and saying, "Let's just call him Peter." Jesus was a Greek name, but his Jewish name was Joshua Bar Joseph. That's what you would have called out if you were trying to find him in a crowd during his lifetime.

"There isn't an awful lot that can be attributed directly to old Joshua. The Sermon on the Mount, and the loaves and fishes trick, but not much more. Most of the mythology, like changing water into wine and dying and being resurrected three days later, came from the Mithra and Bacchus worshippers. You've heard of Bacchus, haven't you?"

"Well, pretty much all I know comes from that scene in Fantasia. Bacchus was the God of wine, the little fat drunk guy with a donkey, wasn't he?"

"Yes, that's accurate enough. Bacchus was the biggest god in Rome at the time the Christian church was trying to take over, and they lifted just about all of his attributes and applied them to Jesus. In the ancient Bacchus story, he was chopped up and boiled by the Titans. He was a god, though, and therefor immortal. Zeus cut his own thigh open and put the pieces in there and sewed up the wound until Bacchus was reborn, popping out three days later. Another case of men wishing they could give birth, I'm afraid.

"The whole Virgin Birth thing was taken from the much older myth of the virgin Isis giving birth to Horus the king. He was just one of the multitude of saviors who was crucified for the redemption of humanity. Here, look at this," she said, shuffling through the stack of books on the table, finally pulling out a huge, thick book entitled The Secret Teachings of All Ages. She skimmed through the bookmarks, various coloured slips of paper, then opened it at a page numbered with roman numerals.

"Right, ah... there!" she said, pointing to a section of the page. "Just read that bit there."

I turned the heavy book around on the tabletop and read, "The list of deathless mortals who suffered for man that he might receive the boon of eternal life..."

That list of the crucified included Prometheus, Adonis, Apollo, Atys, Bacchus, Horus, Mithras, and many more. I read, "Dupuis tells us that Mithra was put to death by crucifixion, and rose again on the 25th of March... your God is risen. His death, his pains, and sufferings, have worked your salvation."

"That was centuries before Jesus," Gwen said. "The early Christian church knew that they couldn't fight that powerful theology, so they absorbed it. The followers of those older religions found the rites and rituals of the new one familiar, so it was an easy transition."

"Wow," I said, thumbing through the book. "And how do you intend to bring down this set of ancient beliefs?"

"By exposing it," she said, stubbing out yet another cigarette. "But you can't just wake people up and take away an institution like that and leave them wandering, dazed and confused. It's like trying to take a stick away from a dog who's intent on chewing it. You have to throw another stick for them to chase.

"Well, I have a whole new mythology, one that doesn't rely on fear of the devil. It's a new idea, but it's built on the most ancient foundations of faith, and that's what people want, something with deep roots to believe in. Have you been following the news lately?"

"Um, not much" I answered. I wasn't sure what she was getting at.

"The States has just sent five thousand troops into South-East Asia to fight communism. It won't work. It's an exercise doomed from the start. Do you know why?" This time it was a rhetorical question. She didn't pause long enough for me to formulate an answer.

"It's because you can't fight a philosophy head-on with conventional weapons. It wouldn't matter whether they sent in five soldiers or five million, all the weapons of the world are useless against an idea. But one poet, in the right place, at the right time, can change people's minds, change the world, with a few well-chosen words. That's something no army with guns or bombs can ever achieve."

"Hmm. And that's something you're going to do this summer in Israel?"

"I think so," she said. "I'll know for sure when I get there. If not there, then somewhere, sometime. I'll know the moment that it happens. When my book comes out, that's when the shit is going to really hit the fan." She lit up another and, breathing out a fresh cloud of smoke as she spoke, said, "Even if they do assassinate me, they can't stop the ideas I'm going to put in motion, once Julian is published."

I think she was quite serious about being assassinated. And, though I could be wrong, I think that was the source of the fear I saw in her eyes on those rare occasions when something, like Mickey running up the path behind us, took her by surprise. Not fear of death, but fear of not getting the word out before death arrived.

"You know that list you just read, the cast of characters who got crucified for the benefit of humanity? I'm going to add the name Julian the Magician to that list!"

She dug her finger into her cigarette package, but they were all gone. I offered her my last one and lit it for her. She took a long, deep drag as if she hadn't had one for days.

"Julian," she said, breathing out smoke as she spoke, "is obsessed with becoming Jesus, like Jesus was obsessed with becoming Prometheus, and so on back to the core of the illness that needs, is addicted to, requires, guilt. It spreads and grows like bacteria, with the infected becoming obsessed with spreading their gospel disease to others. It's kind of like how animals with rabies or movie vampires become obsessed with biting.

"That's all it is," she said, flicking three-quarters of an inch of ash with expert aim into the ashtray, "addiction to feeling guilty results in becoming obsessed with spreading guilt.

"Now that I think about it," she added, "that's probably why so many perverts become priests. They get hooked on the churning-of-the-stomach kick they get from being guilty of something. It's a natural fit.

"But they can also get that fix, give themselves a guilty high, knowing that they could have easily been responsible for Julian too. The big advancement, though, is that Julian doesn't have a devil to fight. His frailties are just plain human." Her cigarette finished, she snuffed it, then began breaking open the butts from the ashtray. She pulled brown fibers away from black char with her fingers, re-rolled this last bit of tobacco in a rolling paper, lit it and took in another deep drag. "Did Bob tell you anything about herbalism?"

"Well, he said that a magician had to be an herbalist, as well as an alchemist and an artist."

"Did he tell you about any herbs people can use to enhance their vision of dark gods?"

"Well, let's see, there was mandrake, belladonna, and I think he said something about mushrooms."

"That devil character is easy enough for anyone to see under the influence of mandrake, an hallucinogenic root, and I suspect that some unscrupulous people have been poisoning congregations with that stuff mixed into the communion bread for centuries. But Julian doesn't need any mandrake, he's just mad enough to be a messiah without it."

She stubbed the butt of this last cigarette out with the words, "In order to wean addicted madmen off their guilt, you have to give them a less destructive madness. A madman is the only thing that madmen will believe in."

Chapter 45
Hot and Hotter

Wednesday morning started off hot, then the temperature rose to sweltering. My T-shirt was wet with sweat even before we boarded the bus for school. Paying attention in class was difficult enough for me at the best of times. Once the afternoon sun swung around and started roasting my back, though, it was just downright brutal. The Teacher took pity on us and organized us into a column, marching two abreast, out the school door and down to the shade under the poplar trees, right at the edge of the Lake. The water was still icy cold, and a slight breeze from the South carried a bit of relief our way as we sat in the sand among the tufts of dune grass and tried to fathom how to covert decimals into fractions.

I was always easily distracted, and the ripple of waves washing the shore were more interesting than arithmetic. Especially when... what was that? I watched, and counted. Five waves, ten, fifteen, and there it was again!

People who don't know the shore talk about how the waves roll up onto the beach, then slide back again. But waves seldom come straight in at the shore. They sweep across it.

I was watching intently as, from West to East, the small waves came in surges across the sand in front of us and there, on the sand immediately behind one of them, there was a glittering, flashing carpet of silver. The smelts were running! With the next wave, just as suddenly, they were gone.

I excitedly told Barry the news when he got home from work and we hauled out the smelt pole and net from under the house.

The pole was fine, and the spreaders were okay, but the net hadn't fared so well. Dampness had gotten to it and it had rotted through in several places. We both knew that the smelts wouldn't be running in really heavy numbers until the second or third day of the run anyway, so the plan was that he'd get a new one in town on Friday, then we'd head down to the Gap on Friday night.

It was so hot that, again, all my blankets went on the floor and I slept under just the sheet. Yeah, I wanted a heat wave, I'd asked for it. But I wanted to be able to sleep, too. I thought to myself that the heat couldn't get any worse than this.

But it could.

Thursday was even hotter, but we didn't have the luxury of a trip to the shore.

When Thursday afternoon recess finished and we took our seats, The Teacher wrote our upcoming assignments on the chalkboard. Homework and reports-due items in large chalk letters double outlined in the upper right-hand corner of the chalkboard. This area was surrounded on all sides with the letters: "PLO", instructions for the janitorial staff to Please Leave On when they washed the chalkboards at night.

He erased two of the previous days lines from this notice section, then wrote: "Monday, Victoria Day, No School."

We quietly cheered

He tapped the chalk beside the words "Friday: Book Report".

"That is due tomorrow," he said.

We groaned.

Next line, "Friday PM, class cancelled."

We cheered.

Last line, "Today:___"

We waited.

He turned, looked around at us. I swear, he wore the facial expression of a cat about to devour a nest full of juicy baby birds.

He wrote: "T", then turned back to face us.

"Your assignment, to read a book," he said, tapping the piece of chalk against the chalkboard beside those words, creating a small puff of chalk dust that burst off the slate surface with each tap, tiny mushroom clouds in an afternoon sunbeam that sliced through the window, "...was assigned two weeks ago. You've had plenty of time to read a library book by now, and reading one will be your homework tonight if you haven't yet. The report is to be at least two hundred words, double-spaced. It has to be about a book of at least a hundred pages..." He glared across to quiet the Snoopies, then went on, "...at least a hundred page book, and, yes, neatness will count..." Then, turning his lighthouse glare upon me, "...and spelling."

His meaning was clear.

"Next." He tapped beside the words: Friday PM, class cancelled, "We're having an afternoon staff meeting tomorrow. The afternoon's classes are cancelled." He left that statement hang out there for a second, letting us relish the extra extension to the long weekend coming up.

There were shouts, as you might expect, of happy cheering.

"Quiet, quiet, keep it down. There's still detention available tomorrow afternoon if need be."

We stopped smirking and tried to sit very still.

"Now, was that all?" He looked at the chalk-written letter "T".

"Oh yes..." he said, as if it had just been recollected, then scratched chalk against slate and followed that letter T with: "est".

"That's right," he said turning back and beginning to hand out stapled bundles of paper as we groaned. "We have a test today. Don't turn them over until I tell you to. Here, take this half and pass them back."

At that moment the sun was obscured by a cloud. The swirl of mesmerizing chalk-dust, unable to find an illuminating sunbeam to dance upon, vanished.

Dink raised his hand.

"Yes, Mike?"

"The book report, for tomorrow?"

"Yes, what about it?"

"That's what we're going to be doing in class tomorrow morning?"

"Yes, that's what I said."

"So, can we go as soon as we hand in the report?"

"What difference would that make?"

"Well, it's just that, you see, if I, that is, if we can hand in the report and go early, then maybe I can make it up to Christie Pits, to see the sprints, on the new track."

"Really?"

"Um, yes sir," Weasel added. "They're opening it up tomorrow. That's what we're going to be running on next year…"

"I heard it back when we had our track and field day," Dink went on.

"Right. And it would help getting off a little earlier because…?"

"Well sir," Weasel continued, "If we can meet the high school coaches that are going to be there, maybe get some pointers..."

"So, in a way, it's kind of like doing homework," Dink said.

The dreaded word created a ripple of groans around the room.

"I mean, like, if we're going to study how to get good at a sport, then we should do some *homework*, (more groans) and learn what the competition knows."

The Teacher just might have been buying this.

"And, if we ride our bikes to school tomorrow, we can bike home and make the twelve o'clock ferry. There isn't another boat after that until one fifteen. We could maybe even get in some practice runs on that new asphalt track."

"They've got asphalt now?" Dooly piped in.

"Yeah. We just don't have any asphalt here to practice on."

The logic of the request seemed to be winning.

"So," The Teacher said, "I guess that we can say that it's an incentive, for prompt completion of your book report..." Would he go with it? "Yes," He finally said, "If you hand in the assignment early, you can have a longer lunch."

There were the sort of mixed murmurs from the class that you might expect.

"So," I asked innocently enough, "When we hand in the book report, we're done for the day?"

"Yes," he answered, not so much suspicious of the intent of my question as irritated that he had to keep repeating it. "When you hand in the book report assignment, you can go. If you bring your bike, then I guess you can go straight home.

"Now, the test before you is three parts..."

"Um, just so I've got this clear," I said, "We can leave tomorrow as soon as we hand in the report?"

He froze for a moment, a faint smile at a private thought seemed to flicker across his face. In an instant it was gone, and he said, as if relenting to my logic, "Okay listen, LISTEN EVERYBODY, if you show up in the morning with your book report done, you can have the rest of the day off.

"Now, as I was saying," he continued, "the test before you is three parts. The first is converting decimals to fractions, the second is fractions to decimals, and the third is a short review of long-division. Don't open them until I tell you to. Use a separate work sheet, don't scribble in the margins. Don't write anything on the test except an X in the box beside the right answer. There may be more than one right answer.

"Did everyone hear that? SOME OF THE QUESTIONS," He resorted to hollering to be heard over the commotion, "WILL HAVE MORE THAN ONE

RIGHT ANSWER! Pick the best answer for the question."
The room was becoming quiet after the last of the test
papers had been distributed. "Turn them over and put your
name on the top sheet... now!"

We all turned the assignment face up.

"You can see that it is multiple choice, check off the
answer that you think is correct. There are fifty questions.
Take your time, you've got the whole period. When you are
done you can hand in your paper and leave, quietly. When
you have handed it in."

A hush fell upon the room. Pencils checked off boxes,
eyes riveted to paper.

The Teacher sat and began to earnestly write a missive of
his own, in longhand, with a fountain pen, on thick, slightly
amber paper.

This test was something I wasn't ready for at all. And I
didn't care. After skimming the first few questions I
realized that anything I checked off was just going to be a
random guess anyway.

I went quickly through all five sheets, checked off all the
answer boxes randomly all down the pages, then opened
my desk and got out my copy of The Dharma Bums and
some foolscap.

Since it still had the library card in the front, I figured that
it would count. But since The Secretary thought it was an
awful book, I figured The Teacher would want to read bad
things about it.

I wrote my report, first stating that: "This book is about a
guy, Smith, who seems to think he's becoming some kind
of holy man. This Smith guy, he ends up sitting in a forest
ranger cabin on a mountain, saying things like: 'God, I love
you' and 'I have fallen in love with you, God' "

I went on to say that the story just didn't seem to go
anywhere, that it was just this guy, who was in this place,
and he was doing this, or that, but that's all there was to it.

And I said that I thought that Smith was drinking way too much red wine. And I couldn't resist writing that the author used a bunch of words like yabyum and Bodhisattva that weren't in the dictionary, so they couldn't be real.

I counted up the words, added a few more comments and, as I still had a fair bit of time, went back to the beginning and tried to erase and re-write here and there to make my handwriting a little more legible.

The sun broke brightly over my left shoulder and I looked up to see if it was illuminating anything interesting in the dorm windows. A flicker of light caught my attention, off to the right, on the chalkboard over The Teacher's shoulder, just about... There! It moved again! What was that?

Heather finished her test and put it on the corner of The Teacher's desk. He didn't look up, no acknowledgement that she even existed as she quietly got her stuff and exited the room.

Peno finished his and repeated her path, then Christine.

I was almost convinced that the flash of light hadn't happened.

But it did.

And there it was again.

The Teacher turned from his letter and, taking the top test from the stack, slid a stiff plastic sheet over it. The bright sun from over my shoulder shone on that piece of plastic and reflected up onto the chalkboard behind him. There were holes punched in that plastic sheet, designed to line up with all the right answers. He started going down the rows with his red pen, putting an X in any box that hadn't been checked off, and all his actions were projected on the white chalk on the black board. Where there was no chalk it was hard to see, but, where the board had been written on and erased several times today, the image of those punch-holes was clear. The answers were in the shadows of the sunlight's reflected glare. I went back to my test.

Okay, I thought, the first problem is:

.75 = A: 1/2

      B: 6/8

      C: 1/4

      D: 3/4

The clock was winding down towards the bell.

Half the room was still writing, half the seats empty.

The correct answers to question one were B and D, and the best was D. And that meant that... he shifted the plastic sheet, turning the test in front of him to the next page. The golden sunlight glow outlined the holes, and that one, there, had to be the shadow made by the answer for question one. So that meant that...

I hurriedly erased my random answers and filled in the blanks on page one to match the patterns on the wall, then realized that he used the same plastic template for each answer page. I filled in the blanks on the rest of the pages following the same pattern.

Wait a minute, that couldn't be right... could .5 equal 3/8? No!

I watched him marking.

First page, second, third, fourth, fifth... Aha!

He'd mark page1, then flip the plastic answer template over, mark 2, flip it again...

So the pattern for one, three and five were the same, and two and four were the mirror image of the pattern.

I hurriedly erased my second set of answers and filled in the correct check boxes.

I wrote a note in large letters on a fresh page, rose from my seat at the same time as Vera and let her go first, following her up to the front of the room to hand in my test. I put my completed answers on the pile and offered him the book report, showing the page with large letters posing the question: "See you on Tuesday?"

He looked at the clean, reasonably neat report of two hundred and sixteen words (including my name). His brow furled, then he hoarsely whispered, "You already did it?"

I whispered back: "I thought the report was due this morning." I tried to look embarrassed, just the right amount.

"So you want all of tomorrow off?"

"Well, the pole vault…"

He looked like he was busy thinking of other things and just waved me off, saying, "Okay, enjoy your weekend," then went back to gliding the nib over the page he was writing.

I had to linger just an extra fraction of a second to admire his ornate, elegant penmanship. Though I can't recall a single word that was on the page as he wrote, I do remember that it was written in a lovely hand.

I do remember, too, that there was no new asphalt running track at Christie Pits.

There was running, yes, but not on a track.

The running that held all the Islanders' attention was Smelts.

Chapter 46
The Embassy

The heat was so intense that the only thing I wanted to do after school was change into my bathing suit and head for the beach.

I have had the opportunity in the course of my life to lay about on a sandy beach in many parts of the world. There is nowhere I've ever been, though, that has sand that feels so good against the skin on a warm, sunny day as the beach sand of Toronto Island. I've heard that the native name for it was Place of Healing Sands.

I think they were right.

I think Flo was also correct when she insisted that I slather on a thick coating of suntan lotion before I left the house.

The heat was intense, but it had come on so suddenly that, like the rest of the kids from school out on the sand that day, I hadn't built up any tan at all. I was totally pasty white. The sand burned my bare feet as I ran, as fast as I could, for a splash in the clear blue water.

After a quick plunge in the icy cold Lake, I turned from pasty white to a shivering pale blue.

Then it was back to the sand, lying down and wiggling my body as deep into its warmth as I could get while talking with Gronk, Dink and the rest of guys about whether or not we should get together and go up to the College Street YMCA on Saturday to play basketball. We could possibly go to Mario's for Pizza afterwards, and formulated a plan for a competition. Whoever could eat the most pizza wouldn't have to pay. Everyone else had to split the bill.

"It might be possible for a guy to cheat," Gronk observed, "if he goes to the can and sticks his finger down his throat."

"Okay, then," Dink said. "You can only go to the can if someone goes with you. Otherwise you're eliminated."

That sounded reasonable, and the pact was made.

We stayed there, alternately baking and roasting in the sun and sand, and dashing into the Lake to cool down and rinse the sand off, until nearly dark.

I finally headed for home for supper and a shower, gritty sand stuck in my hair and under my bathing suit. I really was quite grateful to Flo for her insistence on the suntan lotion, though, when I saw how lobster-red some of the other guys were. They were going to be hurting bad tonight, I thought.

After dinner, with the sun going down and the oppressive heat beginning to subside, I finally had a Thursday night free, with no school on Friday.

"You really should come to the Embassy then," Gwen said when I ran into her on the boat, sort of accidentally on purpose as we neared the dock on the city side (I'd waited and watched three boats leave before I saw her coming to catch this one). She had extremely heavy, black eyeliner under her eyes. I'd never seen her wear that before. I told her that I was going to town looking for something to do and had no school tomorrow.

"It's poetry night tonight, at the Embassy, and I've got something very powerful prepared. I'd love it if you'd come!"

We waited, stayed seated as the ferryboat slid into the dock and roughly nudged the pilings on the starboard and then the port side pilings. A couple of people who had been standing were lurching about, staggering, trying to catch their footing.

Islanders didn't do that. At least not unintentionally. We waited, stayed seated until we were finally satisfied that we weren't going to be getting anymore jolts, Islanders did. When we stood up, we still braced ourselves, ready to dance along a quaking deck so as to not fall down, just in case.

City folk, they rushed for the gate, all in a hurry to get off first, like they were getting on or off of a subway train. Some of them got thrown to their knees, sometimes, and sometimes worse. Only once in a while, mind, but Islanders knew it could happen.

And, somehow, like the way an Islander can know that a rough docking can happen, I sensed that, if I went along with Gwen tonight to this Bohemian Embassy club she talked about, something was likely to happen.

Not necessarily something bad, but something, some kind of emotional upheaval, was possible.

I definitely felt I was up for it and said, "Yeah, okay, maybe I'll do that," then had a sudden question run through my mind: Did I have enough money on me (about three bucks)?

How much would it cost to get in?

I knew that she caught that thought the moment that it occurred to me and she said, "You can get in as my guest, won't cost you a thing, though you might want to buy a coffee or something."

The surging throng of bodies pressed their way off the ferry and along the gangway, disbursing at Queen's Quay in various directions. The heat on the Island had been harsh enough, but here, even an hour after sunset, the blacktop streets still radiated heat like electric stove elements.

I caught the streetcar with her and she told me that Milton was going to meet us there later.

We went up Bay Street and got off at Gerrard, where I stopped at a pay phone to call Flo and tell her that I probably wouldn't be home until late tonight. Then we walked down a street so old it still had cobblestone bricks for pavement. Up a flight of stairs that made me picture the entrance to a prohibition era speak-easy from the movies, then into a depressingly dark room with café tables adorned with red and white checker patterned tablecloths. Multi-coloured candles were stuck in Italian wine bottles wrapped in woven baskets, odd melted-wax rainbows dripped down their sides. Ashtrays that had been dumped out but never washed, caked with layers of ancient cigarette ash.

Gwen had to go talk to somebody and left me there to buy a coffee and look around. The place smelled of stale pipe tobacco and those foul French cigarettes. There was only one other person there, a tall, gangly looking redheaded guy with really thick glasses. He was intent on writing something in a journal. I said, "Hi." He said, "Hi" back and we chatted a bit. His name was Eric.

I noticed a chessboard on one of the tables and asked if he felt like a game.

He said he just wanted to concentrate on what he was writing.

A girl named Nancy, black leotards, black hair, the whole black ensemble, was just coming up the stairs and overheard us. She asked if I wanted to play her and I agreed. As we set up the pieces a gawky looking fellow who introduced himself as Len asked if he could play the winner.

I bought a few more refills of coffee. At some point I needed to use the bathroom and found out, in a rather embarrassing manner, that the door latch didn't work. As I stood there, peeing, the noise of conversation behind me became quite a bit louder. I turned to find myself visible, from the back, to the whole room. I tried to control my aim while twisting about to pull the door shut. I succeeded, not without some spillage, while a few folks snickered. I found the tiny Hercules-store switchblade in my pocket and stuck it into the broken latch to ensure my continued privacy.

On the wall, above the toilet, someone had written:
"I wrote all my poems
On the backs of my eyelids
Until loneliness taught me that

Love
Is an ancient mathematical term
Meaning:
To Share"

I liked that poem. I never did find out who the author was or who scribbled it on the washroom wall, but I liked it so much that, years later, I used it as the quote beside my picture in my high-school yearbook.

While we played I nursed my coffee slowly to make the cup last. The big urn of it had been made long before we arrived and by now it tasted so awful that I didn't want to gulp it down quickly anyway.

It took quite a while, but I beat Nancy. Len beat me and I sat out while they played. The room was filling up with people at tables talking among themselves. Nancy beat Len and I played her again. During this second game against her I noticed that Milt had taken up a seat at a table near a microphone on a stand that had been set up in roughly the centre of the room.

Gwen came back from wherever she'd been and joined him, saw me and gestured for me to come sit with them at their table.

I said, "I'll just finish this game first," and moved my knight into danger, regretting the move as soon as I'd taken my hand off the piece. The game didn't last much longer and I resigned, congratulated Nancy on a good game, took my cup over to buy another refill and then joined them.

Milt was intently studying a hand-written page, occasionally looking to the ceiling and muttering something under his breath. Gwen put her hand on my forearm, leaned to my ear and said, "He likes to concentrate before he goes on."

She took about five sheets of foolscap from her bag, folded them and set them on the table.

I instinctively reached into my pockets, felt no pencil in the left but brought a pen from my right before even wondering if I'd ever get it back again.

She got the gist of the humour in that thought and laughed.

It was odd, the way the thick, black lines under her eyes... no, not really under. Try to picture heavy black lines around the bottoms of her eyes. That's a better way to describe the effect.

Those lines re-shaped the areas of her face under her eyes into horizons and, by letting my eyes just look through instead of at her, sort of the same way that there are pictures that you can only see when you stand and gaze through them, I could see all the way to a distant land beyond her face. She took out a cigarette and her hand visibly shook as she lit it. She was quick, but I noticed. And her knees were trembling too. Not quite a shiver, but...

"Stage jitters," she said. "I still sometimes get them. I just need something else to think about for a bit. A distraction."

"Do you want to play a game?" I asked.

"Sure." she responded with a light laugh.

"Okay, how about this one. The game is called, 'Nicknames'. I've played it dozens of times with the guys, while riding on the ferry or subway."

"Okay, so I've got to guess your nickname?" She asked.

"No," I answered. "We make up nicknames for people we can see around us."

She looked surprised. Then pleased.

"I get to be the Elephant," Milt said. I didn't think he'd been listening.

"Okay, Elephant's taken," she said, taking up the pen and writing.

As the place filled up, we took turns thinking up and writing nicknames for some of the patrons who crammed into the small room.

One table of people became "The Wall". One girl was Crumpet, another Strumpet. There were Dog and G and Priapus from Gwen, Milt added Baubo and Gwen cracked up laughing. I didn't get it.

I put down Squid and The Mole People, and they both saw the resemblance.

It seemed to be taking a long time for the show to get started, and the air was thick and stagnant with smoke that had already been through other people's lungs.

"When does the show begin?" I asked. Just as I got the words out, a gaunt, serious looking fellow, sort of resembling a beardless Abraham Lincoln, went running by behind me, carrying a pie in a tray, shoved past the microphone and crouched down in the far corner.

The bathroom was right in line with the stage, and the door burst open. A bushy-haired man with large, funny looking glasses rushed to the microphone and loudly announced: "I have just written a poem!"

"Yeah, yeah," Milt muttered. He'd obviously heard this one before.

The man at the microphone began to extol the virtues, in a sonorous, trembling monotone, of the Kleenex tissue. He droned on as to how wonderfully this modern miracle was able to handle various forms of snot. I remember horrible lines like: "Snot's the knot that no longer knows my nose. All hail the Mighty Kleenex!"

As he went on and on the fellow with the pie crept up behind him in big, exaggerated tiptoe steps. Someone from behind me called out a warning to the poet, who looked up from his page and questioningly scanned from his left to right, all the while not turning far enough to see the pie bearer who, with index finger of his free hand pressed to his lips to shush the heckler, continued to advance.

The inevitable (and obvious) Marx Brother's moment (pie in poet's face) was about to arrive when, suddenly and swiftly, the guy with the pie swung it down and, narrowly missing the poet, slid it onto the table of the couple next to us.

The poet simultaneously lit a candle with a quick flick of a Zippo lighter, stuck it in the top of the pie, and they both began singing: "Happy Birthday To You," while the cute red-headed woman sitting there smiled and blushed, protesting that it wasn't her birthday.

Gwen laughed a deep, right-from-the-bottom-of-the-belly sort of laugh. Milt roared his approval as applause rolled around the room in waves. "That was new," Milt said to me over the din.

"Usually," Gwen said, adding to his statement, "Don hits himself with the…"

"Good evening ladies and gentlemen," The Pie Man said, taking the microphone from its stand and straightening out the cord. "My name is Don Cullen, and I'd like to thank you all for coming down to the Bohemian Embassy tonight. Don't let our opening poetic offering throw you off, we've got a lot of very talented poets here tonight. I see Milt is here…" there was a strong round of applause, "…along with his child bride, the lovely and equally talented Gwen Acorn" Gwen somehow, while remaining seated, managed to give the impression that she was dipping in a curtsy. "…And Peggy, I believe she's here. Are you there Peggy? Ah, yes there she is, and…" He went on to rattle off a string of names, some of which appeared to be familiar to the audience. There was still a bit of room on the list, he said, if anyone wanted to sign up to read their poetry tonight. Gwen gave me an inquiring look, but I shook my head.

Don Cullen said, "John Robert Colombo usually MC's on Thursdays, but he couldn't be here with us tonight, so, those of you who came out to see him might as well leave now." There were a few chuckles. "Ladies and gentlemen, your host for this evening, Milton Acorn…!" Milt rose from his seat, "…is one of the finest poets on this side of the room… tonight." A smattering of chuckles went around the place as Milt sat back down. "Here he is, the people's poet, Milton Acorn…!" There was a ripple of tentative applause as Milt took a step towards the stage, cut short by: "…because, after all, horses don't read poetry." More chuckles and some outright laughter. Milton was standing right next to him, trying to take the microphone, hesitating, trying again.

"Is he the dog's poet? I say no! Is he the poet of the carrots?"

This time the audience responded with a loud, "No!"

Turning toward Milt, extending his arm, Don said, "Milton Acorn!" and Milt tried again to step up to the mic, but Don went on, "…is he the poet of automobiles and jet airplanes?"

"No!" the crowd roared.

"Is he the poet of dirt and clouds and flowers that you buy your date that wither unwatered in a blue vase on the mantle? No I say, he is not! Because those things don't read poetry. So, whose poet is he?"

"The people's poet!" the audience roared in a single voice

"The peep hole's poet?" Don queried. "Ooo, this show might get dirtier than any of us could ever hope for." There was another roar of laughter. Milt had been patient long enough, and Don had squeezed just about as much comedy from the introduction as he could. "Ladies and gentlemen, I give you… I give you because he's just too precious to sell…"

"You couldn't afford me anyway," Milt hollered.

"I give you, the people's poet, Milton Acorn!"

The place erupted in wild enthusiasm, the cheer taking at least a full minute to die down sufficiently for Milt to continue.

With the back of his left hand on his hip, right hand extended, holding hand written pages before him like a duelist wielding a fencing foil, Milt bellowed the words: "I shout love!" and the crowd exploded again into wild cheers. It was nearly another full minute before the place quieted down enough for him to go on, in dueling stance, with out-thrust page that, tonight at least, really did seem more powerful a weapon in his hand than any sword could have been. Reciting the poem in a voice that varied from ear-splittingly loud to soft as a kitten's purr, he alternated emotions between rage and gentle caress with the smooth, professional ease of a seasoned orator.

Milt then went on to introduce two fellows who's names, I'm sure, are very dear to them. Gwen picked up the pen and dubbed them, "The Hardly's"

I got it immediately.

One rather portly, with a goatee, the other a skinny wiry looking guy in a fedora hat.

I whispered to her "Laurel and Hardly?" She nodded.

They spoke in a language all their own, yet somehow I understood them.

"Skeedilly bop?" the chubby guy asked.

"Skeedilly bop dee boo," the short one replied. They went on for maybe four or five minutes with a wordless dialogue of sounds that, somehow, managed to convey that the guy with the goatee was new in town and looking for... what was it? Either a hotel or a restaurant... and the man in the hat kept giving him false directions.

"Huh, Beats," Milt muttered under his breath without looking up, intent on studying the page in front of him. "Might as well get right to the heart of it and recite: who put the ram in the rama lama ding dong?"

The Hardly's on stage hadn't heard him. They closed the piece with several sounds that resolved into, "Bippity boppity, bippity boppity, bippity boppity boo!" I recognized that as variations on a line from Disney's "Uncle Remus".

Gwen leaned across me and said, "Yeah, like I couldn't see that coming," to Milt as loud applause erupted. It seemed that most of the audience had liked it. "Did you see who just came in?"

"I don't care who just came in," Milt said, eyes still on his page.

"That's Herbert Wittaker, and I think that's Juliette with him."

"I don't care," Milt grumbled.

"Who?" I asked.

"Herbert Wittaker. He writes for the Globe," Gwen said, taking furtive glances over my shoulder. "And Juliet…"

"I know who Juliet is." I did indeed. The catch phrase, "Our pet, Juliet" had worked so well that her celebrity was enormous. So was her hair.

The beat poets at the microphone began another piece, the skinny guy, now without his hat, sat on a stool and slowly, softly, described the sun rising on warm fields of growing grain, using his hands to depict sunshine softly caressing the rising crops. His words were soft and comforting, the room quiet, the scene unfolding, when, suddenly, his partner leapt up and, both feet crashing on the floor in an extraordinarily loud thump, yelled "Boom!" at the top of his lungs.

We jumped in our seats.

Slowly, calmly, as if nothing had happened, the one on the stool carried on, painting a word picture of cattle happily grazing though rich, green hay. Contented cows. There was a brief rumble of chuckling around the room at the reference (an advertising campaign of the day proclaimed that a particular brand of canned milk came only from herds of contented cows). After sufficient time to establish this image of pastoral bliss, the other poet interrupted again, leaping up and pounding the floor, bellowing out another "Boom!"

This time we were ready for it.

The poet on the stool built up image after image, scenes of workers in offices going about their hectic lives, children in schools happily learning their three R's, women in hospitals hopefully popping out babies for the future, while being intermittently interrupted by his large partner's explosive antics. We were all hoping for a future that, the poet concluded, could never be.

Then, in unison, as if they were reading a banner, they recited:

"Russia and France
Can pull down their pants
And blast out their nuclear farts
But most of our fates
Reside with the States
Who explode the most bombs 'round these parts"

The poet on the stool closed with the spoken statement: "There is a nuclear bomb being detonated right now, somewhere in the world. Every single day, someone with an inferiority complex feels the urge, the need, to do another nuclear test. And, so far, the United States remains the only nation in the world which has ever dropped a nuclear weapon on a populated area in anger..." He paused to let his words sink in, then finished with an ominous sounding, "... so far."

There was mixed applause. Their meaning had been clear enough, but the message was so depressing that enthusiasm for the performance was hard to muster.

Milt went back up to the microphone and thanked them, mentioned upcoming shows and other venues where he and some other poets and actors could be seen again. He then introduced a very burly woman in a plaid shirt who told us, in free verse format, about a dream she'd had.

She had dreamed, she said, about buying a brand new couch at Eaton's. It was a white couch. A couch so white and bright that it hurt the eyes to look upon it.

And, she said, she went on to dream that Marilyn Monroe had come to her home and she had offered her tea and allowed her to sit on this brand new, perfectly white couch. The most perfect whiteness that a couch could possibly be.

Marilyn Monroe sat upon her white couch and just wouldn't stop complaining about her cramps, the poet said. And then she, Marilyn Monroe, had started to bleed.

Marilyn Monroe had her period right there on that perfect white couch, then got up and left, her tea only half finished, a large permanent red stain upon the fabric of the new Eaton's store couch.

"In my dreams," she concluded, "I like to sleep on that couch, my crocheted throw over me, watching my cat on the window sill, and rest my head on that place where Marilyn Monroe bled."

While the audience gave their encouraging applause, Milt leaned over and said to Gwen and me, "In her dreams, all right."

I wrote, "Kissercheek" on the list of nicknames.

The room had become almost unbearably stuffy, more patrons coming up the stairs and trying to cram into the small space. There were several more poets who performed, and then one who really sticks in my mind.

He said one word, "Eichmann," then waited and looked back and forth around the room. Everyone became uneasy.

You could here drumming coming from another club not too far away.

"Eichmann," he said again, then, in time to the distant beat, made a request that, when they finally got around to executing Adolph Eichmann, he wanted to have his eyes.

At first there was general revulsion around the room, but he went on.

"When I have Eichmann's eyes," he said, the drums backing up his argument, "I want the doctors to amputate my balls, to remove them, and put Eichmann's eyes in my scrotum in their place."

There was hushed silence, the audience wondering where this was going. There was genuine anger in the room, and

Gwen whispered to me, by way of a warning: "There's a lot of Jews here tonight." The crowd could have turned on him in an instant.

"I want Eichmann's eyes down there," he and the drums continued, "so that I can wander about and randomly pick fights with Jews… and lose. I want Eichmann's eyes so that, when those angry Jews beat me up, when those angry Jews kick me in the crotch, they'll only think that they're kicking me in the balls. But I'll know. I'll know that they're really kicking Eichmann in the eye. And every time that I fight, and lose, I'll smile at the pain, knowing that, even though Eichmann has been executed, I can still go on, giving every Jew I know a chance to give him a damn good kick in the eye…" as he looked up from his hand-written page, the drumming suddenly ceased.

"… and I will smile at the pain."

This had been the chanciest moment of the night, but it had worked and the crowd applauded wildly.

A woman behind Milt leaned over me and, while the poet was still receiving his adulations, told Gwen, "Jewison's here."

"Who? Where?"

"Norman Jewison. Isn't that him over there?"

Gwen looked in the direction of her nod. "I'm not sure."

I felt Milt rise from the seat on the other side of me, returning to the stage.

The woman talking to Gwen leaned closer and asked, "And who's that gorgeous black man with him? Is that Harry Belafonte?"

Another woman behind them leaned into the conversation to ask where, and the first one indicated the far corner of the room. I couldn't see a thing but, oblivious to it all, Milt stepped toward the microphone as Belafonte's name was murmured around the room at the speed of gossip.

Chapter 47
I Was Brilliant

Milt followed the Eichmann's eyes poet with a set of his own. He wove together images of fishermen and farmers, common working folk, with deft and delicate skill. About five poems or so into his set he smiled at me, then, looking beyond the heads of the folks gathered in this hot, stuffy little café, out toward some imaginary horizon, he recited "A BASTARD'S STORY."

And it was more than just a damned good poem, it was my story. I could sense Gwen beside me, reading my thoughts, appreciating my feelings of pride.

Milt was right, the reference to an old man with beautiful hands did make the poem seem like an homage to a life well lived. When he was done my applause was just a little louder, a little more heart-felt than the rest of the audience. But, of course, they didn't know the full story.

"I've got a new piece that I'd like to share with all of you this evening," Milt said as the clapping died down. "I call it: The Necklace."

"I come in peace," he said, then delivered variations on the line that began to sound suspiciously like a beat poem, with the full meaning not in the words, but the sounds of them. I heard in that poem the other things the words might mean because of the way Milt was saying them.

Saying…

No.

Not saying.

It was like he was word-singing them. With a spoken voice resonating an almost musical quality, he was intertwining a double story.

He spoke the words "come" and "peace", and they had double meanings.

As the stanza's continued, the pictures grew, the words speaking of truth and justice being in the hands of the common people... that sort of stuff.

But there was also sex.

The words spoke of truth and justice, but the imagery behind them was the holding of genitals and holding of power, all connected. I felt Gwen squirm in her chair beside me. And there it was, another of those connected moments, and I more than knew, I *understood* what he was saying.

And what he was describing was having sex, with her, putting groins and genitals together and having a raucous good bout of sexual connection. This was mighty adult stuff that probably would have gone right over the heads of most kids my age, but I wasn't that much of a naive innocent, I knew what he meant. The "togetherness" of it was palpable, and I think I actually heard a woman a few tables behind me breathing a barely contained sigh of orgasm. Hell, the whole room was ready to orgasm. Everybody had picked up on this wavelength, this "special" moment. This was one of those times when everything comes together just the right way on stage and the magic happens! I could feel Gwen churn, emotionally, and felt her thoughts.

And what she thought was, "I'm going to have to go on next and follow this!"

And there was true panic right through every fibre of her being.

But there was something more than that.

More than the fear.

I was "reading" her, thinking inside her head, and, suddenly, I was aware that she was aware that... well, you know where that goes. The main thing is, I knew that she had been here before.

To this moment.

Many times.

She had had to follow Milt, and other poets for that matter, on many occasions when their performances had been nothing short of astonishing, when they had, as they say, just killed!

Yes, she felt panic right to her marrow, but panic was no stranger. She had grown, in fact, to love the panic of a moment like this.

He was putting the audience through a huge emotional experience, and she was ready to get up there and top his act!

She was ready!

There was no mistaking that edge, that savvy, experienced soul of a huntress ready to pounce. Like a cat at a mousehole, she was a hunter, a pouncer, and he was casting ripples that would flush out her game. She was after a stray moment, a flicker, a flash in the darkness that can sometimes happen when all the stars line up just right.

I was out of smokes, so I took a half cigarette from the ashtray, one of those foul French ovals, lit it and offered it to her. She smoked it the rest of the way down and her breathing and pulse relaxed. She was ready.

Milt finished with a description of a well-earned string of pearls and the hard working diver who had harvested them. It was an unmistakable metaphor for oral sex and ejaculation.

It was stunning.

Really.

There wasn't any applause, at first.

We all had to, simultaneously, inhale before we could begin to clap. It was that good.

Then the dam burst and the roar of appreciation for a masterful performance was truly deafening.

I could feel Gwen's adrenaline kick in, right at that moment. She was about to get up there and bounce on this emotional trampoline for all she was worth, so high that this room, this world, could not contain her!

It was going to be spectacular!

Milt put his hand to his brow and made a revolving hand gesture.

And Gwen quaked.

I could feel it.

I wondered what was wrong.

She looked at me and sniffed back a tear.

What was wrong?

Milt relinquished the microphone back to Don Cullen, who said: "Wow! What a performance! Okay, we're going to take a little break now. Smoke 'em if you got 'em. Buy lots of coffee, take a cup home for the morning. We're just so desperate for money that you don't even have to drink it, just buy it... Please!

"We're coming back in fifteen minutes with a whole bunch more of really great poets. Believe me, folks, the best is yet to come. Sorry, Gwen, no pun intended... That's right, we've got a lot more coming, including Gwen. You're here with something new tonight, aren't you, Gwen?"

She smiled. Started to rise. If only Don would give her a split second, a chance to...

"Okay, so, don't go 'way, we're coming right back."

He put the microphone back on its stand and everyone in the room struck matches and flicked Zippos and lit up. Milt leaned back in his seat and, amidst the milling swirl of smokey conversation, graciously received congratulations from the numerous admirers who crowded around.

Gwen seethed.

The room was too hot. The air was too thick.

Thick with smoke. Thick with air that had already passed too many times through other people's lungs.

"Well?" Milt queried as folks steadily surged out the door.

"You were brilliant." Gwen replied through clenched teeth.

"Yes," he said, sounding satisfied, "I was brilliant, wasn't I?"

Chapter 48
She Was Brilliant Too

I got another coffee while folks crowded out the door, then, like the whole rest of the audience, stepped out into the sweaty-humid night for a gulp of somewhat fresher air.

After about a fifteen-minute break, I was one of the few who went back in.

There were five performers still on the list to go on, including Gwen. A teen-aged couple right behind me snuggled and giggled.

Don went up to the microphone, spoke a few words of introduction, and Gwen took the stage.

I looked around the mostly empty room. All in all, total, there was Don, me, Milt, Gwen, the other four people waiting to perform their poetry, and eight others. Maybe nine if someone was in the bathroom.

Don stepped out to get some air.

I sat spellbound as Gwen wound word threads that denounced religions and extolled the importance of spelling god with a small "g" and demonstrated a word-sound association that was nothing short of astonishing.

And, yes, in a piece that she made up on the spur of the moment, she responded to Milt's oral sex references in The Necklace with a double-entendre piece of her own. It involved references to a lab in Argentina, but the words sounded odd. The girl at the table behind me hoarsely whispered to her fellow, "She means labia." I made a mental note to look that word up.

She talked of birds, particularly the swallow, "…feathers do get stuck in the throat of the cat, you know you know you know you, you hairball you…" She looked straight at Milt as she said the word "hairball".

She was fixating, captivating, riveting.

Her recitations went on for a good twenty minutes or more. She was giving it her all as if we were the most important audience in the world.

She had been ready for this moment, and it was a loss to those who left that they weren't there to witness it, because she was brilliant too.

The other four performers were pretty good, and then it was time to close. Don asked Milt if he'd like to do one last number to close the show and Milt got up and delivered a hard hitting rendition of "The Fights", expressions like "the brain's the target" swinging and slicing like image punches.

And with that it was time to go.

Don turned out the lights, then shut and locked the door as we preceded him down the stairs. I caught the scent of alcohol on her breath and wondered when and where Gwen had gotten a chance to have a nip? The Embassy didn't serve alcohol.

Chapter 49
Downhill From There

The last Subway train had already made its run and, being Thursday night… well, actually, early Friday morning by now… there weren't likely to be any cabs to be found on Yonge Street. We walked over to Bay in time to see a streetcar rolling away about four blocks to the South. The overnight streetcars were usually about an hour apart but, fortunately, we only had to wait a few minutes; there was another just rumbling down the tracks. This one wasn't on a scheduled run, though. It had a sign in the front window that said "Short Turn". This streetcar was from some other route and was going back to the TTC storage yard. The driver informed us that he'd be turning at Front Street.

Ever the optimist, I asked for a transfer anyway, just in case another Bay car should come along behind. Milt thought that was a pointless waste of paper and said so. Gwen asked the driver for a transfer and glared at Milt, obviously just wanting to be contrary.

We took three separate seats near the doors in the middle of the car, Milt behind Gwen on the left side, me in the seat across from them, just behind the exit doors. He leaned forward and I heard him tell her, in what might have been a sort of a comforting tone, "You were really good tonight."

"Oh, do you think so?" she shot back. The meaning under the words was that his faint praise was the equivalent of a mother telling her daughter that at least *she* thinks she's pretty. It just pissed her off that much more.

We sat in icy silence as the streetcar rumbled and bounced down Bay Street, miraculously hitting all green lights, until it stopped just before Front Street where we had to exit before it squealed its turn and headed off into the night.

The light was red but there weren't any vehicles in sight, so Milt and I crossed Front, then had to wait for Gwen who wouldn't cross against the light. When it finally changed she joined us and we started the fairly steep decline down the sidewalk into the huge maw of the underpass that would get us beyond the overhead railway tracks. Without any traffic on the road, any whispered word would have echoed back and forth in that concrete cavern like a resounding scream.

"What's wrong?" Milt asked, slowing down to walk beside her.

"Nothing, nothing at all," she replied in a tone that clearly indicated that something was, indeed, very wrong. I couldn't believe that he didn't know what it was.

"Seriously, come on," he pleaded, "what is it?"

"You know perfectly well what it is!" she yelled, and the echo: "…perfectly well what it is! …perfectly well what it is! …perfectly well what it is!" bounced back and forth from the walls.

"No! I don't!" he yelled back, those echoes joining the returning sounds of our heels on the pavement.

"Well, if you don't know then you're just plain thick!"

"What? Was it something I said? Come on! Give me a clue!"

"Oh, you're clueless all right!"

"What the hell does that mean? Do you know what she's talking about?" he yelled ahead to me. I just kept my head down and kept walking. I'd seen enough family fights to last me a lifetime and wanted, if at all possible, to stay out of this one.

"You stole my moment!" she hurled at him.

"What? What moment?" He sounded fully and totally confused.

"Don't play the naive innocent with me! You know that you had a brilliant set!" The way she said it made it sound like an accusation.

"Well, yes," he said, conceding the point, "I was brilliant. What else could I possibly be?"

"You could have been gracious. You could have been just a little bit generous. But No! That's not something you could ever really be, could you?"

"What the hell are you talking about? I've been generous to lots of people. And especially you!"

"You arrogant prick!" she screamed, and the words came back over and over: "…arrogant prick! …arrogant prick! …arrogant prick!"

"You're only generous when it suits you, when you know that someone's watching, noticing what a great guy you are!"

"Well now, that's…"

"You looked right at Don and made that gesture! That beckoning gesture that told him to come up and take over on the stage because you were all done!"

"Yeah, so?" We were coming out of the South end of the underpass and the sudden lack of echo somehow made their arguing sound that much louder against the quiet of the night city in these small hours of the morning. Ahead of us a street-sweeping truck was slowly working its way Eastward along Queens Quay.

"You knew he'd call a break and that most of the crowd would leave!"

"Hey, I didn't know he'd do that!"

"YES YOU DID!" The only argument to a statement like that, as any kid who has ever been in a screaming match in a schoolyard knows, is: "Did not!"-"Did so!"-"Did not!"-"Did so!", back and forth until the bell rings or a teacher comes along and breaks it up. This wasn't a schoolyard, there wasn't going to be any bell, and I certainly wasn't the person to try and break it up. I quickened my pace, trying to distance myself just a bit more from the building shitstorm. Family fights weren't new to me, and my defense was always distance, whether physically or mentally.

"What the hell was I supposed to do? My set was finished!"

"You know what you could have done!"

"What? Enlighten me…"

"You just finished laying all our personal things, all our intimate feelings, out there for everybody to see. You could have given me a chance to respond. You could have given me a chance to put my feelings out there too! You could have given me a chance!"

"What do you mean? How could I have…"

"You just don't get it, do you? You got *your* applause, that's all that matters!"

We were getting close to the dock at the foot of York Street. I could see a few people on the other side of the large iron railings sitting there, waiting at the dock, turning their heads our way to see what all the shouting was about.

"That's all you care about, isn't it? As long as you get yours, the rest of the world can go fuck themselves!"

"So I should have introduced you? Is that what this is all about?"

"You know that there are rare, special times when spectacular things can happen! This was one of those times! This was a night when the magic could have happened!"

"You and your god-damned magic!"

"Yes, magic! Stardom! Something spectacular! It could have happened. Right there! Tonight! But you had to have all the glory for yourself, didn't you?"

"Oh, come on now, you know that any given night might turn out to be just as big a turning point in a writer's career as any other. There'll be other audiences, other chances. You know that! You just have to keep plugging away at it, giving it your best!"

"Are you saying that I didn't give it my best?" she hissed.

"Well, no…"

"I gave a fantastic performance tonight, didn't I?" that last part aimed at me.

"Yeah, you really did," I readily agreed.

"And all for just a handful of people while you got to shake up a whole great crowded room!"

"Hey," Milt said, "it's not the size of the audience that counts. It's the…"

"I know, I know. It's the size of the talent in the spotlight. But, damn it all, Milt, there were some real heavyweights there tonight! You know what a struggle it's been to get half-decent sized crowds out for poetry on a Thursday night. And tonight there were *people* there. Important people."

"Hey, nobody's more important than you!"

"Save the soft-soap. I'm way past buying it!"

"Well what the hell am I supposed to do?"

We were at the dock now, a half-dozen folks sitting there, trying to be nonchalant.

"Do you want me to apologize? Is that it?"

"JUST GET THE FUCK AWAY FROM ME!" Gwen went to the far end of the seating area and plunked down on a bench by the farthest jetty, the one nearest the old Skipper restaurant.

It was well past one in the morning. Milt bummed a cigarette off one of the folks who had been waiting there and found out that they had already called John Durnan from the payphone on the side of the RCYC building.

John made a nightly scheduled run at one, and the fare for that was a dollar per person, regardless of how many passengers he had. After that, if you phoned, he'd make a special run, but there was a minimum five-dollar fee. That's what I'd been expecting, to split the fare among the three of us, and still had a one-dollar bill plus three quarters in my pocket.

Since there were more than five people for this run, though, the fare would only be a dollar each. I was going to have an extra seventy-five cents left for tomorrow. At least there was a bit of joy to be found in the situation.

Yep, it was handy that these other folks were going to the Island tonight too.

The problem was, they were going over to join some friends on a boat moored at Hanlan's. It was going to take us about an extra hour to get home. I sat on the top rail, my feet on the middle one, the hot stench of the city wrapped around me like a stinky old blanket, watching the darkness out in the distance for the first glimpse of the water taxi coming.

Chapter 50
The Louise

When sailors look at a boat they talk about her "lines". We learned in math that a straight line is the shortest distance between two points. In science we learned that there is no such thing as a perfectly straight line. In Junior Club we learned that there is no such thing as a straight line in a ship or boat's design that's any damned good. A square box makes a horrible boat.

The way that a hull is curved, the way it's bent and shaped and molded into feminine curves make it all the more understandable that we always referred to a water-going craft as "she".

Of all the boats that had ever been registered for water taxi service in Toronto Harbour, the sleekest, sexiest, most feminine of them all, the one that held the fondest spot in my heart, was the Louise.

My grandfather had owned her for a brief period, and I'd had many trips across the Bay at her helm. Just a small child, but my grandfather had trusted me to steer her true as long as we weren't carrying passengers and he was right there at my elbow.

To describe the lines of the Louise, I'd like you first to picture the head of a single-bladed axe. Now, picture what the imprint of that axe-head would look like if you held it dangling by the handle and pushed it straight down into good, firm packing snow. Now remove the axe and that imprint, that shape, the cutting edge forward, narrow and sharp, curving in and back toward the blunt end, the stern, that was the shape of the Louise. The part of the imprint where the handle comes through the head, where wood inserts into metal, that was her cabin, lined on each side with padded benches for passengers, the skipper's seat forward on her starboard side. She was built for rum-running, probably sometime back in the nineteen-twenties, and cruising around the harbour at low speed was truly a waste of her abilities. She was built to slice, built for speed!

There was one time, out in the open lake, outside the jurisdiction of the Harbour Police, my grandfather opened her up as far as he dared. She went roaring along from the Western gap to a spot roughly in line with Gibraltar point with a huge rooster-tail plume behind, the slight ripple of waves that day feeling like machine gun fast sledge-hammer blows against her bottom. Her throttle just barely past three-quarters open, the wind screaming around the cabin like a full-blown hurricane. He didn't dare push her any faster for fear she'd become airborne and flip. With a stop-watch, estimating a sight line from the trees and houses on shore, he later figured that she'd topped eighty miles an hour!

She gleamed a rich mahogany red through her smooth varnish finish in those days. But now, years later, the wood of her decks and cabin had worn just too thin, she just couldn't be sanded and varnished any more. Her lines, in silhouette as she came around the end of the pier and up toward the jetties at the foot of York Street dock, were just as sleek and sexy, but the darkness mercifully hid her thick new coating of blue-trimmed grey paint.

I was sitting on the steel railing that separated Queen's Quay from the docks.

Milt was halfway through his cigarette.

Gwen got up, walked purposefully up to him, took it from his fingers and walked away smoking it.

"You're welcome!" he bellowed at her back.

It was quite a nice railing, I thought. Sturdy, well made.

"What?" she turned, "I'm supposed to give thanks to the GREAT MAN?"

"Oh, far be it from me to say that the Princess is ungrateful!"

Most likely constructed during the war, probably built to hold up under combat, this railing.

"No, no, being ungrateful is strictly your prerogative! I wouldn't want anyone to think that I was trampling on your territory!"

"When have I ever been ungrateful?"

Yep, this railing was built to last, all right.

"When haven't you? The only one you've ever thanked in your life is yourself: Milton Acorn, the self-made asshole!" She flicked the burning cigarette in a high arc, watching its glowing amber progress to its ultimate demise in the oily water.

Sturdy railing, I thought. Probably way too solid for me to do any real damage to with my tiny knife.

Milt walked part way out the wooden dock, the Louise now less than hundred yards away, the other passengers shuffling out behind him to the loading spot. I could see John Durnan's head sticking out through the starboard side window.

"You're a pig," she yelled, "wallowing in your own filth! I'm tired of finding your filthy shit-stains on the sheets!"

Milt looked puzzled for a second, then yelled back: "Hey, my ass gets itchy!"

"Then scratch it on the fucking snot scales! Isn't that what you pick your nose and stick 'em on the wall for? To scratch your ass on once they're crusty enough for you?!!!"

"All right, we all know that nobody's good enough for you, the Great and Powerful Gwen!" I got the "Wizard of Oz" reference as I fingered the tiny Hercules switchblade in my pocket.

"When you die," she shouted as John eased the Louise toward the slip, second from the East, "...do you know how they'll recognize your body at the morgue, you fucking pig? You'll be the one with an apple in your mouth!"

I took that tiny Hercules switchblade from my pocket, pressed the tiny button, and, "Snick!" there it was. A cute, little, tiny, pointy thing.

"Yeah?" Milt shot back. "Well, before you die, you'll recant!"

"I WILL NOT!"

A very nice railing, I thought. Solid, well made.

"Yes you will!" Milt bellowed at her, "You don't have true belief in your convictions!"

"You take that back!"

A railing made of iron tubing, steel pipes, about four inches in diameter, three rows high. Not too uncomfortable for sitting upon, faced one way or the other. About as solid as a cannon barrel, and probably made in the same foundry where they made cannons, I reckoned.

"You'll renounce everything you've ever learned and kiss a fucking bible and beg for salvation!" He spit the word "salvation" out like it was the filthiest swear word that had ever been uttered.

An iron railing, made of three tiers of pipes about four inches in diameter, with several coats of black paint, the innermost thicknesses of which were probably applied by sailors during the Second World War.

"You take that back! You hear me? YOU TAKE THAT BACK!"

I carved a letter "L" in a lovely script that The Teacher, for all his fancy penmanship, would have admired. Scratched it into the railing's otherwise unmarred black paint.

I did such a bad thing, scratching that letter "L" (in a lovely script, mind you) into that innocent railing, and felt magnificently guilty as soon as I did it.

When boats cruised down this perfectly rectangular body of water between the warehouses, they cast a wake that would echo back and forth, following them. They had to slow long before the docking slips, down to an absolute crawl, in order to not bounce around wildly upon their own wake while loading passengers.

The Louise, though, caused just the merest ripple in this still water as John eased her throttle up a touch in reverse, then stopped her perfectly in place and shifted into neutral. She barely bobbed at all in her berth.

I quickly scratched a further, "...ove..." into the paint after the letter L, hoping that maybe that would make up for my bad deed, then jumped down from the rail, closing the blade of the knife, with thumb and index finger, in mid hop.

I was trying to stow it in my front pocket with one hand while reaching for the Louise's bow line, and that's when the damned knife sprang back open on me, in my hand! I felt a sting as it punctured my palm and instinctively opened my hand, flinging the little Hercules knife and, just like that, instantly, with a tiny splash, it was gone. I wondered what Neptune, snatching it away to sniff and gnaw upon in some dark corner of the deep, would think of the messages it carried.

Milt was on board and seated first, handing John his dollar. John stepped onto the dock as the other folks started to board, handing him their fare. I stood there, holding the bow line so that the current she'd kicked forward wouldn't swing her over near the far side of the slip, waiting for John's signal to cast off.

Now the Louise, as I said, was built in the shape of an axe-head. She was designed for rum running, for slicing smoothly and efficiently through the waves. Her passenger cabin was placed in the aft third of her hull, about where the handle of the axe would pass through the head. Her engine was forward of that, built into a long, smooth bow that took up over half of her over-all length. And, situated forward of the engine compartment in that long expanse of bow, there was an oval shaped seat sunk into her sloping forward deck, just big enough for two. One might presume that she was built in such a way so that a couple of henchmen of an Al Capone sort could stand up there with Tommy guns to keep a lookout for G-men and hijackers.

After the folks going to Hanlan's had gotten on board, John looked at Gwen, fire in her eyes, still standing on the dock. He wasn't about to cross the Bay with these two locked in mortal combat on board.

"You," he commanded Milt, "keep your mouth shut! And you!" pointing at Gwen, hesitating, then taking the dollar bill from her hand, "Go sit up there!"

I offered my hand to steady her step as she crossed the forward deck into the small cockpit opening. Then I let the bow line off the cleat and went back aft and, holding the handgrip that I found easily in the darkness, gave him my buck and swung on board.

The Louise gulped and spat the oily, greasy, grease-ball and grease-soaked-dead-seagull laden water trapped in the Eastern lee side of the slip as John backed her out and around to starboard. As she spewed, gargled, purged and spit the foul scum away from her twin tailpipes I saw, in the outline of the droplets she was coughing, a long plank, maybe a two by twelve, bobbing to our stern. I looked at John as he looked at the plank and juiced her forward just ever so lightly, turning her rudder hard to port. None of the passengers felt any sort of sway at all. She literally just floated around, like a slow, gentle cloud, turning her bow as surely as a needle in a compass. As she turned, her keel hardly varied from pointing constantly straight at the centre of the Earth.

She turned ever so elegantly to the South, toward the far end of the long body of water between the warehouse piers. Then John brought her speed up ever so slightly, cautious of more jetsam lurking in the virtually motionless expanse of the long, straight slip. Going to the Island. Going home.

Chapter 51
Crossing the Bay

We slid by the hundreds of yards of huge warehouse buildings on each side, like walls of an urban Grand Canyon. Up ahead, at the end of the slip, there was the very real chance of another boat zipping across the opening, maybe even Harbour Police in high-speed pursuit. It had been known to happen.

John brought her speed way down again knowing he'd need to see both ways, to be sure that there was no cross-traffic, before he could bring her back up to cruising speed. It would be a few seconds before he'd be able to let her stretch out a little, up to the harbour limit of eleven miles per hour.

We were about to come up abreast of the ends of the piers when...

"I AM SO SICK AND TIRED OF SLEEPING ON THOSE FILTHY FUCKING SHEETS!" Gwen screamed.

"What the hell..." John said, dropping the Louise into neutral while trying to see into the forward seat. The boat was starting to rock as a slow swell of wave action from the larger body of open Bay water reverberated back into the slip.

"Ah, don't mind her," Milt said from his seat behind me.

I tried to peer up past the other passengers who, along with John, were standing up, trying to see what was going on up front.

"I'M GOING TO BURN THOSE FUCKING SHEETS!" she screamed.

"Lorne!" John called.

Elbowing through the other standing passengers I had a fleeting glimpse of potential glory. Maybe John would ask me to take the helm while he went up over the deck to talk to her. I was going to get my Captain's papers next Spring anyway, and already had my learner's application at home on my dresser, all filled out. I was going to file it on my next birthday, just as soon as I turned fourteen...

"I'M SICK AND TIRED OF TRYING TO WASH THEM! I'M GOING TO FUCKING BURN THEM!" she screamed.

Very firmly, in a low voice, hopefully not audible to the other passengers, John looked at me and asked: "Can you make it across that deck without falling overboard?"

"Huff," I scoffed, "of course."

"Okay then, what I want you to do is this, and exactly this. Go over there, talk to her, get her to calm down. I'm going to head West and turn her over to the Harbies. Just keep her in her seat until we get there."

"Huh?"

"The sooner she's off my boat the safer we'll all be."

There was no arguing with John Durnan. He was The Skipper.

I eased my way up, out and around the Starboard side of the cabin, went forward and stepped gently across in front of the windshield until I was midship. I had about six feet of open deck to cross, built in a gentle curve down and away to both sides to facilitate water spray running off.

Like I said, the Louise was a classic, originally built for speed. All of her owners had tried their best to keep her as original as possible. And she didn't originally have proper handrails.

In the expanse of deck in front of me I knew, though they weren't visible in the dim glow coming from her running lights, that there were two hatch covers that came down and fit together in the middle. Those covers, when closed, formed the deck, underneath of which was mounted her enormously powerful engine. There were no handholds to speak of, just two skinny rails designed more to keep the engine hatches from laying flat out on the deck when they were open than for holding onto.

I knew those hatch covers were there, invisible in the darkness of the night, only barely illuminated by the glow of the city reflecting back down from the pollution haze in the sky. And I knew that, because of their age, those hatches weren't all that solid. I'd have to place my feet directly on the centre, distributing my weight evenly between them.

The Louise bobbed a bit in her following wake which, by now, had caught up with us. They were just small swells, but there were lots of them, from both sides. The deck kind of shivered, ever so slightly.

That bit of wave action was passing us, but she was still drifting forward. If I waited for, maybe, ten more seconds, I'd have a straight eye-line both ways and know that there weren't any other boats coming across the opening of the slip.

John tapped on the windshield. I called out "Looking both ways." He heard and waited.

Then… Look left: nothing coming. Look right: nothing coming. The ends of the piers were behind us.

I placed my right foot in the centre, at the seam where the hatches met. I crouched low and placed my left hand on the white life-ring fastened there. Left foot forward and…

"BURN! BURN! FUCKING BURN!!!" Gwen screamed.

I bounced my bum on the deck, got my feet down inside and safely plunked my butt on the padded seat beside her, trying hard to calm my heart down. I gulped a breath and said: "That's pretty loud, you know."

She jolted, sat back, banged her head on the edge of the deck and said, "What the fu...? How'd you…? Ow! You mean you could hear me?"

"Well, yeah, you were pretty loud."

"Oh, sorry. Ow, I hurt my head."

"Here, let me take a look." I reached forward, up into the shelf under the forward deck. Yep, John still kept a flashlight stowed there.

I took a look at her head. There was no blood, but she'd probably have a small bump in the morning.

"John wants to take you over to the Harbies," I said. She looked puzzled. "The Harbour Police dock. They'll, I don't know…"

"Oh, for god's sake, I don't need to be 'turned over to the authorities'." I could actually hear in her voice the set of quotes around the words: "turned over to the authorities." She stood up on the seat, turned and faced the windshield.

"Sorry!" she yelled. "I just needed to vent, there. I didn't think you could hear me, John! Sorry! I'll just sit and be quiet, okay? Sorry!" She dropped back to the seat beside me.

John eased the throttle up and the engine rumbled and roared. The Louise wasn't supposed to sound like that, she was supposed to purr. I turned and kneeled on the seat, stretched my arm into the space behind the backrest and felt the rope ring, gave a good hard pull and snapped the baffle closed. It's really quite amazing how much less of an enormously powerful engine you hear when you've got a good, thick sound baffle closed instead of open.

The smooth hiss of the water of the Bay against the hull was suddenly the loudest sound, except for our own hearts and breathing, and the far away cry of a seagull.

I had to concede that, with the engine so loud at our backs, I could understand how she thought that nobody in the cabin could hear her ranting, and told her so.

"Oh, god! They all think I'm some kind of lunatic, don't they?" she said as she comfortably draped her arm on the deck, one hand resting on the starboard light bracket. That running light cast an eerie green glow on her fingers.

I, in mirror pose, had the port light basking my left arm in a blood-red glow. Smoothly, feeling as if we were at the front of a low-flying airplane, we cruised the smooth surface. There was no sensation of wave or ripple, the air felt like velvet brushes caressing my cheeks and nose, like a refreshingly cool set of hands and fingers massaging every nook and indent of skin on my face and exposed arms.

I felt alive again with the amount of fresh air off the Lake seeping across over the airport to our right. Basking in that breeze was like being cleansed in a shower, a spring. The sweat-soaked armpits of my T-shirt were finally starting to dry. After the itchy-throated scratch from breathing city air, this was oxygen-laden rejuvenation.

We made our turn to line up with the channel marker lights of Hanlan's, then slowed and veered up past the sign at the end of Durnan's Dock. A yellowish glow from the upstairs window indicated that John's sister, Emily, was still awake, waiting at her end beside the short-wave radio transmitter until he finally finished for the night.

Durnan's boathouse was the only place on the Island that the Parks Department couldn't remove by legal force. His family had been here since the eighteen thirties, and they were the only ones who owned their land. Everyone else just leased their lots, and those leases were what the Parks Department were canceling in order to remove them.

For all the summers that I spent living at Hanlan's Point, Durnan's boathouse was my favorite summer playground. Most any warm summer day would find a half-dozen or so Hanlan's kids hanging out at the end of the dock, jumping into the water and swimming back to dive again.

John had a huge sign facing the ferries as they docked, declaring that there were bicycles and canoes for rent here, and comfortable rowboats too. But the antics of us kids jumping and diving into the water, visible to all the tourists coming ashore, drew more business than the sign did. Maybe not everyone wanted to rent bikes or canoes from him, but if those folks from the city wanted to watch us dive, they quickly discovered that, once off the ferry boat, they couldn't see us without coming through the breezeway and out onto Durnan's pier. The boathouse was too wide for them otherwise watch the show.

And if they hung around long enough watching us dive and swim, they'd eventually be lured by the aroma to Emily's concession stand, at the breezeway, for a hot-dog and a glass of orange Honeydew. I spent untold numbers of summer days that way, among a pack of other Hanlan's Point kids diving at the end of the pier, swimming back to the carpeted canoe-launch ramp, then running as fast as we could back out to the end to dive again.

We slowly cruised by the Island Yacht Club on the left, across the end of Long Pond and straight on towards Blockhouse Bay.

We passed by what used to be known as Jones Dock on the right, a slight angle in the retaining wall the only remaining landmark to show where our home used to be. We slowed to a crawl, motored around the bend, the report of sporadic explosions becoming louder. The bright lights of the Filtration Plant came into view though the trees of Miller Island as we came around into Blockhouse Bay.

As we rounded Toothpick Island a cross-chop wave thumped into the Louise's Port side, causing us to lurch slightly sideways as a splash slapped up over the deck. There wasn't any breath of a breeze in the air, but this wave, a big chop, came at us from the shore and, just like that, it was gone.

A small amount of water splashed over me and landed on Gwen's arm and ran down her shirt. The seat got wet too.

John turned on the powerful hand-beam and shone its brilliance toward the shore as we cruised in behind Toothpick. As we circumnavigated Toothpick clockwise, John illuminated the old, decaying hulk of the Trillium to our left, a defunct side-wheel passenger ferry rotting at her tethers against the shore. She was the last remnant of a fleet of paddlewheeler's made up of The Trillium, Primrose, Mayflower and The Bluebell. They were all considerably larger than any of the ferries currently plying the Bay. It was back during their heyday that attendance records were set for numbers of day-tripping tourists flocking to the Island.

Two, three, four people became visible on shore near the Trillium, shielding their eyes against the harsh glare, fishing from the concrete wall near which the old paddlewheeler was moored. They aimed flashlights down at their poles as we cruised slowly on around the bend, the crackle of fireworks now quite a bit louder.

Another twenty or more smelt poles were in the water in front of the Filtration plant, with a crowd of folks on shore tending them. We could see people drinking. There certainly was a good supply of beer, and still a few Roman Candles and other assorted firework explosions going off, but most of that display would have been finished hours ago.

John swung the beam of light around, illuminating the sandy beach of Toothpick Island. To our right, a big rectangular houseboat came into view, nosed up on the shore of Toothpick. Two smelt poles rested in the water off her stern. John turned the big beam on her, shining it up and down, back and forth, then shut it off and stuck his head out of the cabin, on the Starboard side.

"YOU'RE GOING TO HAVE TO PULL THOSE POLES SO I CAN DOCK." He hollered.

"OKAY." "YEAH, ALRIGHT," a couple of guys hollered back.

Two men took the long poles in hand as a couple of women sitting in lawn chairs on the flat top of the houseboat watched them pull them, and their catch, from the depths.

A smelt net is a square of string mesh with half-inch openings, roughly five foot by five foot, stretched flat in a square-shape by spring metal spreaders which are fastened in the centre to a swivel, which is attached to the end of a long pole. When you pull it from the water, (if you're unlucky) it weighs as much as ten pounds, wet. Seven or so after a good shake.

If you're lucky, then when you pull it from the water with a good haul, it might weigh twenty-five or thirty pounds.

If you're lucky. If you just happen to pull the net from the water when a big shoal of smelt are right there in front of you, wriggling about in a breeding frenzy.

That's only, of course, if you're lucky. A big shoal of smelt will also show up, wriggling around in their breeding frenzy, anywhere that a bright light shines into the water. And the lights of the Filtration Plant dock were awfully bright.

Luck doesn't have as much to do with it there.

Plus, unlike other kinds of fishing where you have to be very quiet so as not to frighten the fish away, noise didn't bother the smelts at all. And the smelt run usually happened right around Victoria Day which, throughout all the Dominion, was celebrated with fireworks.

This was the big spring festival on the Island, built around three pillars: smelt fishing, firecrackers and beer.

In the midst of the inner curve of an otherwise sandy-shored bay, there was (and probably still is) this area of rectangular concrete buildings and dock, the Filtration Plant, with its row of bright lights directly over the water and "NO PUBLIC ACCESS" signs. A good number of Islanders quite enjoyed thumbing their noses at such signs.

You could see the thick throng of smelt in the glow that those lights cast into the water. It fairly boiled with them. Somewhere beneath this massive school of fish, underwater where you couldn't see them, there were the outlet ends of pipes that came from the Filtration Plant's storage tanks. Every once in a while an employee would open a valve at the Filtration Plant and dump a sudden surge of water into the lagoon at the center of the area defined by the "NO PUBLIC ACCESS" signs. The result would be a short, sudden wave, which would cascade across to the far shore. That's what had hit us broad side and splashed off our hull as we turned toward this side of Toothpick. They had to add that fresh water when the smelt ran, so they taught us during our week at the Natural Science School, because the Filtration Plant lights attracted so many fish that they'd otherwise use up all the oxygen in this small part of the lagoon and die.

It had been known to happen.

My Grandfather had told of a time when the smelt run was so thick, and the bright lights of the Filtration Plant had drawn them to this spot in such numbers, that they had exhausted the oxygen in the water and died in the millions. The mass of dead fish became so thick that boats could hardly move in the lagoons.

Beyond this dense knot of fish drawn to the lights in front of the Plant, though, still many more millions of them filled the shallows around and behind Toothpick. When smelt were running, fishing was quite good there too.

The houseboat's nose was on the shore, and she was tied off to stout trees on both sides. I figured that John was thinking, if her stern protruded into deep enough water, he could bring the Louise's starboard side stern up to the Houseboat's starboard side stern and let the other passengers, the ones who had called for the water taxi in the first place, get off.

He brought her to a stop, cranked the rudder to port and gave her a wee touch forward, then quickly hard to starboard and a dash of reverse, and the Louise turned, pivoted, and then, with just a wee shot of throttle in reverse, he brought her stern in close enough to throw a line.

The Louise reverberated six times with the clomp of shoes on her stern step as the other folks left, greeted by their friends with boisterous offerings of beer and smelts, pan-fried in a myriad of personal recipes.

John pulled in the line and, with a last shove of his heel as he cast off, continued the turn of the Louise's bow to starboard. He flashed the beam of the bright light along the Filtration plant dock, hollering to see if anyone on shore wanted a taxi.

A small group of guys on the dock waved him over and started getting their poles and buckets ready to load on board. I recognized Andre Philpot, Billy Morrison, Pat Coyle and Frank Oggy among them, all guys from around the Hooper Avenue area. They stowed their long smelt poles along the port side deck where I held them in place with one hand as we pulled away from the dock.

"ARE YOU TWO ALL RIGHT UP THERE?" John hollered to us.

"You all right?" I asked Gwen. "Your seat's a little wet too? Are you cold?"

"Yes, well, a bit."

I felt her hand and it was like ice. John turned the bright glare of the spotlight on us and steam was clearly rising from her wet clothing as she shivered.

"THE SEAT'S A LITTLE WET, BUT WE'RE OKAY," I hollered back. "Here," I said to Gwen, "stand up for a second and hold this for me, would you?"

I handed her the flashlight and got her to put a hand on the forward end of the smelt poles for me. The boat rocked ever so slightly as I managed, easily enough, to pry the padded seat up on its hinges and pull out the thick, grey wool navy blanket that was folded up and stashed there.

I put the seat back down and, as we sat, I wrapped the blanket around her shoulders.

"Aren't you cold too?" she asked.

An older, more knowing version of myself might have chosen to interpret that, rightly or wrongly, as an invitation to join her under the cover, to put my arm around her

shoulder and become, shall we say, closer. But I wasn't yet
that older, more knowledgeable version of myself.

"Naw," I said, "I'm fine."

"Look," she said, "I'm sorry you had to hear all those
things back there? Okay? I'm just…"

"Hey, it's all right, nothing I haven't seen before."

"What? You've seen us fight before? When?"

"No, no, I haven't seen you fight before, not you two. But
I've seen fights, heard swearing before. Sometimes a lot
worse than this."

She pulled the blanket tighter around her shoulders and
gazed out into the dark recesses among the trees as we
cruised by Miller Island to starboard.

Chapter 52
Woulda Coulda Shoulda

The glassy smooth expanse of the lagoon slid away under the Louise's hull as we motored past Jones dock to port. There were so many things I wanted to tell her. I looked across to the row of streetlights that still shone in a line where Lakeshore Avenue used to be.

604 Lakeshore used to stand… right… there!

That was the house where, as a five-year-old child, I had watched through a narrow slit between the planks hurriedly nailed to the front windows as Hurricane Hazel swept houses and lives out into Lake Ontario in the small hours on Saturday morning, October 16, 1954, before dawn. I wanted to tell her how all the Island was prepared for that deadly storm, even though the rest of the city had gone to bed Friday night comforted by reports that this massive storm was on a course to cause trouble in the North Carolina area. Except for the Islanders, everybody else in the city was caught completely off-guard.

Islanders had a natural hatred of authority, and most especially the authority of the city appointed Dog Catcher. There was a web, a system, by which, when someone spotted the Dog Catcher's vehicle coming off the ferry, certain people phoned the certain people who were next on their list. By this means everyone was quickly notified, and virtually no Island dogs were caught.

That same order of communication had worked when, sitting up late at night, one Island person heard radio reports of the devastation happening as a wide swath of Southern Ontario was scoured of homes, with great resultant loss of life. And that killer hurricane was barreling right down on top of us!

That person initiated the "Dog Catcher" warning list, and within minutes my Grandfather was up and out nailing planks and plywood over all the windows and doors, with time enough to go and board up Ivy Thompson's place up the street at 612 Lakeshore as well. There was damage on the Island as a result of Hurricane Hazel, but no loss of life. I wanted to tell her all that. But didn't.

As we came to the bend and turned East, up Long pond, I wanted to tell her about the house we lived in one winter on Hiawatha Avenue, directly in line with Long Pond. That was the year that Barry had worked as the winter watchman at the Island Yacht Club.

Being the only person with authority to be on the property, and not much to do, he had taken to firing his old bolt action .22 calibre Cooey rifle at targets he had set up against the sand dunes.

One sunny winter day while walking along, with Jimmy carrying the gun, we spotted some rusty cans in the snow. Jimmy took a couple of shots and missed. Barry walked over to stand the cans up to give him a better target.

Jimmy wasn't a very good shot, and that was fortunate for the two little black, white and rusty red baby bunnies sitting there that we had mistaken for tin cans.

We took them home, where one died within a few days. The other lived with us for a couple of years. We named him Nipper, because he quite enjoyed hopping onto the bed and chewing on your hair or nibbling on an earlobe when he thought it was time for us to get up.

I didn't tell her any of that either.

John opened the throttle up just ever so slightly. The speed limit was four miles per hour, and we were maybe doing six, but it was unlikely that there would be any Harbour Police boats lying in wait in the shadows at either side of Long Pond at this time of night. I should have spoken up, said something, but the time just did not feel right. She had had her fight, had apologized to me, and was now quiet, lost in her own thoughts.

If she had spoken to me, I could have opened up about so many things. We were passing, over to our right, Donut Island, with its round pond of stagnant water in the middle. Behind it was the series of shallow lagoons we called Five Fingers. Whether it's the result of silting-in or bulldozers, there are only three-fingers of water there now, and the local name for it has changed appropriately. But back then there were five channels of water that ran back from the section of the lagoon that surrounded Donut. The Western most of these was already almost choked closed with a combination of sediment and old boat hulls. That was where derelict hulks were taken and sunk.

We slowed down a bit as we cruised past the old, white bleachers on the right, the only thing remaining of the old Island Canoe Club. Hell, it was the only thing, the only structure of any kind left from the old Centre Island Main Drag days.

The sound of the Louise's exhaust, deep-throated gurgling, spluttering from her stern, echoed back to us as we slid slowly under the Manitou Bridge.

I said nothing.

I could have.

Maybe I should have.

I certainly would have if she'd spoken first, but she didn't.

We went straight on for a ways, passing the petting zoo and display farm on the left, then around the bend to the left, then to the right, and there we were at the dock next to Philpot's boathouse.

John swung the Louise hard to port, then backed her in, stern first, swinging her starboard side in to the dock. As he let the guys that he'd picked up at the Filtration plant step off, I passed them their smelt poles. There was a chance that Gwen might get bonked on the head as I lifted them across from the Port to the Starboard side, so she got up out of her seat, onto the dock. She walked down the dock, to the stern and got back into the cabin to sit with Milt.

We cruised on down the lagoon, under the Algonquin Bridge and on to Ward's, small groups of Mallard ducks slowly parting to make way for us to pass.

By the time we pulled in at the side of the ferry dock at Ward's, Gwen and Milt seemed to be reconciled.

Sort of.

Milt solemnly vowed, as we walked across the path towards Channel Avenue, that he would give Gwen her chance, her shot. He would put her on a stage in front of the world, he promised, even if he had to stand at the corner of Yonge and Bay and scream his lungs out to do it.

But Yonge and Bay run parallel to each other, there is no such corner. I didn't know if he was aware of his mistake or not, but I wasn't about to get involved by correcting him.

I did know, though, that something was broken between them. A rift had been opened up that could never be mended.

I have heard it said that time heals all wounds.

I know that that saying isn't true.

No, healing all wounds simply is not possible. But time can do many strange and wonderful things. Time and heat.

I slid the key out from under the mat and quietly let myself into the dark house, softly holding the spring loaded latch so that it didn't click as the screen door closed behind me, then shut the inside door.

I stepped softly around to the right and used the bathroom. Then, just in case, checked the grey paint.

It was dry!

Odorless and hard-as-a-bowling-ball dry!

Epilogue

My Grandfather finally finished the whole case of
whiskey. When it was gone, he shakily crawled out of the
bed he'd been crapping and barfing in for two weeks,
showered and shaved, got into his best clothes and headed
for the city to buy beer. My Grandmother, as usual, cleaned
up his mess and tried to pretend that the whole thing never
happened.

*****

There was a silly law on the books in Toronto, which
prohibited reading poetry aloud in any city park. Milt read
poetry as loud as he could in city parks, gathering crowds
and getting arrested, garnering headlines until he caused the
city to repeal that law. It was not, however, enough to win
for Gwen the amount of attention he owed her.

She went to Israel that summer, and came back quite
changed.

I am put in mind of the droves of would-be stars that
flock to Hollywood, certain that their talent will be obvious
and they'll be *discovered*. It seems that very few of them
are.

Many wild-eyed would-be messiahs also flock to Israel
hoping that their faith will be obvious and they'll be
discovered. It seems that very few of them are.

Gwen certainly wasn't. All she was seen as was a wanton
Western woman, alone, so it was assumed she was on the
make.

She just barely escaped being raped.

*****

Deja vu one more time, about a year later, on the Thomas
Rennie. As the engines rumbled deep in her belly and
voices were raised to be heard above the throaty din, on our

way from the city to the Island, Peggy wondered wherever Sam could have ended up.

"Well," Barry said, "he used to follow us up and down the street. It was like taking a dog for a walk."

"But then he followed us out to the gap when we went smelt fishing..." I interrupted.

"Let Barry tell the story," Flo said.

"So," Barry went on as the capacity crowd of standing non-islanders swayed with the turning of the ship, "he followed us out to the Gap last spring. He was just sitting there beside us, big and white and snooty as if he owned the whole world, and I was straining to pull up the net. I could feel that it was pretty full..."

"And that's when I said, 'Dump it on him!' " I said.

"Right. So I did, and you should have seen him jump!"

"He was suddenly buried in about five pounds of live smelts!"

"He must have leapt about ten feet in the air!"

"Funniest thing I've ever seen!"

"So anyway," Barry went on, with a glower that meant 'let *me* tell the story', "He cautiously came inching his way back to the pile of fish,"

"While I was picking them up and tossing them in the bucket," I said.

"Right. And he sniffed at one, then bit its head. Then another."

"He didn't want the whole fish."

"Nope, just the brains."

"And we cut the heads off when we cleaned them anyway."

"So he sat there beside us the rest of the night, biting the heads, eating just the brains, and after that..."

"After that he wouldn't eat canned cat food at all!"

"He always was a finicky eater."

"We couldn't even get him to eat steak unless you offered it to him with your fingers."

"And then only if it was very rare." Barry looked at Flo. "He did eat canned tuna though, didn't he?"

"Just a little." Flo said. "I threw away more stale, crusty cat food that went hard in the dish. He didn't like any brand of dry or even the most expensive wet cat food from a can."

"But he sure liked fresh, live smelts," Barry said.

"Well, their brains anyway," I added.

"Right. So this Spring, when the smelts were running, he just took off and didn't come home any more."

"But I saw him..."

"That's right, Lorne saw him down at the shore behind Jimmy's new place on Third. So I went over to see and, sure enough, there was big old Sam, sitting on a rock at the water's edge, staring down and wiggling one paw in the water. I watched for a couple of minutes and suddenly, swipe! He clawed a tiny fish out onto the bank and pounced on it."

"Just ate the brains!" I added.

"He looked really good, very healthy, with a shiny looking white coat. None of that hanging belly fat that he'd built up over the winter. All muscle."

"And fast!"

"Yeah. When we went up to him he bolted, ran away through Coleman's yard and gone!"

"But there were over a dozen small headless fish on the shore."

"Well," Peggy said as the ferry gently bumped its way into the Ward's dock, "I guess, if he's healthy and happy, then that's all that really matters."

"Oh, he's healthy all right," Barry said.

"And he sure looks happy," I said. "And it looks like he's found a friend. That cat of Mrs. Acorn's? Lucifer? A big black cat with a tuft of white fur right at the tip of his tail? Well, I've seen him with Sam several times. I think they're hunting together"

*****

When Gwen returned from Israel, she and Milt parted ways, loudly, vehemently and permanently.

She dropped the "Acorn" last name, publishing instead as Gwendolyn MacEwen. Her maiden name had been McEwen, but she told me that the Mac prefix denoted a person of greater importance. She let me read the galley draft of Julian the Magician before it was published. Her main question, when I finished it, was, "Did you get the part about the Mandrake?"

Yes, I did.

But I think, now, that she missed the mark. She was too late. The opportunity for Julian to succeed, the way she wanted him to, had passed.

Just as Julian the Magician was starting to move off bookshelves, with reasonably good critical acclaim, John F. Kennedy, the President of the United States, was assassinated, and there was a fundamental shift in the things that people were searching for.

Looking back on it now I think that, if Julian the Magician had been published three, maybe four years earlier, when she first wrote it, then it may have had a chance to do what she intended.

Right from the start there was a lot of controversy, and many conspiracy theories, everyone wondering who really killed President Kennedy.

Regardless of who pulled the trigger, I think that John Wayne was responsible. It was John Wayne, as the man who shot Liberty Valance, who made it possible for a sniper with a rifle hiding in the shadows to believe that he was one of the good guys.

*****

Bob Mallory moved in with Gwen at 10 Second Street, staying on in the house long after she left the Island a couple of years later. We played many a game of chess on winter nights while he slowly became more and more detached from reality. I brought him gifts of firewood as often as I could, but the pile of books, and the stack of drawings that he and Gwen had made was steadily diminishing.

Oil paintings give a surprising amount of heat for a short time, though they stink terribly. Poetry doesn't smell as bad but doesn't last as long. As sacrificial offerings, they didn't seem to help him at all.

He started wearing a layer of tinfoil on his head, "to block out *their* signal," he said.

"The aliens," he said, "have a base for their flying saucers on the floor of the ocean at the North Pole." He was certain that he had become so attuned to the workings of the universe that he could hear their signals and, for that, they were hunting him. Aliens, and the Masons.

He wore a turban over the tinfoil so people wouldn't stare. Turban or not, people would always stare at Bob Mallory. Someone tagged him with the nickname "Bozo" and it stuck.

Not a scrap of his, Gwen's or Milt's poetry or art remained there by the time the house was demolished.

*****

The rest of the Island houses didn't get torn down in six years, as promised by the Parks Department. I found some old paint and touched up the "Save Island Homes" graffiti on the Algonquin Island breakwater, just in case. I have no idea whether or not the paint is still there.

But, at the time of this writing, about two hundred of the houses are. They don't have to rely on septic tanks anymore, they've all been hooked up to a proper sanitary sewer system.

*****

Whether I could actually do it or not, I stopped trying to influence the weather. If I couldn't do it, which is most likely the case, then I was at risk of becoming as delusional as Bob and all the religious devotees that he so derided.

If I could, which is highly unlikely, then I simply could not afford the consequences. The price was just too high.

*****

Milt died on August 20th, 1986. He was much older than Gwen, and had lived in such a derelict state for so many years, sleeping in seedy flop houses and soaking up beer in cheap dives that his death came as no great surprise. In his last days he invited an Anglican minister to his bedside, kissed a bible and begged for salvation.

Gwen died on November 30th, 1987. She was found on the floor, an apple on the counter. She had taken one bite, and was dead before she could take another.

The coroner listed the cause of death as metabolic acidosis. Although there was no alcohol in her system, nor any trace of any drugs, it was assumed that she had been a long time alcoholic who had quit cold turkey, resulting in a fatal imbalance to her system.

There was no criminal investigation.

Why should there be?

There was no known reason why foul play should be suspected in the death of a well-respected poet and novelist, at forty-six years of age.

*****

I graduated from the Island Public School and, years later, as I walked out of High School on the day that I completed my last Grade 12 exam, I lit up a smoke and realized that I only had a half pack left. That wasn't going to last me very long. My habit was up to 3 packs a day. I went into a store at the corner of Wellesley and Church and bought a fresh pack of my favorite brand.

As I stepped outside into the bright afternoon sunshine, it occurred to me that the stars were all aligned, the time was right, this was one of those moments when mysterious and powerful things can happen.

I looked at that new package and, because it was something that I wanted so badly, I recognized it as something else: the perfect sacrifice.

I didn't even unwrap the cellophane.

I tossed it, along with the half-pack from my pocket, into a garbage can and walked away.

It's been over four decades, and I still have no desire to ever smoke another cigarette.

*****

I looked at that box full of pieces of paper that were oh-so-important, a quarter century before her death. I thought of those speech exercises, saying "ahhhhh" and "ummmm" in an attempt to quit stuttering by substituting one speech impediment for another, and it made me think of Gwen offering up Julian as a sort of Jesus-Lite, trying to substitute one affliction for another.

Some things, sometimes, simply must be done. Sometimes a cardboard box that has become slightly sodden and likely to crumble has to be dealt with.

Sometimes, well, sometimes you just have to climb down from the attic and put a box of musty old papers into the recycling bin, while resisting the urge to toss them into a fire.

>>>end<<<

Suggested further reading:

More Than an Island by Sally Gibson

Shadow Maker: The Life of Gwendolyn MacEwen by
Rosemary Sullivan

Milton Acorn In Love and Anger by Richard Lemm

The Northern Red Oak, Poems for and about Milton Acorn
by various contributors edited and with introduction by
James Deahl

The Bohemian Embassy: Memories And Poems by Don
Cullen

The Louise